Damn his presumptuous orders.

She would tell him exactly where he could go tomorrow at one o'clock and what he could do with his marriage proposal when he got there.

Zach paused on the porch step, his back to her. Shoulders as broad as the doorway dropped, his head falling forward. "Julia," he said, the single word whispering a need that had sent her running to his house barely twenty-four hours ago.

All those damning curses within Julia dried up. Her mouth closed. She waited. Wanted.

What she wanted, she didn't exactly know, but she stood on the edge of something scary. Life would change for her based on what she decided in the next few seconds. "What, Zach?"

"I guess I needed you more than I realized."

His soft-spoken words rumbled with more of that need, tipping her over the edge. Come one o'clock, Julia knew she would stand beside him in hell itself if he asked.

Dear Reader,

A new year has begun, so why not celebrate with six exciting new titles from Silhouette Intimate Moments? *What a Man's Gotta Do* is the newest from Karen Templeton, reuniting the one-time good girl, now a single mom, with the former bad boy who always made her heart pound, even though he never once sent a smile her way. Until now.

Kylie Brant introduces THE TREMAINE TRADITION with *Alias Smith and Jones,* an exciting novel about two people hiding everything about themselves—except the way they feel about each other. There's still TROUBLE IN EDEN in Virginia Kantra's *All a Man Can Ask,* in which an undercover assignment leads (predictably) to danger and (*un*predictably) to love. By now you know that the WINGMEN WARRIORS flash means you're about to experience top-notch military romance, courtesy of Catherine Mann. *Under Siege,* a marriage-of-inconvenience tale, won't disappoint. Who wouldn't like *A Kiss in the Dark* from a handsome hero? So run—don't walk—to pick up the book of the same name by rising star Jenna Mills. Finally, enjoy the winter chill—and the cozy cuddling that drives it away—in *Northern Exposure,* by Debra Lee Brown, who sends her heroine to Alaska to find love.

And, of course, we'll be back next month with six more of the best and most exciting romances around, so be sure not to miss a single one.

Enjoy!

Leslie J. Wainger
Executive Senior Editor

Under Siege
CATHERINE MANN

Silhouette®

INTIMATE MOMENTS™

Published by Silhouette Books

America's Publisher of Contemporary Romance

SILHOUETTE BOOKS

ISBN 0-373-27268-5

UNDER SIEGE

Copyright © 2003 by Catherine Mann

Books by Catherine Mann

Silhouette Intimate Moments

Wedding at White Sands #1158
*Grayson's Surrender #1175
*Taking Cover #1187
*Under Siege #1198

*Wingmen Warriors

CATHERINE MANN

began her romance-writing career at twelve and recently uncovered that first effort while cleaning out her grandmother's garage. After working for a small-town newspaper, teaching on the university level and serving as a theater school director, she has returned to her original dream of writing romance. Now an award-winning author, Catherine is especially pleased to add a nomination for the prestigious Maggie Award to her contest credits. Following her air-force-aviator husband around the United States with four children and a beagle in tow gives Catherine a wealth of experience from which to draw her plots. Catherine invites you to learn more about her work by visiting her Web site: http://catherinemann.com.

Dedication:
To Colonel and Mrs. James Furman Fowler, USAF Ret.
Thanks, Granddaddy, for teaching me a girl could hang
out in a workshop, too, and for teaching me the
all-important life lesson, "Measure twice, cut once."
Thanks, Grandma, for giving me such a beautiful
example of how to love a man called to fly.

Acknowledgments:
Thanks to Colonel David Hesp, USAF Ret.,
and Patti Hesp, for the technical advice and the
warm military welcome to the neighborhood.

And as always, thanks to my very own "major,"
Major Mann.

Chapter 1

Lieutenant Colonel Zach Dawson liked to think he'd learned a few lessons after sixteen years in the Air Force, ninety-seven combat missions, two weeks as an Iraqi POW and one very speedy divorce. More important, he'd learned that *being* him was a hell of a lot easier than being *married* to him.

And today, being Zach Dawson was tougher than snow removal in Thule, Greenland.

Zach scooped his LMR—land mobile radio—from the front seat of his truck and loped across the steamy South Carolina hospital parking lot at a slow jog. Nineteen minutes left until visiting hours ended.

Nineteen more minutes, then his longest Friday on record would be over.

Duty dictated he pay a courtesy call to new mother Julia Sinclair, the widow of one of his pilots. Conscience insisted her loss couldn't be repaid with any simple hospital visit. But for today, that's all he could do, give her nineteen inadequate minutes of his time as if it might somehow erase her past eight months alone.

If only the radio gripped in his hand would stay silent. Zach clutched the LMR tighter, sprinting past a decorative pond toward the glass doors.

As commander of a Charleston Air Force Base C-17 squadron, he kept that radio plastered to his side—his walkie-talkie "pipeline to the flight line." Since the radio was tailor-made, with frequencies acceptable even in a hospital, Zach never slipped out of range. He even slept with the thing. Not much of a life to offer someone else.

Nope, he didn't blame his ex in the least for walking. He did, however, resent like hell that she'd abandoned their children when she'd strolled off with her cooking instructor boyfriend.

Ruined Zach's lifelong penchant for brownies—and robbed his two daughters of their mother.

He swallowed a curse as the hospital doors swooshed open to release a blast of cool, antiseptic air. Normally, he didn't let Pam's leaving get to him. His father had shown him well how anger had a way of leveling everything it touched faster than a SCUD missile. Zach had too many people counting on him to indulge in a momentary vent that wouldn't accomplish anything constructive.

But as he entered the hospital to visit Julia Sinclair and her fatherless son, thoughts of children missing a parent just hit Zach damned wrong.

He flipped his wrist to check his watch. Seventeen minutes left and—

The radio crackled. "Wolf One, this is Command Post. Over."

Wolf One, radio code for the Squadron Commander, which meant trouble. He'd checked in with the control tower before leaving. While he couldn't be off-line, he'd requested non-emergency questions be directed to Wolf Two, his second in command.

Zach shifted his focus to work-mode and answered without breaking stride. No need to change course until he assessed the situation. "Wolf One here, go ahead, Command Post."

"Sir, this is Lieutenant Walker. I have a phone patch from Moose two-zero. Please initiate."

"Roger, Command Post. Break, break," he answered, chanting the lingo to change who he was speaking to as he rounded the reception desk. He mentally scanned the day's flight schedule. The mission flying under the call sign Moose two-zero would be—Captain Tanner "Bronco" Bennett's crew. A crew not scheduled to land until 0100 hours. The early call could only mean an in-flight problem. "Moose two-zero, this is Wolf One. Go ahead."

"Roger, Wolf One." The connection buzzed with interference from the plane's roaring engines. "This is Bronco. Moose two-zero is aborting the mission due to equipment malfunction. Nose gear's stuck in the Up position. We've tried everything, sir. We're currently holding ten miles east of the field while waiting for word on what to do next."

Damn. The day from hell had just plunged to a level lower than even old Dante could have penned. Zach twined around a couple carrying flowers, past the gift shop, toward the elevators. "Roger, Bronco. Put a call through to the aircraft's manufacturer for further input on options."

"Yes, sir. I'd like to do just that, but Command Post refused our request to speak with the technicians on-call at the manufacturer."

Disbelief slowed Zach's steps. "Say again."

"Command Post refuses to place the call."

Disbelief gave way to a slow burn. Zach stopped in front of the elevator, stabbing the Up button. "Break, break," he called to switch speakers. "Command Post, I assume you have a good reason for denying my man's perfectly reasonable request."

Bronco might be a new aircraft commander, but he had

solid air sense, a gifted set of flying hands and top-notch knowledge of the aircraft. And all that could only haul him through so far if he didn't have the proper ground support, support Zach would make sure became available.

No way in hell was he losing another crew on his watch. Never again would he tell a woman her husband wasn't coming home. Julia Sinclair's eyes full of restrained tears still haunted his waking as well as sleeping hours. "Well, Lieutenant?"

"Sir, Training Flight is already reading through the tech manuals to find a solution."

That burn simmered hotter, firing Zach's determination. Not that he would let it overheat. Once the shouting started, the battle was lost. "Let me get this straight. While my flyers are up there tooling around the skies with busted nose gear, you're telling them not to worry because you've got folks holding a study session with the instruction manual? Lieutenant, if my man Bronco says he's tried everything, then that's exactly what he's done. Time to look for answers outside our base."

"The Wing Commander says we're over budget. No unnecessary consultation calls. We can handle this one in-house."

Zach stepped into the elevator, ignoring the curious stares from an elderly couple wearing Proud Grandparent pins. "Now maybe I'm just slow on the uptake today, Lieutenant, but I have a question," he drawled, taking his sweet Texas time to let the quiet heat of his words steam through the radio waves. "Do you really think the Wing Commander meant that to save five thousand dollars on a consultation call we're gonna land a plane nose gear up and do half a million dollars worth of damage? Do you think that's what the Wing Commander meant about saving money?"

Silence crackled for three elevator dings. "Sir, I'm just repeating what Wolf Two said. He gave the order."

Frustration bubbled closer to the surface. He should have known his second in command was behind this, a narrow-minded, micro-managing ass who couldn't see the big picture if it swallowed him whole. All the more reason Zach couldn't relinquish control of his squadron for even a second.

"And this is Wolf One overriding that command," Zach enunciated softly, slowly. He would take the hit from the Wing Commander later without hesitation. "I assume full responsibility, *Lieutenant.* Place the call."

"Dialing now, sir."

Zach exhaled with the swoosh of the opening elevator doors. "Roger, Lieutenant. Expect me on the runway in—" He glanced at his watch as he plowed into the hall. "Forty minutes."

That would give him ten minutes with Julia Sinclair and still have him back at base well before they put that plane down. No need to leave now. There was nothing he could do on the runway until Bronco landed. Time management was everything in his job. He couldn't fritter away valuable minutes waiting around, because he would undoubtedly need them for some other emergency in the morning.

Seeing Julia wouldn't be any easier tomorrow anyway.

He checked the arrows directing him toward her room number and turned left. So much for finishing up early enough to enjoy a video and popcorn with his kids.

The crisis made for a fitting end to a hell of a day. A day that had started with a memorandum stating the Inspector General's intent to reopen the investigation into the fatal crash of one of Zach's crews eight months ago.

And now it was time to face Lance Sinclair's widow, a woman as much Zach's responsibility as any of his aviators. A woman who needed the one thing he could never give her back.

A father for her child.

* * *

Julia Sinclair had never hurt so much in her life. If she didn't get some help from the nursing support group soon, her breasts would explode.

Sitting on her hospital bed with a pillow in her lap, Julia jostled her son and tried to urge his face into the correct nursing position. At least, she thought it was right from everything she'd studied in childbirth classes.

Breastfeeding had seemed so easy, so natural—in theory. Hadn't women been doing this since the beginning of time? Apparently her son didn't know that. After twenty minutes of unproductive attempts, he'd fallen asleep.

Julia burrowed her hand under the baby blanket to tickle his toes. Patrick tucked his tiny knees into the swaddling and snoozed on.

"Headstrong little guy, aren't you?" Her watery laugh tripped over itself. Tears blurred the soothing birthing room decor of mauve and forest-green to pure gray.

She wanted this so damned much. Just a simple wish, to nurse her child, likely the only baby she would ever have.

One persistent tear eked free. Julia knuckled it aside with a determined swipe. "Stupid hormones."

It had to be the hormones, because crying wasn't her style. She sniffled, willing away the blue cloud threatening to rain tears on Patrick's special day. Her son deserved a happy welcome, not one full of mourning.

She would think of her husband later. In the darkened quiet of her own home, she would allow herself to imagine what this day could have been like with Lance beside her. A fleeting image of him whispered through anyway, so handsome and blond, wearing his flight suit and best playful grin.

At least she had his baby.

Julia skimmed a kiss along the white knit cap covering Patrick's head and snuggled him closer to her chest, his butter-soft cheek precious against her skin. She resolved to concentrate on blessings, and the baby in her arms was undoubtedly her greatest blessing.

A stubborn, non-nursing, snoozing blessing.

Two quick knocks sounded at the door, replacing her urge to cry with a welcome swell of relief. Julia readjusted her loosened pajama top over Patrick's head so she wouldn't be exposed to any hallway passersby, but didn't button it. Why bother when she would only have to unbutton it again in minutes? "Come in."

The door opened.

But not to Susan from the breastfeeding support group.

A tall, flight-suit-clad body filled the doorway. For a funky, time-fugue kind of moment, Julia thought her husband stood in front of her after all. Her breath snagged on an ache so powerful it stole the air from her room.

Eight months faded to a time of promise for a fresh start with a baby. That new beginning for her marriage had ended the day she'd pulled into her driveway after work to find every military wife's worst nightmare. An ominous, uniformed trio of chaplain, doctor and commander had waited on her front porch. She'd known before being told by the Squadron Commander.

Her husband would never come home.

The commander. Reality dispersed her dreams like bubbles hitching a ride on an afternoon breeze.

The superimposed image of Lance faded, Squadron Commander Zach Dawson easing into focus. His rangy body towered until his head just missed brushing the doorway.

How could she have mistaken the two men for even a second? The shorter Lance had been built more like a wrestler as opposed to the commander's lean runner's frame.

No, he wasn't Lance. But he was here and in her doorway for a visit. Time to piece together some composure and quit gawking at the man before she proved once again what a flop she was at being a reserved Air Force wife. No surprise, since she'd never fit the white-glove mold from day one. Those barefoot childhood years in the commune had left their indelible stamp on her.

"Hello, Colonel," she said, dropping the lieutenant part of his rank as protocol demanded in conversation, just another inexplicable quirk of military lingo. They may have developed a surprising friendship over the last few months, but even so, protocol stood.

He cleared his throat, but didn't move. The normally confident man hesitated. "Sorry. Didn't mean to interrupt the baby's, uh, eating."

A tingle of realization prickled at her scalp.

Uh-oh. Worse than barefoot, she'd forgotten she was also too darn close to being bare-breasted.

Heat crawled all the way from her toes straight up over her half-covered chest to her nose. Thank goodness Patrick's snoozing face covered as much as any bathing suit. "He's just sleeping, not eating, I mean not yet anyway."

The commander's gaze darted everywhere around the room—everywhere she wasn't. "I can come back later."

Julia stifled the urge to shout a resounding acceptance of his offer to hightail it to the nearest elevator. Women breastfed in public every day, after all. "Don't go. Just give me a second to..." Get dressed? Put away her breasts? "Just give me a second."

"Sure, no problem." He turned, his profile backlit by the fluorescent glow from the hall.

The hard angles of his face shadowed forbiddingly, another difference from Lance. Her husband had been light-hearted, easygoing—and so blasted good-looking some had labeled him downright pretty.

No one would ever dare call Zach Dawson pretty.

Rugged. Magnetic. Starkly attractive like the no-nonsense Texas desert he hailed from. But never pretty.

Julia jerked her gaze away. The poor guy would fall asleep standing in her doorway if she didn't stop daydreaming. She secured the last button and cradled Patrick in her arms. "All set. Sorry about that."

He pivoted on his boot heel toward her again. "No need to apologize or be embarrassed." A half smile tipped his craggy face as he circled around a discarded IV pole. "It hasn't been so long since Shelby and Ivy were that size nursing round the clock."

Great. Even Zach Dawson knew more about breastfeeding than she did.

Julia gave herself a mental shake. She refused to surrender to self-pity in front of him. Maybe the best way to ward off those weepy hormones might be to resort to the teasing that had become the hallmark of their relationship over the last few months. "Thanks. You're a doll to make me feel better."

"A doll?" One brow arched up into his coal-dark hairline.

This man was far from being anyone's kewpie doll, but it was fun wringing a smile from him. And she could use some fun today. "Absolutely. Hasn't anyone ever called you that before?"

He leaned back, one boot braced against the wall, his arms crossed over his chest. "I'm sure they've called me plenty of names around the squadron, but I feel downright confident Colonel Doll wasn't one of them."

"That's too bad. It's catchy, far more cuddly and approachable than Wolf One, don't you think?"

"Demoted from Colonel Doll to Colonel Cuddly?" A low chuckle rumbled free along with his mock wince. "Now that has a ring to it I'm sure the crewdogs will appreciate. But I think we can save those cute and cuddly labels for the little fella you're holding."

She relaxed into her pillows, grateful the awkwardness of her "flasher" moment had dissolved and the ease of their friendship had returned—a friendship no doubt born of obligation on his part.

He'd been so hell-bent on helping her lately. She felt like an ingrate for resenting him when he mowed her lawn. Changed a tire. Removed a squirrel from her chimney.

She'd done everything in her power to become strong and independent for her baby. She was proud of taking her woodworking to a new, professional level with her playhouse-manufacturing division in the company. It galled her to accept help that could well be a threat to her newfound independence.

And here Zach Dawson was again, fulfilling his obligation by visiting her. God, she hated being anyone's obligation.

Julia rubbed her wrist over the Band-Aid covering a tender IV puncture wound. "Colonel, please don't think I'm not grateful for your visit, but don't you have anything better to do on a Friday night than hang out with a lactating new mother?"

"Can't think of a single thing." His thumb sawed absently back and forth against the radio clutched in his hand.

"Surely you'd rather be back on base at the club with the guys." Her eyes narrowed as she realized he might well have very different plans. He was an attractive bachelor after all, probably not more than thirty-seven or thirty-eight. Of course she was only thirty-one, but felt closer to ninety-one some days. "Or out on a hot date."

All hints of a smile faded as he held up his radio. "Not unless she's willing to meet me on the flight line in an hour when the next plane lands."

Flight line. Planes. Fearless pilots.

Without warning, that blue cloud threatened a proverbial thunderstorm. She needed Zach Dawson to take his flight suit, military radio and all other reminders of the Air Force out of her room before she totally lost it.

The guy already carried that sense of obligation to the extreme. She didn't need to make it worse with a crying jag that would have him changing her oil by sunrise. "I appreciate your stopping by, but it's late and you probably want to finish up at the flight line in time to say good-night to your girls."

"I do need to head out soon. But before I forget, I have something for you from Ivy." He swung his boot up onto the chair and unzipped the thigh pocket. Zach tugged free a folded piece of paper. "Doc Bennett's call about your delivery came just before the kids left for school. Ivy drew this for you."

Julia tucked Patrick to her chest as she leaned to take the homemade card. Neon marker colors sketched out a rainbow over a playhouse with a little boy on the steps, a playhouse just like the one Julia had designed at work the month before. How like quiet Ivy to remember from a brief stop at Julia's office on their way to the mall.

Shopping trips with the Dawson girls had been a welcome distraction lately. And she'd soon discovered the only way Zach would let her pay him back for all his help was through his daughters.

"Thank you," she said, tracing a finger over the arch. That rainbow tugged at her. Peacemaker Ivy always plastered rainbows over everything, an endless task given the year those girls had weathered after their mother walked out. "You've got a great kid there, Colonel."

"Blind luck on my part, but yeah, she sure is." He smiled again. Lieutenant Colonel Dawson didn't smile often, but mention of his children reliably earned his lopsided grin.

"Tell Ivy the card will go in Patrick's baby book at home." Julia inched up in the bed, wincing at aches in more places than she could have predicted. "For now, I'm going to give it a center-stage spot with the other cards and flowers."

"No need to get up. You should take it easy while you can." He reached for the card. "Tell me where you want—"

Their fingers brushed.

Just the tips, not much of a touch, but it zipped a spark through her she'd never expected to feel again. She certainly hadn't expected to feel it thirteen hours after giving birth.

Surely the reaction was only a byproduct of an emotional day and the crazy intimacy of that moment when he'd opened the door. After eight lonely months, her body craved the comfort of human touch.

Except the spark searing her fingertips had very little to do with comfort.

She might want that comfort, even the spark too in about six weeks, but she didn't want all the baggage that came with it. She'd fought a draining battle to salvage something with Lance because she'd made a commitment to the marriage, only to lose him anyway.

Never again would she risk offering her bruised heart to any man but her son. Patrick needed a steady environment and a strong mother to thrive.

Julia snatched her hand away. The paper crackled in her tight grip. "I can do it. The doctor said it's good for me to walk."

She sneaked a look at the silent man in front of her and wondered if he'd noticed her momentary insanity. If so, that inscrutable expression of his probably covered horrified shock. Like he would actually go into testosterone meltdown over a puffy, post-partum woman in purple pajama shorts.

"Okay, then." He set his LMR on the bedside table and held out his hands, palms up. "At least let me take the little guy in case you're shaky."

Thoughts of sparks and comfort cooled. Her arms tightened instinctively around the bundled baby.

Zach waited, hands unwavering. "I haven't dropped one yet. Promise."

Julia pulled a small smile, but couldn't make herself let go. She wasn't ready. She didn't want to share Patrick.

Or face the inevitable questions.

For just a moment longer, she wanted this day to be as normal as possible. She'd endured enough consolations and platitudes the past eight months to fill the Atlantic. She couldn't stomach any more.

In spite of what others might think, she refused to see Patrick's birth as anything other than a blessing. How could anyone use a harsh word like *defect* in regards to her child? To her, he was perfect.

Which meant she needed to set an open, positive tone up front. She would show Patrick a world full of possibility, not limitations. Her son wouldn't be sheltered. Protected definitely, but never hidden away.

"Thanks, Colonel. Just be extra careful with his head." With hands a little shakier than she would have liked, Julia passed over the sleeping infant into Lieutenant Colonel Dawson's callused hands.

She made damn sure she didn't touch him in the process.

Swinging her legs from under the blanket, Julia kept her eyes trained on her toes and waited for the commander's reaction. Should she have simply told him? Maybe it wasn't fair to expect unconditional acceptance when he hadn't been prepared.

Why wouldn't he say something? Anything? Even question her?

She respected, trusted this man's integrity so much. If he didn't react with grace and composure, what could she expect from the rest of the world?

Her heart filled with a fierce protectiveness for her baby. Damn it, she would down a mountain lion for her kid.

Even take on one daunting "wolf" if need be.

Chin tipped defensively for battle, she looked up to find Zach's steady hands cradling her son against his shoulder.

Those hands palmed Patrick's back and head like a sea-soned veteran.

Maybe she would find the reassurance in his face as well as his hands. Letting her gaze travel farther, she sought Zach Dawson's brown eyes and found them...

Not staring at Patrick, but at Julia's bare legs.

Chapter 2

Zach couldn't drag his eyes off Julia Sinclair's legs propped atop the sterile white hospital blankets.

The allure of those legs blindsided him like a bogey from his six o'clock. Granted, they were mighty incredible. Likely the best he'd ever seen—long, slim, with just the right mix of toned muscle and soft curves.

Awesome legs he had no business checking out.

His gaze snapped up to her face—her very surprised face. And she didn't know the half of it. One hint of all the images churning through his head, and she would bash him over the head with a flower arrangement.

One hint that he was mired in an investigation of her husband, and she would do more than bash him over the head.

Zach looked away, studying the It's a Boy balloon bobbing beside a plastic pitcher as if it held a full flight plan inscribed on its blue surface. He didn't speak. Apologizing for his unguarded stare could only make the situation more awkward.

Julia eased to her feet, standing almost eye-level with him, a novelty for Zach as he usually developed a crick in his neck from leaning when he talked to a woman.

Or kissed a woman.

The bogey was damned persistent today.

Julia spiked her fingers through her short blond waves. A flicker of confusion shifted through her dewy green eyes before she turned from him. ''Ivy's card will look just right tucked between the roses from the Clarks and the plant from the squadron.''

Zach exhaled. ''They're…uh…nice.''

''All those flowers are wonderful for masking the hospital smell.'' She inched across the private recovery room, bracing a hand on a rolling tray for support. Leaning to place the card between a vase of yellow roses and a spidering fern, she rambled about who had sent each card and arrangement.

What the hell was he thinking letting his eyes wander right back to those legs the minute she wasn't looking? The woman had just given birth, for crying out loud. She was a widow of less than a year.

He should bash himself over the head.

The lack of sex must be cutting off oxygen to his brain. That and the whole awkward way he'd walked into the room messed with his control. Her glow of maternal beauty, the subtle curve of her breast had stopped him dead, stirring him more than any flagrant exposure.

He forced himself to turn away.

Zach secured the baby against his shoulder and walked to the window. The half-empty parking lot made for safer viewing anyway. ''See that clear sky, Patrick? It's a great night for flying.'' He patted the baby's back, speaking softly in his ear. ''Sun's going down, but that's okay. We're just about the only Air Force in the world that flies and trains at night. We like the protection, the stealth of a dark sky. Day or night, it's all the same in the cockpit thanks to our electronics.''

Lance Sinclair had died at night. His instruments had been in prime condition and still he'd hit a mountain.

Zach carefully pushed aside the thought, continuing to mumble about planes and flying, all the things Lance would have told his boy. "When you go to flight school, little fella, they're gonna try to talk you into one of those pretty fighters. But don't you listen. You want to fly the heavies. You want to fly with a crew. With guys to watch your back. Friends to share their cookies.''

The baby stirred against Zach's shoulder, one thin leg kicking free of the blanket. Julia stepped forward as if to grab her son back.

Zach shifted Patrick from his shoulder to the crook of his arm. "It's okay. I have him.''

He slid his finger along the tiny palm for the baby to grab hold and tried not to think about how the boy's father should be here.

Instead, the boy would only have a few medals and war stories as mementos of his dad. Zach owed it to this child to clear Lance's name so those stories were good ones. "Your daddy was a great guy, Patrick. Top-notch flyer. A friend to everyone. He always shared his time and his cookies.''

The baby blinked, staring up with that unfocused newborn gaze Zach recognized. Yeah, he remembered those first days with his girls, talking to them, walking the floors, repeatedly counting fingers and toes to check yet again that all was well—

Zach frowned.

He looked at Patrick again, closer. The parental alarm in his head went on red alert. He'd read every baby book on the shelves during both of Pam's pregnancies. Even now he had a book on troubled teens by his bed. He would be prepared for anything, know all the warning signs....

Like the flat facial profile beneath a white hospital cap. The excessive space between the front and second toe of the little foot kicking outside the blanket. The small skin folds around upward-slanted eyes peering back at him.

Already certain what he would find, Zach crooked his finger to open the small fist—and traced a single, deep crease across the center of the baby's palm.

All characteristics of—

"Down syndrome," Julia said softly, standing just beside him. "Patrick has Down syndrome."

Her words thundered in Zach's head as he studied the newborn staring so trustingly back up. His arms tightened protectively around this boy who would never fly planes, but would face battles far tougher than any Zach had seen.

He'd made it his mission to protect, defend, even put his life on the line for others when called upon. Yet now, when it mattered most, he had no idea what he could do.

But by God, he would do something.

He faced Julia. "What do you need?"

"Excuse me?"

"Tell me what you and Patrick need from the base, I'll make it happen. Medical benefits, family services, you name it. What red tape do you need slashed? Who should I lean on?"

Julia shook her head, wavy curls dancing above her solemn eyes. "There's nothing for you to do. I'm keyed in with a local group for EIS, early infant stimulation. We're fine with medical. He's blessedly healthy. Half of babies with Down syndrome are born with a heart defect, but not Patrick. We're very lucky."

She reached for her son.

Zach tucked Patrick closer. "Sounds like you've done your homework. When did you find out?"

Julia paused for a guilty second. "My second trimester."

"That long ago." The squadron patch on the sleeve of his flight suit seemed to burn a tattoo into his arm.

Anything. Anywhere. Anytime.

The stitched motto mocked him. He'd failed the Sinclair family on all three counts if Julia had felt she couldn't turn to him. "So you've had *months* to prepare."

"The alpha-feto protein test came back low in my fourth month. An amniocentesis confirmed it."

A shot of anger pierced his defenses. "You should have told me."

"So you could do what?" She forked her hand through her rumpled hair. "Rotate my tires? Clean leaves from my gutters at 6:00 a.m. again?"

What was wrong with wanting to help? "I could have placed some of those calls for you. Paved the way. Made things easier. Been there."

"There's nothing you could have done that I couldn't do for myself. He's *my* son, and I'm a single parent. I'm on my own with this one. Thank you for caring, but I'm not your obligation." Her hand fluttered toward his arm, then stopped just shy of touching him. Her hand drifted back to her side. "This is life, Colonel, and I intend to make sure Patrick has the best one any child could wish for."

"I'm sure you will."

"Damn straight." She met his gaze dead-on.

"I believe you."

"But you still want to rotate my tires."

The familiar playful glimmer in her eyes crackled over him with an unfamiliar intensity, like St. Elmo's Fire zipping through the cockpit. Dangerous. Exciting.

He wanted his perspective back. He flat-out didn't have time for hormonal insanity, especially with a woman who needed a helluva lot more than tire rotation.

"Stop it, Julia. I don't feel much like laughing right now. I'm…" Mad. Frustrated. In need of a wall to punch. "You should have told me."

She could insist all day long that he wasn't obligated, and it wouldn't change a thing. Regardless of why Lance

Sinclair's plane had gone down, Zach knew he would never stop feeling responsible. It had nothing to do with guilt and everything to do with duty. Honor.

That plane had smacked a mountain on his watch, which made Zach responsible for the family left behind.

Julia gently grasped Patrick's flailing foot. "I understand you don't feel like smiling, but you're going to do it for me anyway. Because I'm asking you, and you know that in spite of everything you've done for me, I've never actually asked you for anything."

His jaw clenched. "Julia—"

"Well, I'm asking now. I want Patrick to see flowers and smiles. I want him to hear laughter and songs, everything a baby deserves for a welcome." The playful glint faded altogether. "Can you do that for me? For Patrick."

He still didn't feel much like smiling, but she was right in thinking he would. Because she'd asked and those glistening green eyes had haunted his dreams.

Zach nodded, letting his face pull up in his one-sided grin.

"Thank you," she whispered, gifting him with a smile in return so damned sweet it twisted the knife in his gut a double rotation.

He wanted to pull her to him, and not because of any hormones, but because he somehow knew that in spite of all of her bravado, she needed to be held.

"Colonel?"

"Yeah, Julia?"

"I'll take him back now."

He gave her a brusque nod and waited for her to sit on the edge of the bed. He passed the baby with careful hands, reluctant to let the little guy go.

Zach was careful not to touch the little guy's mama.

A solid knock on the door punctured the silence, and he winged a prayer of gratitude for the interruption.

"Come in," Julia called with a voice huskier than it should have been.

The door swooshed open, admitting Doctor Kathleen Bennett, a flight surgeon from the base. Bennett made a sharp officer in her spit-polished combat boots and camouflage BDUs—maternity-sized.

Major Kathleen Bennett, the very pregnant wife of Captain Tanner Bennett, who was stranded in the air with busted nose gear.

Zach's eyes darted to the radio. He couldn't have requested a more effective dousing for the strange impulses that had gripped him since he'd walked in on Julia Sinclair nursing her son. This scenario held too much similarity to the one eight months ago. A pregnant military wife with a husband in the air in a potentially dangerous situation.

Not that he could tell Kathleen Bennett a thing now. No need to worry her when he would make damned sure that plane landed safely.

The radio cackled from beside the rolling bassinet. "Wolf One, Command Post. Over."

Zach snatched up the LMR before it blared info neither of these women needed to hear. "Wolf One, hold please. Over." He reached for the door. "That's my cue to leave. Bennett, you're heading home after this, right?" he asked, hoping he wouldn't have to use the information to contact her.

"This is my last stop on rounds, sir."

"Good." He nodded. "Julia, call me if you need anything. I mean it now. Anything."

"My tires are under warranty." Julia held up a hand before he could speak. "But thank you for offering. I'll let you know."

He flashed a thumbs-up and strode out the door. If only he could close the door as easily on the vision burned in his brain of Julia's mile-long legs and tear-filled eyes.

*   *   *

Julia watched the door hiss shut behind Zach. Sounds from the hall muted—the rattle of a medicine cart, a television blaring laughter.

The fading echo of his boots thudding on tile.

She'd imagined a kazillion times what his reaction would be when he found out about Patrick. Never had she imagined she would want him to hold her. She'd accepted the reality of those test results months ago and faced any grief over the trials her child would face.

So where had the urge to tuck herself against Zach's broad chest come from? It was a reckless urge that would only lead her into accepting more of his help.

Julia turned to Kathleen, her military doctor since flight surgeons treated flyers as well as their families. Kathleen wasn't an ob/gyn, but she had consulted through Julia's pregnancy. Beyond that, Kathleen had lent support, even standing in as a coach during the delivery.

Somehow that support seemed easier to accept when it didn't come packaged in a lanky, too-tempting lieutenant colonel's body. "Thanks for driving over. You really shouldn't have—but I'm glad you did."

"I had rounds anyway and couldn't resist sneaking another peek at this precious baby." Kathleen skimmed a knuckle along Patrick's cheek, her other hand resting on her belly. "Makes me impatient to see my own."

"Shouldn't you be home putting your feet up?"

"I can do that here just as easily." Kathleen lowered herself into a chair and swung her boots up onto another chair. "The house is too quiet anyway, and Tanner's not due to land for another few hours."

Julia understood all about quiet houses. The lonely silence grew every day. As a child, she'd longed for peace and privacy amid the chaos of her parents' commune. Now, she found that stillness strangling.

Kathleen grasped Julia's wrist to check her pulse. The

doctor frowned. "A bit fast. What did Colonel Dawson do?"

Julia tucked her hand under her hip to hide the racing pulse that betrayed her. "Excuse me?"

"What did he do when you finally told him? I assume that's why your pulse is elevated."

"Oh, uh, he insisted I should have said something sooner. You were right. He didn't like being left out of the loop. He was..."

"Pissed?"

"Not exactly. He doesn't get mad. Ever. But man, was his jaw tight. He doesn't seem to understand he's not responsible for Patrick and me." She forced herself to say, "It's not like I'm a military wife anymore."

"Stop right there." Kathleen straightened, her eyes sparking with her legendary redhead's temper. "Regulations state you're an Air Force dependant until you remarry. Even after that, you're still one of us for life."

Their husbands had been more than just part of the same squadron. They had often crewed together until a couple of months before Lance's plane had crashed. While Julia grieved over the other crew members who had died as well, she thanked God none of them had had wives and children. Especially not a pregnant wife.

"It's just.... Sometimes I feel as though if I see another flight suit, I'm going to scream." Julia pulled her hand from under her hip and held it up to stop Kathleen from interrupting. "I know! Cutting off the Air Force isn't going to help me get over losing Lance, but I need a break from it all."

The temper doused from Kathleen's eyes. "Do you want me to leave?"

"No! No." Julia waved for her to stay seated. "I must sound like an ungrateful brat."

"Not at all. Just a woman who's been through a hell of a year." Kathleen rubbed a hand over her stomach absently, all five months of pregnancy very apparent on her petite frame. "How do you feel? Honestly."

"Like my breasts are going to explode if this kid doesn't eat soon. And if he doesn't feed within a couple of hours, they're going to give him another tube feeding."

She'd read all the literature on breastfeeding a baby with Down syndrome, how his larger tongue in relation to mouth size, weaker sucking reflex and muscle tone could make breastfeeding a challenge. But somehow, she'd hoped that wouldn't apply to her.

Kathleen pushed to her feet. "That, I can take care of. I'll hustle up some help at the nurses' station, and I won't leave until we have this fella settled."

An inelegant snort of laughter tripped free, and Julia hugged her stubborn little non-nurser closer. "How late did you say Tanner would be out?"

"He's not scheduled to land until one, but don't worry. I bet I beat him home." Kathleen tugged open the door. "I'll be right back with the cavalry."

"Thanks," Julia called to the closing door.

She relaxed into her pillows. How many nights had she waited up for Lance? How many nights had she spent worrying? Somalia. Afghanistan. And then Sentavo. She'd rejoiced when his short leave time from the conflict had lengthened into a surprise rotation out of combat. How ironic. All those months with the war, she'd waited and feared, only to lose him in a routine peacetime mission.

Anything. Anywhere. Anytime. Like the motto of his C-17 squadron, her husband had promised he would always be there for her.

Julia thought of Zach Dawson's demand that she call him if she needed anything. A tempting offer from an intriguing man, no doubt.

But she'd learned the hard way it was safer not to depend on anyone for anything ever again.

* * *

Zach pulled into the driveway of his brick base house. Two in the morning. The longest Friday had slipped into Saturday.

The day Julia would bring home her son.

Shoving aside thoughts of her, Zach turned off the engine. She'd made it clear she didn't want his help.

He might not have given her what she needed, but at least he'd made it through the day with everyone alive. The in-flight call to the manufacturer had netted results. Landing gear restored, Moose two-zero had skimmed to the ground flawlessly.

Radio in hand, Zach shut his truck door quietly so as not to disturb his sleeping neighbors. A muggy fall breeze whispered through the pines, the only sound on the deserted road. He glanced across the street at the ranch-style base house where the Bennetts lived. Bronco's car was already parked in the driveway behind his wife's.

Zach nudged a scooter aside with his boot. Heaven help him when the quick-tempered flight surgeon discovered he'd held back information about her husband's in-flight emergency. She would demand a pound of flesh at Zach's next physical.

Not that he would have handled it any differently.

Walking through the carport, Zach wove around his motorcycle. His hand trailed along the seat of his vintage Harley Electra Glide. "Been a long time, huh, girl? I haven't forgotten about you though."

If he timed his day right, he could give the bike a tune-up while Ivy was at ballet, Shelby at her band retreat. Time alone was a rarity for any single parent.

As Julia Sinclair would soon discover.

What kind of day would she face when she brought her son home to an empty house?

It's not your problem. Hadn't the lady said as much? Let it go and enjoy the weekend.

Zach traced the lettering on the bike's gas tank.

Wildcatter. A holdover from the days when he'd followed his dad around the oil rigs to earn money for college.

The name had stuck once he'd entered Texas A & M, later becoming his original Air Force call sign back in simpler times when he could fly his plane and come home to his family at a reasonable hour. Before he'd been given the new name with his new job.

Not that he would change. His job was…not just a job. It was a calling he couldn't ignore if he tried. Even to save his marriage.

Zach patted the leather seat a final time before pivoting away. He unlocked the side door—and almost stumbled back outside. The house reeked of burnt cheese.

"What the hell?" Zach sprinted into the cramped kitchen to find the inside of the microwave looked like a nuclear slime experiment. Tension easing somewhat from his shoulders, he placed the radio on the counter and grabbed a rag.

"Hey, Colonel," Shelby shouted from the family room. "You busted curfew. I'm gonna have to take away your phone privileges for a week. And then there's your language…"

"I'll be glad to get rid of the phones anytime, Shel. Just say the word." He slammed the microwave shut.

Scrubbing a hand across his left cheek, he worked to waken the groggy muscles that had never completely rejuvenated since the battering his face had taken in Iraq. He carried a crooked smile as a reminder of the benefits of controlling his emotions. As if he could forget.

Zach crossed to the family room and leaned against the doorframe. His sixteen-year-old daughter sprawled on the sectional sofa watching MTV with her golden retriever, Aggie. As usual, Shelby wore a cropped shirt and low-slung jeans to showcase her belly-button ring.

If ever Zach had wanted to lose his temper, it had been over that piercing. Julia had told him to be grateful Shelby hadn't dyed her black hair purple. Or pierced her eyebrow, her lip or heaven forbid, her tongue. "Thanks for watching Ivy. Everything go okay?"

"Germany called."

Germany. So Pam was in Germany now. Shelby never referred to her mother by name, just by her latest port of call. "Any message?"

"Nope."

Pam and her chef husband had signed on for a Tour-Europe cooking course eight months ago. To her daughter, Pam changed names like a Rand McNally road-trip. Sometimes she took the time to call her kids and let them know where she'd relocated. Other times a food product landed on their doorstep with a foreign shipping label.

Over the months, his daughters' mother had become depersonalized to nothing more than a country. And of course, food.

France. Brie.

Switzerland. Chocolates.

Zach watched Shelby hack away with a paring knife at the latest priority postage offering.

Germany. Sausage.

Shelby pitched a chunk to Aggie.

Zach glanced over at the TV. The multi-pierced performers confirmed Julia's observations of worse scenarios. His gaze fell to the videotape poking half out of the VCR in the entertainment center. "Sorry about missing the movie."

"Like I care. It was just some lame kiddie ballet thing for Ivy. I didn't expect you to actually show."

"Shel, not tonight."

She flipped another piece of sausage to the dog, not even bothering to look at her father. "Our little optimist thought you'd make it home right up to the minute you called. Of course, she still thinks Germany will come home for her birthday."

Aggie caught the next bite before it hit the rug.

Thanks to Pam, Aggie was the best-fed dog in all of South Carolina. Aggie grew fat while Shelby grew bitter.

"Shel, I know this is a tough—"

The teen rolled off the sofa and to her feet. "As much as I'm enjoying our delayed family hour, I think I'll go to bed. Don't worry about carting me to band camp tomorrow. John's gonna pick me up."

"Okay," Zach agreed since it wouldn't do any good to say he'd actually looked forward to the time with her.

"Sorry the kitchen's a mess. Ivy exploded the cheese in the microwave," Shelby said over her shoulder, leading her dog by the collar as she walked toward her room. "No big loss though. Brie really sucks on nachos."

It wasn't that hot on grilled cheese either, but he'd choked down one of those sandwiches because Ivy had wanted him to. His youngest daughter seemed to think if they ate all that food, her mother would somehow be with them. God help him when Pam got to Greece because he hated olives.

He hated what was happening to his kids even more.

"'Night, Shel."

She shut her door without answering. Not even a slightly surly "'Night, Colonel." Just the sound of her fish tank gurgling. The guinea pig churning its wheel.

Zach walked toward Ivy's half-open door, his footsteps echoing along the hardwood floors. Eight-year-old Ivy slept curled on her daybed. Pink ballet shoes dangled from the iron bedpost. Such little shoes.

An image of other small feet kicking free from a baby blanket tugged him. His kids had problems, sure, but they were healthy. He needed to remember that at times like these.

Stopping outside his own bedroom, Zach hooked a hand overhead on the doorframe. His empty bed swallowed the room.

Those first weeks he and Pam had brought their babies

home from the hospital had been hectic—and the best part of his marriage. He and Pam would lie side by side, baby between them. For hours, they would stare at the miracle they'd made together.

Suddenly the image of Julia Sinclair dropped itself smack into his unmade bed, those long legs tangled in his rumpled plaid comforter. Julia, gifting Patrick with all those smiles.

Sharing a few with Zach.

Damn. Definitely deadly testosterone build-up messing with his mind.

Zach turned his back on the image, opting for his trashed kitchen instead. He pitched the sausage in the garbage and pulled a block of frozen hamburger out of the freezer. Domino's pizza and chili had become his best line of defense against Pam's postal packages.

At least Friday was over. He would toss together a Crock-Pot of chili for the weekend. Spend some time with his kids, then his bike. Julia didn't want his help, and he sure as hell didn't have the extra time.

That didn't mean he could stop himself from giving it now any more than he'd been able to the past eight months.

Zach stared through the kitchen window at his Harley and knew it wouldn't be getting the tune-up after all. No way could he let Julia bring her son home to an empty house.

Chapter 3

Julia glanced in her car visor mirror for the fiftieth time to check Patrick in back. Not that she could actually see him in his rear-facing infant seat. But every now and again, a spindly arm or leg flailed reassurance.

A Mickey Mouse diaper bag perched beside her where once a portfolio full of architectural designs for her playhouses would have rested.

The bag looked good there.

Cars whipped past on the bridge out to her barrier island bungalow. The hospital had demanded she sign a waiver before releasing her without someone to drive her home. Somehow it had been important to do this herself.

Of course Kathleen would be blazing mad when she received the message that Julia had left alone. Any number of people would have driven her.

Like a certain tall, dark and studly Lieutenant Colonel Dawson.

Julia shoved an image of his broad shoulders right out of her mind and turned down the narrow street into her beach subdivision. Clapboard houses on stilts lined both sides of the streets. Older homes of Charleston natives claimed the waterfront property. Newer homes made to look like the old sprawled into the rest of the housing development where Julia lived.

Rounding a corner, she tapped the brakes, freshly painted toenails sparkling from her sandals. Seeing her toes again proved a real treat. Her glitter-specked rosy pedicure shone with a touch of femininity she needed after months of bloated pregnancy. She'd packed polish in her hospital bag with just that in mind. Except the simple pampering ritual had brought a greater resurgence of femininity than she'd expected.

Surely not because of Zach's hungry stare at her legs.

Her toes glistened a mocking contradiction she didn't want. There'd been a certain comfort in the numbness that had followed her initial grief. Perhaps she wasn't ready to wake up.

Too bad a six-foot-four testosterone-oozing alarm clock sat waiting on her porch.

Julia inched down the street. She shouldn't be surprised to see Zach Dawson there. No doubt he had called the hospital to check on her and they'd caved to his request for information in spite of regulations.

The man was persistent. Countless times over the past eight months she'd come home to find Zach in her yard tackling some fix-it project. The guy couldn't seem to get it through his head that she knew how to wield a hammer with the best of them. And, of course, there was the first time she'd come home to find him on her porch eight months ago—

Julia sliced off that depressing thought.

She slid her car into the driveway beside his red truck. Zach stood, slowly unfolding himself until he towered beneath her shaded porch. Yeah, his jeans and T-shirt rather than a flight suit made it easy to forget that other visit.

Dangerously easy.

"Hi, Colonel," she said as she stepped from her car, using his title as a reminder for distance.

He balanced his radio on the banister. Another reminder of his job. Did the man ever go anywhere without that thing?

Julia spun away, her achy legs protesting the fast move. More careful of her tender body, she unbuckled the car seat with her now-sleeping son inside. She couldn't resist pressing a kiss to the tiny sock-clad foot.

"Welcome home, sweetie." Lifting out the seat, Julia called over her shoulder, "Where are the girls?"

"Ballet and band. I figured you didn't need them climbing all over you just yet. We'll save their visit for when you're settled." He stopped beside her, taking the infant seat.

No choice but to face him, she straightened. "I guess I would be wasting my breath telling you this isn't necessary."

"Smart woman. Unlock the front door and I'll unload the flower shop in your back seat."

She smiled her thanks and followed his commander-like order since it would be childish to argue anyway.

Fitting the key in the front door, her hands began to tremble. She shoved the door wide, but her feet stayed planted on the porch. She wasn't ready to step inside her empty house. Not yet.

"Uh, Colonel, everything can go in the hall." For once grateful he wouldn't even consider letting her help, she sagged into a wooden porch rocker. "Patrick and I will sit here and enjoy the breeze."

"Perfect." Zach placed the car seat beside her before loping down the steps to the car.

"How did Ivy's ballet auditions go?"

"Graduated a level." He hefted out her suitcase.

"She made it up on pointe?"

"You mean all that torturing her toes stuff?" His cowboy boots thudded up the steps. "Yeah."

"Good for her!" Julia cheered, taking refuge in their safe territory of familiar discussions about his girls. She did not need to think about all that lanky appeal encased in soft, faded denim. Her hand draped over the armrest to rock Patrick's car seat while Zach carried load after load of roses, carnations and daisies. "How's Shelby?"

"Don't ask." He battled a bouquet of balloons from her passenger seat.

"That good, huh?"

"You got it." A salty breeze gusted off the ocean, dragging the balloons behind him as he took the steps in two strides. He looped the dangling ribbons around a post into a slip knot and tucked his hands in his back pockets.

Nothing left in her trunk, no safe territory remaining to explore, Julia's gaze skittered from the gaping door of her empty house, back to the too-intriguing man on her porch. "Uh, do you want to sit for a minute? Patrick should sleep for at least another hour."

"You need to rest."

"I can rest in the rocker."

He checked his watch. "Sure. I have another few minutes before I have to pick up Ivy."

Zach hitched up onto the porch rail across from her. Palmetto trees rustled in the silence, a barge horn blaring in the distance.

He jerked a thumb toward the casserole dish on the top step. "I brought chili. Light on the spices since you're— uh—nursing."

"Oh. Thanks." Heat tingled up her face, an answering tingle settling in her breasts as she even thought of nursing. Of Zach seeing her. Let-down reflex, of course. Nothing more, she reassured herself. "You didn't have to, but we'll be gracious receivers. Patrick and I can't very well live off my one claim to culinary fame. Slice-'n'-bake cookies."

"Last I heard," Zach said, his drawl twining around her like the warm fall breeze, "gourmet cooking skills weren't on St. Peter's list of mandatory requirements for passing through the pearly gates."

"Good thing."

Twenty-four hours ago, they would have shared a laugh and now she couldn't even meet his eyes. She missed the comfort of their unlikely friendship. Needing the precious reassurance of her baby in her arms more than ever, Julia bent to unbuckle Patrick.

Baby nestled on her shoulder, she kicked off her sandals, her head lolling back to rest. She propped her feet on the bottom brace of her porch rail and rocked, arching and flexing her bare feet.

Zach's gaze fell to her legs, then her feet, lingering on her painted toenails.

Uh-oh.

Before she could blink, he reached, grabbed the porch eave and hefted himself up. Swinging a leg onto the roof, he disappeared overhead. Heavy footsteps thudded from above.

"Colonel?"

Had she imagined his momentary glance due to leftover wishful musings from her midnight pedicure? Julia stood as quickly as her aching body would allow and padded barefoot down the four steps into her yard so she could look up at him. "What are you doing?"

"Last week's storm tore up your trees."

Shading her eyes, she watched him stomp across the roof punting branches to the ground. "Please be careful. I don't have the energy to cart you to the ER."

"Not a chance. Walking around up here's nothing. I was scaling oil rigs while other kids were climbing monkey bars. Kinda like flyin' without the plane if you swing out just right."

She couldn't miss the edge of excitement in his voice as

it rumbled out over her yard, or how at home he looked that much closer to the sky even now.

He scooped a handful of leaves out of her gutters and sent them fluttering to the ground. "I'll head back over later and clear out the rest of these."

"Do you ever sit still for more than two minutes, Colonel?"

"Nope. Waste of time. Call me Zach."

"Relaxing's never a waste of time, Colo— What did you say?"

"Call me Zach."

Standing on her roof, feet braced, sun at his back he'd never looked less like a Zach and more like a commander. He towered, inky-black hair as dark as the shadow he cast across her slate roof. His frown equally as dark. The whole image so fascinating she would call him the Easter Bunny if he asked.

Julia snuggled her son closer as a reminder for safer thoughts. As much as she might be tempted to toss caution off like a pair of sandals, she wouldn't let herself fantasize about gazing out on the world from the roof with Zach.

Zach.

She shivered at the intimacy implied by the name. An intimacy she had no intention of exploring.

Zach stared down from the roof at Julia below him and thanked heaven for his sure-footed instincts gained from years of climbing oil rigs.

She looked so damned beautiful. Sun glistened off her wheat-colored curls. Her flowing dress—made out of that scrunchy fabric—swirled around her, twisted and molded to her mile-long legs.

Except she wouldn't be exchanging pleasantries with him if she knew what topped his schedule Monday morning when he began an extensive review of her husband's flight history.

Julia shifted under his scrutiny, her bare feet tracing a restless dance in the grass. God, he would far rather stare at her than think about what he had to do. Those surprisingly sexy painted toes had sent him vaulting off the porch before he fell into a repeat gape of the night before.

What color polish did she wear? He hadn't allowed himself the indulgence of finding out. Now he couldn't tell for certain from such a distance and for some reason he had to know.

Zach scaled to the ground, landing beside her. Overgrown lawn masked her toes. Damn. "You said back at the hospital you aren't my obligation. Fine. So forget I was your husband's boss. I'm your friend helping out which means you can stop calling me Colonel and start calling me Zach."

"Okay."

He waited. Where had the whole name request come from in the first place? Strange, but he hadn't thought much about the fact that not many people used his given name anymore. As he had climbed the ranks, his circle of familiars narrowed. And then with the divorce…

He wanted to hear his name. From Julia.

She shuffled, scratching her toes over the top of her other foot. Pink. The polish was pink. Soft, pretty pink—with those damned alluring sparkles. A lot like her.

"Well, Julia?"

"Thank you for the chili and the welcome-home smile…Zach."

His name whispered from her mouth and right through him.

Ah, damn.

What the hell had he done? Drawn a dumb-ass line in the sand that she'd stepped right over. And now there was no going back.

Julia stared at Zach, his name still warm on her tongue and swirling in her mind. Patrick stirred against her shoulder, reminding Julia of her priorities. Flirting factored way down on the list.

Determined to climb those steps, Julia secured her hold on her baby and herself. If only she could jump straight from the porch into Patrick's farm-theme nursery, the only room in the house that didn't carry memories of living there with Lance.

Zach's steady bootsteps followed. His shadow lengthened over her as she crossed into her living room.

For about ninety seconds, she thought everything would be fine. The familiarity of her home embraced her. Two overstuffed sofas in slate-blues and buttercup-yellows bracketed the fireplace. Frothy sheers allowed light to filter through and caress the honey-warm tones of oak furniture, some things her own work, such as a miniature playhouse under the window. Other pieces lovingly chosen flea-market finds, like the pie safe.

With her wedding picture on top.

In full-dress uniform, Lance smiled out of the crystal frame.

Her stomach gnawed on itself like the grinding tug of a saw chewing at a piece of hardwood. She was truly alone. Alone to bring up a precious child totally dependent on her for so much more than most children.

The awesome responsibility washed over her—along with a surprise surge of anger at her husband.

If only Lance hadn't convinced her to forgive him for doing the unforgivable, then died before she could finish reconciling her feelings. She had managed to accept that he'd had an affair. She hadn't, however, been granted time to find a way to forgive him for loving the other woman. The kind of woman he should have married.

Knowing her feelings were unreasonable didn't stop her from shifting some of that pent-up anger at Zach. How could he tempt her with thoughts of what it would be like to share responsibilities with someone again? To trust someone again—even if only with friendship?

She didn't dare think about the desire to touch him in a way that had nothing to do with friendship.

"Zach," she said his name, trying to ignore the thrill of it tripping off her tongue. "Please don't take this the wrong way, because I do think of you as a friend. One who's become too important. You have to go. We'll work something out later for the girls to see the baby like I promised, but you have to stop coming here."

"Damn it, Julia," he sighed with uncharacteristic impatience. "You can't do everything alone."

"I'm not." Already, his stoic face tugged at her. "My parents are coming for a couple of weeks. My friend Lori's flying in for another."

She scrambled for a persuasive reason to give him for why she would accept help from others, but not him. Her eyes landed on Lance's picture, providing her with an excuse not far from the truth. "It hurts too much having you around. Even without the flight suit or rank, there's no mistaking who you are. You're the Colonel. You carry yourself with the bearing of an Air Force officer. You walk with the confidence—hell the cockiness—of a jet jock, and I can't take the reminders right now."

Waiting for him to speak, she wondered if he might scavenge an argument that could sway her. Did she want him to? "It's not you. It's what you represent that I can't be around."

He took a barely discernable step back. But from a man who shared little of his feelings the gesture relayed bucketsful of how she'd rattled him. Forcing him out of her life hurt more than she expected.

Zach began shaking his head, and Julia braced herself for an argument from a man who could convince troops to follow him into hell.

His cell phone chirped in his back pocket.

As if in response, the military radio blared from the porch through the open door.

For once, Zach didn't bolt to answer.

"Shouldn't you—"

"That's why they make caller ID," he assured her, maybe trying to assure himself as well. He cricked his neck to the side until his shoulders lowered. "All right. I have to respect your decision, but you have to respect where I'm coming from too. You've been there for my girls, and I want to be there for this little guy. There's no shame in a new mother asking for help."

Zach smoothed a hand along Patrick's back. His hand continued up to palm her cheek. "Just know you can call me. Anytime. Anywhere. For anything."

She squeezed her eyes shut. Why did he have to pick now to use those words?

With her eyes closed, her senses heightened, betraying her resolve. Zach's callused skin against her cheek reminded her of unsanded oak, rough, natural. Strong.

Just as she weakened, ready to tip her face into the sheltering heat, into the power and strength of his touch, his hand fell away.

The heat lingered.

Her eyes drifted open. He reached for his phone as he turned to the door, military bearing ingrained in his stride.

Once the door clicked behind him, she allowed herself to move. To breathe.

Swaying from side to side to soothe her baby and perhaps steal a little of that comfort for herself, Julia listened to Zach's truck growl out of her driveway. A part of her grieved over ordering him to leave. Another part of her realized that grief and separation would be short-lived.

"Well, Patrick," she whispered in his tiny shell ear. "I may not have known he climbed oil rigs as a kid. But I've learned more than a little about Zach Dawson during the past eight months."

As good as the man was at giving orders, he could be really rotten at following them.

"That's an order, Lieutenant," Zach barked over the headset to the copilot, his hand steady as he flew the C-17, in spite of his irritation.

Not anger, he reassured himself. Just irritation. Six weeks worth of pent-up *irritation* building since he'd left Julia's house.

Miles of ocean and sky stretched in front of his windscreen as he piloted the plane back from a two-week training deployment to Guam. He needed to get home to his kids before the sitter lost her mind—and to check on Julia before his head exploded from frustration over her self-imposed exile. "Do you copy, Renshaw? Over."

"Roger, Colonel," answered First Lieutenant Darcy "Wren" Renshaw, the newest addition to his squadron, currently sitting beside him in the cockpit. "But I can pull another hour in the co's seat, no problem."

"I'm sure you can, Renshaw, but you don't have to. An eighteen-hour mission makes for plenty of flight time to go around." His hand tightened around the stick. No yoke steering for the C-17 Globemaster III. The mammoth cargo aircraft possessed the same stick and grace as the A-10 he used to fly. "Head on back to the bunk and sleep. Bronco will relieve you."

Captain Tanner "Bronco" Bennett piped onto the headset from the seat behind Renshaw. "Hey, Wren, quit grousing and take your turn in the rack so I can have mine next. I'm an old expectant father and I need my beauty sleep."

Renshaw snorted. "I don't think this mission's long enough to help you on that one, Bronco."

"Ouch! Mortal blow to the ego!"

"Yeah, yeah, my heart bleeds for you." She unbuckled and stood. "All yours, Bronco."

Zach waited until Renshaw disappeared through the

bulkhead and Bronco strapped his linebacker-sized body into the copilot's seat before pushing the private interphone button. "How's Wren doing?"

"Good, Colonel. Real good. Makes my job as aircraft commander a cakewalk. She's a damn fine copilot, fits right in with the rest of the crewdogs. If anything, she tries too hard. Probably feels the need to live up to that impressive Air Force pedigree of hers."

"Could be."

Renshaw's father had called to check on his "little girl" just last week, tossing those general's stars around to make sure his baby was being careful in Guam. Zach cared more about his people than stars. Renshaw didn't need cosseting. She deserved the chance to prove herself and advance her career.

Julia's voice echoed in his mind with her insistence she didn't need his help.

Zach shrugged off the thought. Different matter altogether. "Glad to hear she's working out."

Settling into the comfort of routine and silence broken only by the occasional radio call buzzing over the headset, Zach flew. Just flew. Nothing like it—him, his plane and miles of sky.

Flying across the Pacific provided an extra thrill of isolation. With Atlantic flights, a landing site could always be found within two hours. Other planes crowded the Atlantic airways. Not so over the broader Pacific. The wide expanse of ocean offered complete freedom from the rest of the world.

Zach inched the stick left, nipping the plane closer to the clouds flicking past. Tighter, he slipped alongside a cloud.

Hugging a cloud allowed him to gauge visually how fast he flew, optimizing the awesome effect of hurtling through the sky. One of his favorite flying games.

God, he loved his plane. Not many people had a hundred-and-twenty-five-million-dollar toy to take for a spin, complete with all the latest bells and whistles. He'd come a long way from his teenage years scavenging rides off anything with wings to log flight hours. Gliders. Crop dusters. Even hiring out to make runs for the local coroner.

Anything to touch the clouds.

Closer. Closer. Closer he inched until his wingtip disappeared into the nimbus.

"Colonel." Bronco's voice slid through the headset and Zach's concentration. "Could we switch back to private interphone?"

Commander instincts overriding, Zach nodded, tapping the button on his stick. "Done. Speak to me, Bronco."

"I received a call this week from an accident review board."

Zach forced his grip to stay loose on the stick. "And?"

"When did they re-open the investigation into Lance's crash?"

"About six weeks ago." Six weeks and three days ago, to be exact. Patrick Sinclair's birthday. "What did they want to know?"

"His state of mind at the time of the crash. His performance during the months leading up to the crash. All sorts of questions I sure as hell never wanted tossed my way. We scheduled a time to talk when I get back." Bronco shifted in his seat, his restlessness impossible to miss in the confined cockpit. "Sir, what am I supposed to say?"

Zach kept his eyes trained forward. "The truth."

"That he was one of the best pilots I've ever flown with, but yeah, his concentration was shaky? That his marriage was on the rocks, so maybe he wasn't up to speed?"

Zach's fingers clenched around the stick. At least the plane didn't bobble. All the same, he had to rein himself in. He'd never been one for emotional displays. A waste of time.

Relaxing's never a waste of time, Colonel.

Julia's voice drifted through his mind like one of those whispery clouds keeping pace alongside.

Tucking the plane's nose, Zach dipped below the clouds and abandoned games. He would leave emotional displays and front-porch relaxing to free spirits like Julia. He understood what he needed to do to keep his life in order. "If that's the way it happened with Lance, then that's what you tell them."

"Even at half speed, Lance could fly circles around most of the squadron. Except I know how those boards work and they won't hear that part."

Hell, Julia wouldn't want *him* hearing the part about her shaky marriage. But it was his job and as Pam would have bitterly reminded him, he always did his job. "What part *will* they want to hear?"

"That his wife was considering walking because he'd been seeing someone else. No way in hell do I condone the mess Lance made out of his personal life, but in the air…I know in my gut that crash wasn't his fault."

Zach's gut agreed with Bronco's.

At least he thought it did. Doubts didn't come often to Zach, but he couldn't help questioning his objectivity on this one because of his attraction to a sexy pair of legs, sparkling toenails—and winsome green eyes.

"Well, Colonel? What should I say?"

The pilot in him wanted to advise Bronco to blow off the board. The commander in him knew he couldn't.

And what about the man within him? He wanted to hang Lance Sinclair out to dry for hurting Julia. For giving her all the more reason to shut out reminders of the Air Force.

As always, the commander finished in first place. "Answer their questions. You don't have to hand them Lance on a silver platter, but give them what they ask for."

Bronco's exhale echoed. "Yes, sir."

The ping of a TACAN navigational aid locking in dragged Zach's focus back to work, where he intended to keep it until he landed. Only two hundred miles to the California coast.

In the homestretch, he would see Charleston again within six hours. Zach changed radio frequencies until he had California's Travis Air Force Base Command Post on the line. "Reach one-two-two here, requesting landing weather for 2300 Zulu time at Charleston Air Force Base."

"Roger that, Reach one-two-two." Low static buzzed until the voice returned. "Charleston weather for 2300 Zulu. Ceiling, one hundred feet. Visibility, a quarter mile. Thunderstorms in the area for at least five hours."

Thunderstorms. The homestretch lengthened. He wouldn't see home today. Or Julia.

His hand itched on the stick, trying to convince him to press on. He'd managed to fly through worse in battle conditions.

Too bad he recognized the itch well. It originated from the deadly disease flyers called get-home-itis. It made pilots do stupid things, like fly through mud-soup thunderstorms just to hug a wife or kid goodnight.

His girls couldn't afford to lose another parent.

"Roger, Travis. I'm gonna need a phone patch to Charleston AFB Command Post." He recited his home phone number to the Charleston controller and waited for the connection to complete. A sampling of his chaotic home life would be broadcast over the airwaves for anyone from the Pacific across the whole United States on the same frequency to hear.

Charleston Command Post responded, "Reach one-two-two, party's on the line. Initiate phone patch."

Zach depressed the button. "Break. Break. Colonel Dawson here."

"Hello, Colonel," his daughters' sitter, Mrs. Middleton, answered. "The girls are fine. Ivy's already planned a special meal for you. We're cooking some of the rigatoni that came in yesterday's mail."

Rigatoni. Italy. Pam. Great.

"There's a problem with weather, and I won't make it in tonight after all."

"Oh, Colonel, I'm sorry, but that just won't work. My daughter-in-law's being induced in the morning. I'm catching the red-eye flight out tonight. You'll have to find other arrangements."

Frustration kicked into overdrive. The finality of her tone left him with no doubts. She would pull out of that driveway even if it meant leaving his children alone.

"I'll come up with something, Mrs. Middleton. Just don't leave until I call you back." He switched buttons. "Command Post, Reach one-two-two terminating phone patch."

Bronco drummed his fingers on the control panel. "Kathleen's TDY to Shaw AFB and won't be driving home from Sumter until tomorrow afternoon or she'd help."

"I know." Zach clicked through his dwindling options, not a lengthy task. He shied away from asking other members of his squadron or their wives as it could sound too much like an order. A coercion of sorts. And he didn't want his daughters facing a stranger at the door.

Without question, the best answer for his kids would be to call Julia.

Except what about Julia's wishes for distance? Didn't she have an overloaded plate of her own?

She would be the first to say his children's safety took priority. He would have to ask her.

Even thinking of hearing her voice jolted through him with too much excitement. An excitement he couldn't afford.

He stunk at long-term relationships. Julia wasn't the fling sort. Even if he could somehow convince himself to try something more substantial, a doubtful prospect, they weren't suited. Her free-spirited personality would wither

under his more somber outlook. Together, they would be
an emotional crash in the making.

Besides, he couldn't risk subjecting his kids to more turmoil.

"Command Post, initiate a second phone patch. This one
to Julia Sinclair." Again, he recited the number from memory, eliciting a pair of raised eyebrows from Bronco.

"Yes, sir," Charleston Command Post answered.
Crackle. Crackle. "Party's on the line. Initiate phone
patch."

He pressed the button and spoke to Julia with the whole
world listening in. "Break. Break. Colonel Dawson here."

"Zach, is something wrong?"

Zach. His name echoed over the headset with a husky
sensuality that could stir a man into a damned lethal case
of get-home-itis.

And apparently he wasn't the only one who noticed.

All background chitchat on the headset ceased. Bronco
sat up straighter, even went so far as to press his ear piece
to secure the seal. Bronco, the one dubbed King Cupid at
last year's Valentine's Ball because of his infamous match-
making. Between him and the other listening ears, gossip
would saturate the base by sunrise.

Zach reminded himself his daughters needed Julia. And
for the moment, so did he. "Julia, I need your help."

Chapter 4

"Ack! Can somebody help me with this fudge, please?" Gripping the designer pot, Julia huffed a lock off her brow. Her hair flopped right back, limp from all the steam pumping through the kitchen.

Hot fudge avalanched over the side of the pot toward the edges of the pan. Julia rushed to stem the tide with a useless high-tech spatula left behind from Pam's gourmet kitchen. The last thing she needed was to send the stuff splattering onto the stark white cabinets. Of course the mess wouldn't even come close to the chaos of her emotions as she waited for Zach to walk through that door any minute.

Ivy shot to her feet, hopscotching over the scattered pieces of her science project littering the floor. "Pour slower, maybe."

Kathleen started to swing her spit-polished boots from the chair across from her then stopped. Her camouflage uniform stretched across her stomach. She sank back into her seat at the white spindle table and hitched Patrick up on her shoulder. "Can you two handle it? By the time I manage to roll out of this chair, that fudge will have petrified.''

Ivy steadied the pan under the stream, her chestnut ponytail swaying as she adjusted. ''We've got it. Right, Julia?''

''You betcha.'' Julia smiled down at a miniature version of Zach's face. All those angular features that looked so strong on a man made a tough handle for a little girl, but Ivy would grow into a stunning woman.

Julia risked a glance at Kathleen to check her son. ''Stay put, Kathleen. You've already done plenty coming straight over after your drive to help out. Just keep holding Patrick while we talk.'' She continued the steady stream of words in time with the pouring chocolate. ''Everything I've learned in Early Infant Stimulation classes says talking to him nonstop is the best thing I can do to help his language stay as close to on track as possible. The week after my folks and Lori left, I talked myself hoarse. So talk. Please!''

''That, I can do.''

Soft baby coos in response swirled through the kitchen, and Julia tried not to think of how much she would miss those reassuring sounds when she returned to work.

Kathleen lifted Patrick nose-to-nose. ''Too bad we don't have my chatty hubby around for that one, huh? He could gab your ear off.''

Julia's laugh was cut short by Ivy's squawk. ''Hey! Watch out!''

''Oops, sorry.'' Julia slowed the stream of chocolate to a trickle and reminded herself not, under any circumstances, to look through the screen door again at the driveway—at the empty spot Zach's truck would soon fill.

Too bad the window over the sink offered an eyeful of the darkened street. Ivory lace curtains framed her view. Rows of near-identical military brick houses lined the road with porch lights blazing a welcome home. Families waited inside, trusting that their person would walk up those steps just as she had trusted one time too many almost ten months ago.

Hands trembling, Julia set the pot back on the counter to hunt for a larger spatula, desperate for anything to do to stay busy and distracted. Since rushing to Zach's house the night before, there had barely been a free second to breathe. With school and homework all today, it seemed there hadn't been time to think.

Now, with him due home soon, she couldn't do anything but think about his voice reaching to her through the telephone. The most capable man she'd ever met uttering words she'd never expected to hear from him.

I need your help.

Enticing words. Seductive words.

Dangerous as hell words.

Don't think. Stay busy.

Julia rifled through the drawer, but Pam had left precious little of her favorite cooking utensils behind. All that remained was an abandoned mishmash of gourmet gadgetry—tiny pastry brushes, a grapefruit knife, an egg-poacher. Where was an old fashioned, cheapo spatula for a clueless fudge cook?

Ivy swiped a dribble from the side of the pot and sucked it off her finger. "Umm. Good. Hey, maybe we could crunch some candy canes on top. That would be kinda like Mom's triple-layer mint brownies."

"Maybe I should call Shelby to do this part." Or turn over the whole dang pot to Shelby so she could feed it to the dog. "We should work on your science project anyway. How about we build another level for your nature habitat?"

Man, she would rather tinker with a hammer, some nails and a block of pine, instead of fudge as gritty as sandpaper.

Another fast shake of Ivy's head sent her hair swishing. "We should finish this first. I like cooking with you."

Of course she did, but then any female mother-figure

would have fit the bill. Poor kid. "Me too, sweetie. This was fun."

Julia swirled the grapefruit knife through the unmelted blobs of marshmallow cream. Okay, not too bad, even appetizing with all those unmixed marshmallow swirls marbleizing the effect.

Ivy chewed her lip. "Maybe if we keep it in the refrigerator."

A snort sounded from Shelby in the family room. "More like the freezer."

Julia glanced over her shoulder at Shelby strolling to a stop in the doorway. The teen pitched pretzels into her mouth. Aggie trailed, pitiful puppy eyes tracking every bite.

Shelby plastered an expression of boredom across her face with more masking perfection than an Estee Lauder makeover. Except Estee Lauder ladies didn't usually have a silver stud through an eyebrow.

Stifling a groan, Julia scratched her own brow. As if things weren't already going to be awkward enough when Zach walked through the door.

When he saw what Shelby had done…

Julia's rebellious eyes snuck another peek at the driveway. His truck still wasn't there, but the lean lines of his Harley offered too potent a reminder of the man anyway. She wanted to see him, had been lonely for his towering presence and brooding smile for the past six weeks.

Too much so.

She needed some of that chocolate. Now.

Julia whipped open a drawer and scooped out a handful of spoons. "Let's just eat it as is, kinda like raw cookie dough."

"Cool!" Ivy squealed, bouncing on her toes. "I hardly ever get to lick the bowl since Mom always scrapes it clean like the recipe says."

Julia padded barefoot across the kitchen, passing a spoon to Ivy and pitching one to Shelby. "Well, hon, I've never been one for following the recipe since it usually doesn't work out anyhow. I'm a make-it-up-as-I-go type.''

Kathleen placed the sleeping infant in his car seat and extended a hand. ''Don't I get one?''

Grinning wickedly, Julia dangled the spoon just out of reach. ''You told me not to eat junk food when I was pregnant.''

''I told you to limit junk food, and believe me, Tanner's limiting my junk food just fine. I swear, I'm going to burn all those pregnancy books he's reading,'' she said, her grumbling completely negated by a smile. ''You'd think he would know I have the darn things memorized. Now, give me a spoon.''

''Yes, ma'am!'' Julia passed the spoon over Patrick still snoozing away in his car seat. She brushed a quick kiss across his brow, savoring her last days with him before her maternity leave ended. He might be six weeks old, but she recalled those pregnancy cravings well.

Six weeks since she'd seen Zach.

Or he'd seen her.

The sitter had been the one to bring the girls over to meet Patrick. Never Zach.

What would he think of her trimmed-down body? Not that he could even see it in her baggy clothes. The khaki overalls had seemed logical when she'd packed. Practical, comfy. Safe. And they were her favorites even if they made her look like a blob. She didn't want to change herself for a man ever again.

Even one with sleepy bedroom eyes and endless lanky appeal.

''On second thought…'' Julia whipped the bag of pretzels from Shelby's hand, poured a pile on the table and scooped one through the chocolate. ''Who needs a spoon?''

She plopped into a chair, drawing her legs up and sitting cross-legged. She popped the chocolate-covered pretzel into her mouth. Her eyes slid closed. Euphoria melted through her in a tide of warm chocolate.

If only life could always be this simple, friends and junk food. But Zach wasn't a simple man to understand.

Julia, I need your help.

Her heart stuttered. Another bite of chocolate soothed the unsteady beat.

Shelby clicked a fingernail against the stud in her eyebrow. "Is it true that chocolate is the next best thing to sex?"

Julia dropped a pretzel in the pan.

Kathleen coughed, twice, then hefted herself from the chair with surprising speed to pitch her spoon in the sink.

Clearing her throat, Julia turned to Ivy. "Hon, would you run back into your father's room and look through the diaper bag for Patrick's pacifier?"

"But he's not cranky."

"Better to be prepared."

"Sure." Ivy sighed. Ponytail swinging, she tiptoed around a poster, markers and wooden box full of cactuses on her way out of the kitchen.

Julia waited for Ivy to clear the room then turned back to Shelby. "Do you think that was really appropriate to say around your little sister?"

The teen shrugged. "Well, she's gone now. So? Is it? The next best thing to sex?"

Julia longed for simpler problems, like diapers and feedings. Even if she wanted to answer that question, which she absolutely did *not,* she wasn't sure she could. It had been so long since she'd had a man and chocolate in her bed at the same time for comparison.

She willed herself not to think about the past night she'd spent in Zach's bed. Alone, but so very aware of the man.

Where else could she have slept other than the sectional sofa? Not that she'd slept much wrapped in blankets that smelled too much like the man who used them.

Shelby quirked a pierced brow. "Well?"

Julia looked to Kathleen at the sink for help, but her traitorous friend had suddenly decided to wash her hands. She pumped soap from a dispenser with intense concentration.

Weren't doctors supposed to have training in answering these sorts of questions? Julia pulled a weak smile. "I guess I should be grateful you don't already know the answer."

Shelby rolled her eyes. "Forget it."

"Wait. You just surprised me."

"Never mind. I mean, come on, as if you'd really tell me anyway."

Way to go, Jules. "Okay, let's talk about it then."

Shelby pulled her term paper from under the pan. "I just said it to get a rise out of you anyhow. Lucky I didn't ask the Colonel, huh? He would have had a stroke."

Understatement of the year.

The teenager skulked toward the refrigerator, ten pounds of attitude dragging her steps. How had life become so complicated for all of them in the span of one year?

A truck rumbled on the street.

Julia curled her toes, tucking their painted tips out of sight. Her eyes shot straight to the window over the sink. It could be anyone's vehicle. Lots of people drove trucks. Red trucks. Slowing.

And pulling into the driveway.

No time left to wonder if Zach's reaction to her after Patrick's birth had been a fluke.

Time to find out.

Zach shut off the engine, stared at the porch light and wondered when he'd turned into a coward.

Geez, why couldn't he do something simple, like fly combat, dodge some missiles, deliver enough supplies to feed a third-world nation? But no. He had to walk into that house and find out if the rogue attraction to Julia had been an anomaly, and the timing couldn't be any worse.

Flying always left him restless, pumped with excess adrenaline, in need of the very best release for all that testosterone slugging through him, in need of a bed and a woman for a few uninterrupted hours. And for the past six weeks, the only woman who came to mind was Julia. One hint of that mind-blowing image would send her long legs sprinting away from him and his girls again.

Of course, who said he had to let Julia know how he felt? He wasn't some teenager ruled by his libido. Although he felt damned close at the moment.

She might not want the military in her life, but she needed him as much as he needed her. Time to set their friendship back on its old path.

Zach slammed his truck door closed just as the side door to the house swung open.

"Daaa-dy!" Ivy sprinted out the kitchen door, one of Patrick's pacifiers clutched in her hand. Sailing from the porch step in a leap that would have made her ballet instructor proud, she flung herself at her father.

"Hey, kiddo. I was only gone for a couple of weeks."

"Missed you."

"I missed you too." He hugged her, amazed for probably the millionth time at how much he could love another person. Until Shelby was born, he'd never had a clue. He glanced through the open door. His older daughter buried her head in the fridge.

"Hey, Shel."

Not even bothering to turn toward him, she waggled a wave over her shoulder, already headed for the hall with a soda can in hand. "'Night, Colonel."

Okay, so it wasn't enthusiastic, but at least she'd kept the normal Shelby-zinger to herself.

Zach swung Ivy to his back. She looped her arms around

his neck, hanging like a monkey as she'd done countless times. He lumbered up the steps and into the house.

Tossing his helmet bag and radio onto the counter, he lowered Ivy to the ground and prepped himself to face Julia for the first time in six weeks. He turned, not a hundred percent sure if he wanted the attraction to have been an aberration or not.

She sat at his table.

Just sat. No special or seductive pose. Just Julia in khaki overalls sitting cross-legged, her tangled curls pulled back from her face by some kind of band behind her ears. Chocolate smudged her cheek, exhaustion smudged her eyes. She was a mess. She was gorgeous.

Then she smiled.

Ah, hell. Beyond gorgeous. Not even a full-out smile this time, just a half grin pulled at her full lips, lips trembling at the corners.

Something shifted inside him, something he'd cemented into place years ago out of a need for survival so strong nothing should have shaken it loose. The hell of it was, he could swear he saw an answering attraction in her eyes.

"Colonel?"

Zach's gaze snapped to the other woman in the room. How had he missed Kathleen Bennett sitting at the table too? "Evening, Major." He tugged Ivy's ponytail. "It's late, kiddo. How about you get ready for bed while I thank these ladies for helping out. I'll be back in a few minutes to tuck you in."

"Story?"

"One chapter."

"Three."

"Two."

"Roger that, Papa Wolf."

"Roger, Cub Pilot." He shot a thumbs-up.

Ivy paused in the doorway. "Julia?"

"Yeah, honey?"

"Don't forget to tell me goodbye before you go, okay?"

"Of course I won't forget."

But Pam had. She'd bolted in the middle of the night, packed up, stormed out, leaving him to explain everything to their children in the morning. Four weeks later, Pam had resurfaced from a cooking cruise with hugs, a new boy-friend and a box of saltwater taffy for the girls.

Julia had been the one to take Shelby shopping for a prom dress, the one to twist Ivy's hair up into that ballet recital hairnet thing. Julia had been all that kept his family from falling apart.

Zach scrubbed his hand over his jaw, scratching the numbed nerves awake. He could do this, pretend to be un-affected by those toes she tucked out of sight. He could pretend he didn't notice the curve of her breast outlined in a stretchy T-shirt just showing in the gaping side of her overalls. "Hi, Julia."

"Zach."

He knelt beside Patrick, cupping a hand over the pale, fine hair. "He's grown into quite a bruiser."

"He's a happy baby." She shifted, one foot poking free. Purple polish. Silver sparkles right at eye level.

Zach stood. "Major, thanks for stopping over to help so soon after coming home from a TDY yourself."

"Nothing to it, Colonel. I just hung out and enjoyed the pizza and fudge. A pregnant woman's idea of heaven." Kathleen bumped the pan toward him. "It's really good stuff. You ought to try some."

Julia dropped the bag of pretzels. "There's pizza in the fridge."

He reached for a spoon. "Great. I'll get to that too later. Flying always makes me hungry."

Among other things he damned well didn't want to think about right now. Fudge offered a poor substitute for what he really wanted after a flight, but it was better than nothing.

Zach scooped through the chocolate and ate. "Good stuff. Who made it?"

"Uh," Julia squeaked, then continued, "that would be me."

"Damn good stuff. Is there more? This doesn't stand a chance of lasting much longer." He turned to the pregnant woman choking on a laugh behind her hand. "Did you want some, Major?"

"No thanks. I'm getting plenty at home."

Julia shot from the table. "Kathleen, isn't that Tanner's car pulling into your driveway?"

Kathleen braced a hand on the edge of the table to rise. "I should go then. After a flight, he's usually pretty, uh, hungry too. G'night, Colonel," she said as she waddled out the door.

Quiet settled over the kitchen.

Julia grabbed the pan. She wound around Ivy's spilled bag of toothpicks and a bag of aquarium rocks as she whipped past to toss it in the sink. "Sorry about the clutter everywhere."

"Leave it." Zach stopped behind Julia, closer than he'd meant to. Too close. "I'll put it all away later."

"Yeah, well…" She kept her back to him, twisting on the faucet and filling the pan with water. "There's leftover pizza in the fridge if you're still, uh, hungry, and some iced tea." Her voice drifted off as the water trickled to a stop. Still she didn't turn.

Zack stayed behind her, unmoving, but she didn't move either, just stood in front of him while they looked out the window and exchanged body heat. He breathed in the mix of strawberry shampoo, baby lotion and chocolate.

The soft curve of Julia's neck begged to be kissed. Zach forced his eyes somewhere safer, like back to the window. Tanner Bennett jogged across the street, meeting Kathleen at the edge of the driveway. With a whoop, the big lug scooped his pregnant wife off her feet and kissed her as if they'd been separated for a year rather than just two weeks. He dropped another kiss to her rounded stomach.

A sigh whispered from Julia. "They look good together."

She sounded so wistful, Zach couldn't help himself. He had to touch her. His hands fell to rest on her shoulders. His thumbs stroked the curve of her neck, her skin even silkier than he'd imagined.

She swayed under his touch, shoulders dropped, head lolled forward. Her body started a lean back that would bring her flush against him, her hair to his face, her bottom nestled snug against him. Damn it, she did feel that tug between them too.

His arm started the glide around to draw her closer.

Julia ducked from under his hands. "I should gather my stuff and go."

Yes, she should, but he didn't want her to and couldn't stop the urge to keep her talking so she would stay. Pizza and Julia looked a helluva lot better in his kitchen than the chili and solitude he'd been facing the past year. "Everything go okay with the girls?"

Julia scratched her eyebrow, then dried the wet spot with her wrist as she backed out of the kitchen. "Uhm, yes, homework's almost done. We built a cage for Ivy's desert habitat project. Shelby's in her room typing in corrections on her term paper. And there's pizza in the fridge."

"Yeah, you told me already."

"Oh, right. I'll just say goodbye to Ivy first before she falls asleep." Julia spun away, darting down the hall.

Zach slumped against the counter in his wrecked kitchen, not too different from his wrecked libido after standing so close to Julia. He glanced around the trashed room full of pizza boxes, dishes in the sink, Ivy's science project on the floor. At least he would have something to do to burn off the restless energy from his flight. Not that he minded the mess in the least. For the first time in too long, his house felt...

Normal.

He wanted someone who would be there for his kids. And from where he was standing, the scene in front of him fit the bill too damned perfectly. Of course he was far from being the perfect man for Julia Sinclair or her son.

Zach knelt beside the baby. "Hey, little man. Good nap?"

Patrick stretched stiff-backed in his car seat.

"Good. Glad to hear it." The kid deserved the best. Grabbing a sleeper-clad foot, Zach tweaked the baby's toes. "You go easy on your mama tonight, okay, Bruiser? She needs her sleep and there isn't anybody around to help her with those night feedings."

Would there have been even if Lance had lived?

Zach frowned. Where had that thought come from? Still, he couldn't stop wondering if the already rocky Sinclair marriage would have lasted. Did Julia still love the guy?

A moot point anyway.

Zach stared at the tiny foot in his hand and forced himself to be honest. He was trying to justify the possibility he could be finding the man guilty of negligence on the job. If Julia didn't still have feelings for Lance, then she wouldn't resent Zach for what he had to do if the results of Bronco's interview with the board went wrong.

Yeah, right.

Regardless of how Julia felt about her cheating husband, he was still the father of her child. Just as Pam was the mother of Zach's children. And even as pissed as he was at Pam, he wanted his children to have good memories of their mom.

No way in hell would Julia understand him tainting Lance Sinclair's memory.

Time for her to pack up before he found himself sharing more than a spoonful of fudge with her tonight.

Chapter 5

Shelby pushed once, twice, a third time on the screen to her bedroom window. White, ruffled curtains flapped in the breeze. She so hated those curtains. She'd wanted purple, but her mother had said neutral colors matched better in any house wherever they moved.

Screw moving. Shelby thumped the screen again with the heel of her hand. Finally, it slipped loose.

Freedom.

Swinging one leg over the sill, she waved goodbye over her shoulder to her fish and favorite hunk poster. Shelby landed in her backyard with a muffled thud, easy enough since she had the routine down pat. She could shimmy out that window, past Ivy's swing set and into the pine forest behind her house with a stealth that would have impressed her dad's airmen doing maneuvers.

But the last thing she wanted was more attention.

Headlights rounded the corner. Shelby flattened herself to an oak tree. Bark scratched her bare arms, but she held still until...the car...passed.

She exhaled, darting deeper into the stretch of trees to a dirt path. Her running shoes crunched dry leaves. A cool breeze kept her from getting sweaty without freezing her out. The moon streaked just enough light through the branches for her to run without tripping.

And she couldn't run fast enough away from that house.

Being the Colonel's daughter totally sucks, she thought for the hundredth time. She might as well be in the Air Force too. She didn't have a real life.

They lived in a military house. Bought their groceries at the commissary. Went to the base chapel. Even her doctor wore cammo.

She couldn't breathe crooked without someone reporting it to her dad. When he was even home, which was next to never since he always had a world to save. Countries to feed. Messes to clean up overseas. Sure would have been nice if he'd ever take time to clean up his mess of a life at home.

Except now he had Julia to take care of that for him.

Shelby tucked around another pine tree onto the base golf course. Almost there. Too bad the escape couldn't be forever.

Geez, even her lame mom had figured out how to get away for good. Shelby's chest tightened, like when the bell for first period rang and she hadn't done her homework. She gulped in night air as she jogged, but the pain wouldn't go away.

Probably just that rigatoni giving her heartburn. Mrs. Middleton had made her eat it the night before.

Shelby slipped on a slick patch of pine straw, grabbed for a tree, steadied before taking off again. She didn't get a say in anything. Even what she ate.

Well, she would get her way tonight.

A flash of orange blinked in the distance—John's favorite sweatshirt.

John. He slouched against a tree, tall and lanky with his dark hair loose to his shoulders just the way she loved.

Waiting.

For her.

The stitch in her side eased.

Ducking and weaving, Shelby sprinted across the golf course straight against John's chest. "Sorry I'm late."

He stumbled backward, but his hold stayed tight around her. "I wasn't sure you were gonna make it tonight."

"Me neither."

He ran his hands up her arms. "Hey, you shoulda brought a jacket."

"I didn't want to wait." Or risk going back into the hall where her father could see her pierced eyebrow. "It's not that cold."

November in Charleston never was, not like the five other places she'd lived. She'd be moving to city number seven next summer, thanks to her dad's job and some to-die-for assignment in Alabama.

No choices.

The stitch came back.

John pulled away, whipping off his sweatshirt. "Here. Wear mine anyway."

He slipped it over her head. All that concern and cotton slid right over her too until the tightness in her chest lessened.

Shelby tucked back into his arms and rubbed her cheek against his T-shirt. She wanted to stand like this forever. No demands. No rigatoni or goodbyes.

She tipped her face up and pulled John's head down to hers and could have sworn she tasted chocolate.

Julia backed out of Ivy's room, blowing a kiss as she closed the door. Stalling in the hall, she traced the first in a cluster of framed baby pictures of the girls lining the walls, followed by school pictures, all marching time along to the present.

She eyed Shelby's door, fish tank gurgling in the silence, and considered whether or not to knock. Probably best to leave well-enough alone for now. No need to push her luck after the chocolate incident.

Which she would have to tell Zach about along with the newly pierced eyebrow. But not tonight. Let him get a good night's sleep first.

In that big, warm bed of his.

Julia slumped against the wall. Definitely better to wait until tomorrow to discuss it with him.

Talk to him tomorrow?

What had happened to keeping Zach's hot body and aviator wings out of her life? Was she making excuses to see him again? Maybe. But she couldn't face more time with Zach tonight without caving and doing something impulsive.

Not to mention stupid.

Julia pushed away from the wall and walked toward the kitchen. The cool parquet floors against her bare feet helped temper a heat that had begun flaming through her the minute Zach started wolfing down all that fudge.

She stepped into the kitchen—and stopped short.

Zach knelt beside the baby car seat, grinning down at Patrick. A floor of ice wouldn't be cold enough to chill the warm tide of emotions flooding through her. That enticing half smile kicked up one side of Zach's face as he played piggies with baby toes, such an incongruous image.

Erase the car seat and Zach personified the warrior spirit, protector of his country whatever the cost. A five-o'clock shadow peppered the harsh angles of his jaw. Miles of lean muscle telegraphed strength encased in a forest-green flight suit and black leather combat boots. He even had a survival knife tucked in one of those boots.

More than a little fearsome.

Completely awesome.

And playing "This Little Piggy" on a six-week-old's toes with a gentleness totally at odds with all that restrained power. She definitely needed to pack her baby and her bags, and make tracks back to her house. "Zach?"

Zach looked from the baby up to the boy's mother standing silhouetted in the open doorway. Julia's feet shuffled a restless dance. No doubt she was ready to go, and who knew when he and the girls would see her again?

He braced a hand on his knee and stood. "Thank you for coming over when I called yesterday. I know this wasn't easy for you. I wouldn't have asked if there had been any other way."

"I know that. And you're welcome. I owe you—"

"No. Don't ever say you owe me a thing. What I do for you is no strings attached. No obligations." He needed her to leave, but didn't want her running so far this time. A tough balance to strike, but he would do it. "This isn't about you and me or debts. This is about what the kids need and my kids needed you."

Her feet stilled. "I had fun with the girls and Kathleen and the whole laid-back schedule. Next week, my maternity leave's up. I'll understand soon enough what it's like to balance child care and job demands as a single parent." Clouds shifted through her eyes for a flash until the ready sparkle returned. "Before you thank me, you should check what happened to the back hedges when Ivy gave us an impromptu performance of *Swan Lake*."

"That bad huh?"

"Let's just say Aggie wasn't interested in joining the cast."

Chuckling, Zach hitched a shoulder on the doorframe. Yeah, he'd moved closer to Julia but no problem now that they were back on familiar ground just as he'd planned. No need to rush her out the door now.

Think again, dumb ass. Still, he couldn't stop himself

from enjoying a moment of the friendship he'd missed too much the past six weeks. "Thanks for making it sound like this wasn't a colossal imposition."

"It wasn't."

"Yeah, right. Every woman with a six-week-old baby wants to take on two more kids to watch and pick up after."

"You must be joking about the picking-up part." She swept a curl off her brow. "It looks like I ran through your house with a lawnmower."

"It's not that bad." Well, it was, but that didn't matter. Julia brought laughter for his girls along with all that chaos. "Just looks like y'all had fun."

"You should have seen it before they helped me clean."

Zach snorted. "My kids? Help clean? You forget, I've seen their rooms."

"Really. They did."

"Either you're a great liar or a miracle worker."

"I'm not their parent so it's no fun playing the martyred kid with me."

"Too true."

Her laugh joined his with too much ease. Too much power. Too much. Period.

With adrenaline rising as fast as his resistance fell, he needed to stop playing with fire. Even if that fire promised to be more exciting than any game of cloud chasing. "Point me toward your bag and I'll load it in the car."

"In your bedroom."

He did *not* need to hear that. His imagination took a fantasy flight right into sharing that bed with Julia.

She spun away, padding barefoot down his hall while Zach strode behind her. If he helped, she would leave all the sooner. Right? He wasn't actually following her into his bedroom for any reason other than that.

Ah, hell.

He pivoted on his heel and went back for Patrick. Snagging the car-seat handle, Zach hefted along his very own pint-sized chaperone. "No napping now, Bruiser. You hear that? I'm gonna need all the back-up I can get. You'll be my wingman and watch for bogies looking to blast us out of the sky. Got it?"

Patrick gurgled a spit bubble.

"Yeah, just like that. Keep 'em coming if that'll help you stay awake." Zach cruised to a stop in the doorway.

Julia darted around the room like a firefly, stuffing sweat pants, a brush, shampoo into her bag.

She'd slept in his bed.

His sheets would carry her scent when he slept there later.

Zach secured his grip on the car seat. "Need any help?"

"There's not much, but yes, please carry the Portacrib." She reached across the bed and picked up an oversized T-shirt, revealing—

Panties. An orange thong.

Ah, man, he was so not going to get any sleep tonight.

He tried not to look at Julia, but then he would have to look at that underwear. Better to look at her.

Her cheeks pinkened.

Julia wasn't a particularly bashful woman. A holdover, she'd once claimed, from her days growing up in a commune. No privacy had quickly translated into little modesty.

An image blared in his mind, full blown and fully unwelcome, a memory of going to the base pool to check on his girls and make sure they weren't imposing on Julia while he worked through a Saturday afternoon.

Instead of a worn-out pregnant woman he'd found Julia in a bikini, glowing and magnificent even at seven months pregnant. Hot as hell.

Objectively speaking, of course.

More than a few male heads had turned to admire the sensual earth mother, Amazon goddess strolling to the snack bar.

For the first time, Zach questioned how objective he

could have been if he remembered the day so clearly. Apparently, the memory had stored itself away just waiting for a weak moment to flatten his sorry butt.

Zach stuffed the thoughts away as quickly as Julia jammed those panties he'd never get to see up close and personal into her bag.

She tugged on socks and shoved her feet into sandals in record time before crossing to him. ''Thanks, Zach.''

She dropped the bag at his feet beside the folded Portacrib. Julia grabbed the car seat from him and dashed down the hall without ever once glancing at him.

He followed, watching the glide of her long legs. Thinking back to that poolside moment.

Unwise. Wrong. Impossible to ignore.

Tucking his radio under his arm on his way out, Zach called over his shoulder, ''Ivy, hang tough kiddo, and I'll be back in a few minutes for those chapters. Shel, keep an ear out for Ivy.''

The screen door banged shut behind him, leaving Zach in the carport. Alone. With only Julia and a yard full of crickets.

She popped the trunk, and he welcomed the excuse to focus on something else. He tossed the crib and bag inside and slammed it shut. Circling around the car, he perched the radio on the seat of his Harley. ''You look good, Julia.''

Ah hell, again. Where had that come from?

His mouth had apparently staged a rebellion against his better judgment.

Julia buckled Patrick's car seat in the back without turning. ''Thank you.''

Actually, she looked incredible, so hot he wanted to take her inside to his bedroom and close the door on the rest of the world. ''I mean it. You look great. No one would guess you just had a kid.''

She draped and smoothed a blanket over Patrick. For the third time. ''Thanks, Colonel.''

"Zach."

She ducked out of the car and faced him, sparks from her eyes showering all over him like anti-aircraft fire. "Okay, *Zach,* what the hell are you trying to do?"

Adrenaline abandoned him in a snap. He leaned against the car. "I don't know, Julia. I just know I've missed you."

All those sparks dispersed from her eyes. She sagged against the car beside him. "I've missed you, too."

He tried not to think about that day at the pool when he'd seen those long legs. Tried not to think about how damn worried he'd been seeing her rounding belly and knowing she would face parenthood alone.

And tried like hell not to be mad now because he hadn't known the half of it that day.

In spite of all their talk of being friends, she hadn't told him the outcome of those tests. She'd carried around the knowledge that her child had Down syndrome for months and never once told him.

Whatever he'd done to make her hold back, he would fix it. He had to, for the little bruiser in the back seat. For his kids inside. And yeah, maybe even for himself so he could sleep again without dreaming about her and her orange thong. "I want us to be friends again."

"Really?"

"Yeah." God yes, he did. And he didn't.

"Me too."

"So we'll just do it. Backtrack a few months and pick up from there."

"I'm not so sure I can do that."

"Why the hell not?"

"Because you're looking damned fine to me too."

Blown out of the sky and he never even saw the missile coming.

Zach exhaled, long and slow. It was one thing suspecting she felt the attraction too. But hearing it. Well, that was a-whole-nother pack of trouble altogether. ''No chance of anyone accusing you of holding things back.''

She turned her head and smiled, soft and womanly and close. Only a few inches separated them, a hand span maybe. Even less space separated their mouths. It would be so easy to reach, so easy to grasp her arm and tug her to him. Her body language shouted a very firm go-ahead.

But her smile faded, her eyes blaring an unmistakable wary message, *Please, don't hurt me.*

Damn Lance Sinclair.

Damn himself too for wanting something so obviously wrong for both of them.

Zach shoved away from the car. ''Go home, Julia. We're both tired and too lonely to be having this conversation now.''

He opened the driver's door and stood aside. He never knew what to expect next with Julia. Anything from impromptu whittling lessons for Ivy to defiantly baring her pregnant body to a pool full of onlookers.

Zach prepped himself for anything.

Except her touch. There was no way in hell to steel himself against that.

Julia cupped his face in her hand, the numb side, frustrating him all the more with the diluted sensation. His brain knew her soft palm was there, and he felt the slightest pressure. But he wanted it all—the full-out feeling of her hands on him, and he had to settle for a phantom caress.

Her hand fell away. ''Good night, Zach.''

He held the door wide for her, tucking her inside and out of arm's reach before making tracks for the house. He forced himself not to look back. Eight hours of sleep and a solid morning of work and he'd be back on track. He gripped the doorknob.

Why hadn't she turned on the car?

He glanced over his shoulder and found Julia Sinclair doing the very last thing he expected.

Crying.

Not wracking, dramatic sobs like Pam had poured all over their arguments, but slow, leaking tears. Her whole body trembled as if from the mammoth effort of holding back.

Those few tears hammered him more than open floodgates.

The past year had been beyond hell for her, but never once had he seen anything more than those restrained tears. Even at her husband's funeral, she'd been pale but composed when Zach, Bronco, Cutter and Tag had walked past carrying the casket out of the church. Zach could still feel the weight of her dead husband in his hands, the weight of her constrained grief on his shoulders.

And none of it came close to the ten-ton thud on his soul as he saw a tear slide off her nose.

Zach charged down the steps. He'd spent the past months hell-bent on making sure Julia had whatever she needed. Damned if he would fail her now.

Julia clenched the steering wheel until her palms slicked with sweat. The muscles in her arms vibrated with tension. She would not cry. She would not cry.

Two tears did not count as crying!

Julia swiped both drops from the end of her nose. Damn Zach for making her vulnerable with all that concern tearing down her defenses.

Count blessings. Her son was happy, the most important blessing of all. Even one of his precious baby smiles cancelled out anything else.

Yet, as much as she wanted to believe raising a happy child was her only goal, she knew Patrick needed so much more from her than smiles, especially during this first year. Another tear eked free. Between work and Patrick's packed schedule of doctor appointments, therapy sessions and support meetings, when would she have time just to smile with her baby?

The car door clicked just before it opened.

She didn't even have to look. She could feel him there. Zach. Tall, strong and always there for her no matter how shrewish she was as she sent him on his way because she couldn't handle a few silly hormones.

Zach knelt beside her. He pulled her into his arms and God help her, she didn't have the will to say no. She would steal just a few minutes to relax against his chest, a chest even more wonderful than she'd dreamed it would be. And man, had she ever savored some secret dreams about that chest over the last six weeks. Musk and man swirled through her senses.

Comfort break officially over.

Julia inched away. "I don't cry."

Zach held firm. "I know."

Maybe she could stay another minute. "I won't cry now."

"Of course not."

"Life's all about attitude." Since she'd already tossed control to the wind for the moment, Julia allowed her fingers the pleasure of exploring the rough texture along his hairline, bristly hair trimmed short into a tapered military cut. "Crying doesn't fix anything but smiles can move mountains."

Or this man could, by sheer force of his will.

Zach didn't speak, his silent acceptance of her need to vent wearing down her resistance more than a thousand platitudes.

"I probably just need a good night's sleep."

"Babies have a way of making that tough."

Julia pulled free and tried to ignore the urge to climb back into his arms. "No, Patrick's not any trouble. He's such an easy baby, eats and sleeps most of the time. Sure, he has his moments, like when he doesn't want his feet uncovered. But he's such a blessing."

Zach nodded. "Yes, ma'am, he is."

"It's just…" Her restless hands landed on a poofy bear that had spilled from the diaper bag. Her thumb stroked a silky patch, soft like Patrick's tiny hands. "He demands so little but needs so much from me. I want his life to be normal, except I know I have to face reality too. He has some practical needs beyond what other mothers expect from their babies for the first year."

"Like what?"

She hesitated. Would he try to be there for those too? The man already had stretched his time paper-thin with his own life.

"Julia?"

His tone left no room for argument, not that it really mattered. She knew well enough already that if she didn't tell him, he would find out anyway.

"Early intervention is important. Patrick's educational program calls for more than just talking myself hoarse to stimulate language. The appointments are mind-boggling, physical therapy, occupational therapy, along with the pediatric speech therapist. Zach, he probably won't walk until around twenty-four months. And then there's learning to talk, to feed himself, dress himself, so many milestones other parents expect to pass with ease."

Her thumb stroked comfort from the silky toy like a talisman. "This first year is crucial for helping Patrick reach his full potential."

She held up a hand to stop Zach from saying something that would launch her into another teary moment—and right back against that perfect chest.

"I know, Zach. I know. I'm really lucky."

He braced his forearm on the doorframe and leaned his head against it, sealing off the opening with his shoulders. Somehow he sealed off the rest of the world too until all she could see was Zach, his chest and those chocolate eyes that melted over her with warmth, comfort and damn it yes, excitement.

"Lady, from where I'm looking, you've had a helluva year," he drawled. "You've lost your husband. Had a baby alone. And now you have some very real concerns for your kid. Nobody's going to think less of you if you want to scream down the whole neighborhood. Definitely a helluva year."

A watery snort tripped free. "I've had better." She scrubbed her nose and wished for a pair of form-fitting jeans and a nose that didn't resemble a clown's. "I try to focus on the blessings, and there really are so many. Money's not an object. Even though the life insurance was eaten up with old debts, I still have a great job I enjoy. I can afford the best child care. And believe me, child care for a special-needs baby costs major bucks."

Julia hugged the bear to her stomach. "The thing is, I want to take care of it all myself. Is that so wrong? I want to be with him every step of the way this year, see and rejoice over every one of those milestones and somehow find time between all those appointments and work just to hold him."

A fresh spurt of frustration stabbed through her at Lance for leaving her behind, at the military for taking him when their baby needed him most. "Is it so wrong for me to want a few months more to hold my baby?"

Warm chocolate eyes darkened, deepening with a determination she'd come to recognize. The commander had a plan of action. What should have been an impossible situation would work out because this man willed it so.

A part of her niggled, reminding her of hard-won independence, her resolve to be strong and fix her own problems. But time was running out. With her son's welfare in the balance, could she really afford to say no to whatever Zach suggested?

He ducked to eye level with Julia, clasping her hand in his as he pinned her to the seat with nothing more than the magnetism of his gaze and the power of his determination.

"Marry me."

Chapter 6

What the hell?

He'd planned to offer her a job as his girls' nanny so she could have more time with Patrick. Instead, a marriage proposal had fallen out of his mouth.

Now those words floated between them, and he found himself actually considering it. He couldn't pay enough for her to maintain her house, and if she moved in as a full-time nanny there would be talk. The base community was tight. Gossip would flow. The whole base had known he and Pam had split before she made it to the security gate.

How ironic people well-versed in keeping top-secret military intel couldn't hold onto a piece of gossip for more than thirty seconds.

No, he and Julia couldn't share a house without a ring and an official piece of paper. She would have those months with Patrick, and he could finish out his tour as commander without the roof caving.

"Marry me," Zach repeated, course set. His job never

allowed him the luxury of time wasted wavering. Decision made. Move forward.

He waited for her reaction. Readied for battle by prepping his rebuttals. Thought through a dozen possible scenarios from Julia.

Except laughter.

She slapped a hand over her mouth.

Then smacked his arm. "You always do know how to cheer me up. Thanks for making me smile."

Zach swiped a hand over his face. "Damn, Julia, good thing I have a mighty healthy ego or that could have set me back a step."

Her laughs trickled to a stop. Green eyes widened. "You're not joking?"

He shook his head slowly until her hand gravitated to her mouth again. No laughs this time. "Marry you?"

Time for those persuasive arguments before she poked a finger through the bear's stuffing. "A temporary marriage. Until the end of the summer when I transfer to Air War College in Alabama. You'll have your months with Patrick and I'll be able to finish out my tour as commander without my family falling apart."

"But isn't marriage going a little overboard? We could just help each other more."

He planted a boot on the running board, elbow on his knee as he leaned toward her. "That won't fix the fundamental problems. You want to be a hundred percent available for Patrick these next few months and I need someone I can count on to be there for the girls twenty-four/seven. My job has insane hours: TDYs like the Guam deployment, midnight calls from the flight line. God, can you imagine what it was like arranging day care for my kids from the middle of the Pacific Ocean via phone patch?"

The more he thought about it, the more the proposal made sense. "My kids deserve better. My squadron deserves better."

And he couldn't afford to give his second in command a toehold for pulling more stunts like he had with Bronco's nose gear six weeks ago. More than his peace of mind rested on this decision. The safety of his kids and an entire squadron hung on one simple word from Julia.

Yes.

He willed her to say it, and when she didn't, he charged ahead full-throttle. "We're already friends. The girls are used to you. You know their routine. Patrick will have even more support with all the extra hands and smiles around here. You can rent out your house. Beach property always fills, and your place will be there waiting for you afterward. Think about it, Julia."

He could see the wheels churning, and his instincts told him he was making headway. The promise of victory surged through him.

Her eyes narrowed. "What about sex?"

Victory leapt backward.

Leave it to Julia to spell it out, but then he'd always liked that about her. No games. No artifice. Just Julia. Too bad he didn't know the right answer to her question.

Honestly, he wanted her. Not a chance could he see himself turning down an offer to have those long legs and her husky laugh wrapping around him. But if her acceptance hinged on a no-sex agreement, he would lock up those thoughts so tight she would never know.

"What about sex?"

"I'm afraid I misled you with what I said earlier, about finding you attractive. I do. Find you attractive, I mean." A smile whispered over her mouth. "Really attractive. But." The smile vanished. "I'm not ready to have a man, any man, in my bed again."

"Julia, I understand you just had a baby. I realize your body needs time to heal."

"That's not what I meant. It's been the requisite six weeks. My body may have healed, but my heart..."

Straight up and honest, she met his gaze. "It's a long way from ready, and right now, I can't imagine a time when I'll ever be ready to open myself up to any kind of relationship again."

Disappointment chugged through him, but he wouldn't let that rock his determination. "All right, then. We'll make it a platonic thing. I'll put a daybed for myself in the computer room. You take the master bedroom since it's large enough for the crib too."

"For nearly a year?" She laughed again, a short snort of disbelief. "Get real, Zach. I don't expect you to stay celibate that long because I have some hang-ups." She clutched the bear to her stomach like a lifeline. "Call me crazy, but if we did marry, even a no-sex kinda thing, I couldn't take it if you slept with someone else."

Bronco's words earlier about Lance's affair burned into Zach's brain. Damn Lance Sinclair and his ability to reach beyond the grave to hurt Julia.

Zach chose his words with care, strategy never more mission-essential than now. What he said became important beyond convincing her to marry him. He needed to heal those fears for her and reassure her that some men could be trusted. *He* could be trusted. "Julia, I've already gone without sex for over a year and it hasn't killed me yet."

Although there were times—like now—when he suspected it might.

"You have?"

"You know my schedule. When has there been time? Every spare second, and there haven't been many, I've spent with my kids."

Her gaze skittered around the car, anywhere but toward him. "I figured that maybe during TDYs..."

She'd thought about his sex life before now? A promising, exciting as hell, admission. Except the woman was busy listing all the reasons she couldn't sleep with him.

Wings level. Stay the course. "Keeping crewdogs out of

trouble on TDY is a full-time job. There isn't time for anything else."

Her gaze landed flat-out on him. "Give me a break."

There came that directness of hers again, which meant she would respect honesty in return. "Julia, I'm a regular guy with a healthy sex drive." A hundred percent healthy at the moment, not that she needed that much honesty. "But I've had years to practice controlling myself. You know how much time cargo fliers spend away from home. Not once did I ever cheat on Pam."

Julia's thumbs stroked over the bear's ears. "I'm not Pam."

Thank God, for him and for his girls. "I know." He tugged the toy from her and took her hand. He brushed her wrist with his thumb as she'd stroked the stuffed animal. "But married is married, regardless of the conditions when those vows are taken, no matter what the time frame. I'm a man who keeps his word and as long as we're married, I won't touch another woman. You can trust me."

He pushed aside the thought that he wasn't being completely honest with her about Lance's accident. The commander voice inside told him it didn't matter. That was classified business so it didn't concern the here and now with Julia.

She stared at their clasped hands. "You'll actually consider that long without sex, when you've already gone over a year without?"

His libido offered a shout of protest.

Which Zach ignored. No time to waver now, because even if he backed down he couldn't envision any other woman he wanted in his bed.

Besides, there was nothing to say he couldn't try to persuade her later. "You're an incredible woman, Julia, and I won't lie to you. I want you. If you change your mind about sleeping together, I certainly won't turn you down, but the call's yours to make."

Her brows pulled together. "How can you be so sure that if I change my mind, you will still want me in your bed for as long as we stay married? We've never even kissed."

Zach knew an invitation when he heard one, and there was no mistaking her gentle sway forward. All the restless adrenaline from his flight stirred to life. "Instinct. It's everything to fliers. We learn early on to trust what it tells us, and my instincts tell me we will be good together. Very good."

He lifted her hand and pressed his mouth to her wrist without ever looking away from her face. Her pulse leapt approval under his lips. Zach tucked her hand against his chest and slid his fingers along the back of her neck, up into her hair and coaxed her head forward. He might be willing to marry again for his kids, make any sacrifice for their well-being, but this moment was for him.

And Julia.

Julia.

One last time he checked for hesitation. He found a flash of wariness, but longing overrode it by a mile. Her bottom lip fell open just a hint, all the confirmation he needed. Right or wrong, she wanted this too.

No more waiting.

He skimmed the corner of her mouth once, twice, drawing her bottom lip between his teeth until she whimpered. Her lashes drifting closed, she turned her face toward him, bringing their mouths closer. "Please."

"Not yet." Zach shifted his attention to her jaw, up to her ear. With so much riding on a single kiss, he planned to take his time and make that kiss so persuasive she wouldn't be able to walk away. So persuasive she would be too weak-kneed to walk. Period.

He outlined the delicate shell before pausing to whisper, "I haven't kissed you, Julia, not yet, but I still know I want you. Just you."

Her head fell back, exposing a stretch of neck he couldn't resist, didn't have to resist for once. His mouth found the pulse he'd traced earlier with his thumbs, but still he didn't kiss her. He continued his determined assault on her senses, trying to ignore the undeniable effect she had on his own in the process.

He traced his way back up until his mouth rested against her temple while he held her. "We still haven't kissed, Julia." He breathed against her skin. "But you know too."

A moan vibrated through her throat.

His forehead fell to rest against hers. "Julia?"

Her lashes fluttered open. "What?"

Zach stared into her sleepy eyes, needing to hear her say she wanted him too, praying she would admit it soon because he wasn't sure how much longer he could hold back. "Trust those instincts, Julia. You know too, don't you?"

"Yes, Zach, I know. Now kiss me, and please make it as awesome as I think it's going to be. Make me forget everything else for just a while."

He'd never been one to turn down a challenge.

Zach took her mouth, fully. His tongue swept inside, deeper, chocolate, Julia and heat flooding his senses. Her fingers glided up to his face, cupped, caressed until he could almost swear she revived nerves long dead. He tried to hold back and shower her with gentle enticement.

But she was having none of that.

He should have known better.

Julia threw herself into the kiss with all the exuberance he'd come to recognize she devoted to every second of life. Her arms locked around his neck, her lips parting, inviting. Demanding. And he planned to accept the invitation as well as the challenge.

She moaned into his mouth, her hands running down his back and drawing him closer. Soft breasts to solid chest, she strained to get as close as they could without him pulling her out of that car or laying her down inside. Need pulsed through him—hot, thick and urgent. No half measures, he wanted all of her now.

That commander voice of reason within him insisted he was losing control. Somehow, his calculated persuasion had backfired, because kissing Julia, taking that kiss beyond and finishing became too important. That was unacceptable. He forced his hands to ease their hold around her.

Rustling sounded from the back seat, followed by a squawk.

Patrick.

Reality splashed over Zach like the ice-cold shower he would be taking in a few short minutes. He pulled back. What the hell had he been thinking? He hadn't been thinking at all. One kiss from Julia, and he'd forgotten about the sleeping baby in the back and the other two children inside the house liable to burst out at any moment. Not to mention an entire neighborhood full of people.

No ma'am, he hadn't been thinking of anything except Julia.

Zach rested his forehead against hers. Their ragged breaths battered the air between them. He'd made thousands of snap decisions in the air as well as on the ground and never once doubted his judgment.

Until tonight.

She'd been dead-on correct that he should have kissed her before proposing, because now he knew a marriage between them could never work. If one kiss from Julia could so shake his focus, months of her in his bed—should he be so lucky as to lure her there—would blast away any hope of control over himself, his feelings and his life.

There had to be another option. And he would find one as soon as he could breathe right again.

He pumped air into his lungs until lights sparked in front of his eyes. Lights? Zach frowned, turned, finding…

Car lights swept across him as the base security police

pulled into his driveway. Not just any cop, but the chief master sergeant in charge of security sat behind the wheel.

Not good.

Zach glanced at the silent radio perched on his motorcycle and wondered what could have gone wrong if he hadn't been called. No matter what the chief had to say, it couldn't be positive for him to have driven over.

Then he saw the huddled figure in the back seat and his mind exploded with the worst possible scenario, one he never would have expected.

He stared through the windshield at his daughter.

Disbelief stunned him for half a second before anger gripped him, which he allowed for a satisfying three seconds then shoved it aside and stood. He wouldn't be like his father. He'd worked too long to offer his girls a childhood different from his own. No raging scenes. No alcoholic outbursts. His girls would have as much stability as he could give them.

And still he stood in his driveway with the cops bringing his kid home.

Again that persistent anger clawed at him, anger at Pam for leaving, anger at himself for not being able to make her stay. Damned useless since that wouldn't have solved the problem in front of him. He shoved aside his own needs. His first instinct to marry Julia had been right and he needed to stick to his course.

Control never more important, he shut down his emotions, prepping himself for whatever Shelby had to dish out this time.

Oh, God. Julia sank into the bucket seat. She'd forgotten to tell Zach about Shelby's pierced eyebrow.

Julia stifled the hysterical urge to laugh.

A pierced eyebrow was the least of her worries, but she couldn't wrap her mind around rational thoughts just yet thanks to a kiss that fired so hot it threatened to melt her toenail polish.

Marry me.

She pressed trembling fingers to her lips. She might want to jump the man's bones, but no way did she ever want to remarry. So she'd better dump all those feelings and focus on the mess at hand.

Stepping from the car, Julia gasped in night air, stalling by studying the nightmare-in-the-making unfolding in the Dawson driveway. The corded muscles along Zach's neck broadcast restrained anger. Shelby angled out of the back seat to stand beside a cop wearing BDUs and a blue beret.

As if that wasn't enough, a door opened across the street. Tanner Bennett trotted out of his house carrying a garbage bag. Shorn blond hair shining under his porch light, he stumbled to a stop for a telling three seconds before hustling to dump the trash pronto.

The pulse in Zach's temple double-timed.

The situation threatened to explode into an argument that could permanently damage an already faltering father-daughter relationship. No time to think about her own screwed-up life, she had to do something. As Zach had said, the children came first.

Julia started toward the car. "Shelby, hon, what's going on?"

Zach's arm shot in front of Julia. "Evening, Chief." He nodded to the uniformed security cop, never looking at his daughter. "Shel, go inside."

Hurt flashed beneath that pierced brow, quickly replaced by attitude. "What do you care what I do, anyway? It's just one less kid to worry about."

"Shelby Lynn," he said, his voice low and tight. "Inside. Now."

"I mean, geez, you can't even keep up with both of us. I'll bet you don't know Ivy wanted to try out for the lead in the *Nutcracker* but you wouldn't be able to drive her to the extra rehearsals.'' Shelby strolled to a stop in front of her father until he had no choice but to look at her.

Julia saw the very minute Zach noticed Shelby's latest jewelry addition. Not that he said a word. His eyes narrowed, a tiny tic twitching. Julia couldn't help but wonder if that look of hundred-percent commander might be covering a flash of hurt very similar to the one she'd seen in Shelby.

Finally, the teen broke eye contact and spun away. She flounced toward the door in a theatrical huff, mumbling, ''It's so not fair that you two are the only ones allowed to make out in public places. I mean, geez, I saw you all over each other the minute we rounded the corner.''

The door slammed behind her.

Zach pivoted on his boot heel to the security cop. ''Evening, Chief. What do you have for me?''

''Well, Colonel…'' The chief hooked his thumbs in his gun belt looking like he'd rather battle a pack of renegade rebels than deal with one curfew-busting teen of a senior officer. ''The sergeant patrolling the golf course found your daughter and a young fella she says is her boyfriend tucked away in a patch of pine trees. The sergeant called to check with me, given who the young lady is and all.''

Zach shifted his attention to the night sky, scrubbing a hand along his jaw. Julia stepped up to give him time to absorb what he'd heard.

''And John Murdoch?'' Julia asked, then held her breath, praying it had been John with Shelby because heaven help them if Shelby had any more surprises for her father tonight.

''The sergeant escorted young Murdoch home. There wasn't alcohol or illegal substances involved, so there's no reason why we can't keep this a friendly visit. No need for an official report.''

Zach nodded. ''Thank you, Chief. I appreciate your making the special trip out.''

"No problem, sir. Since we're all finished here, I'll just call it a night." Saluting, the uniformed cop snapped to attention

Zach returned the salute. "Have a good evening, Chief."

"Good night, Colonel." He nodded to Julia. "Ma'am." He stepped back into his patrol car.

Julia stayed quiet until he pulled out of the driveway. No matter how much she wanted to run hard and fast from all the turmoil brought on by one incredible kiss, she couldn't walk away from Zach now. Not with those broad shoulders so tense.

At the very least, she should see him through the next few minutes. "Do you want me to go inside with you while you talk to her?"

He shook his head, jaw so tight he could have flattened nails. Did the guy ever lose control? He strode to his motorcycle and swiped the radio off the seat.

Julia stuffed her hands into her pockets to keep from stroking the trenches from his brow. "I don't mind if you think it would help."

"No. Thank you." He paced through the carport, boots pounding an angry tattoo against the cement. "One conversation isn't going to fix this and if the past is anything to go by, she won't talk for another day at least."

He nudged aside a stray bicycle helmet with his boot. "I'll ground her. Take away phone privileges."

His boot tapped a bucket of sidewalk chalk into a corner, his words picking up speed, his every step heavier. "She'll roll her eyes, slam her door then pierce another damned body part the minute she's not grounded anymore."

He kicked the wall. Julia winced.

His shoulders rose and fell with each erratic breath, finally slowing. He turned to face her, his face impassive. Except for that small tic. He stalked toward her, carefully stepping over a scooter. "So, what's your answer? Will you marry me?"

"I don't think now—"

"I know we're not much of a prize," he plowed ahead. "A messed-up teen and an eight-year-old Betty Crocker wannabe who breaks my heart she's so damned wary. And then there's me." He thumped his chest with a splayed hand. "I know I make a sorry excuse for a husband, but I like to think my friendship is rock-solid. If you take us on, I'll do my best by you and Patrick."

In spite of a thousand logical reasons crowding her brain and telling her this was a bad, bad idea, she weakened. Even Patrick chipped away at her already crumbling resolve with a gurgle from the car.

Zach edged forward as if sensing his advantage and pressed ahead. "The kids need us and what we can give them together, now more than ever."

She knew he was right, although she resented his using the all-out impact of that charismatic will to convince her. How could she turn away from those two girls who'd already worked their way into her heart with their vulnerable eyes? How could she say no to the sweet baby cooing such trust from the back seat?

Yet a part of her wanted something more from this proposal, some indication that he needed *her* and not just the role she filled for his children.

A dangerous wish since she wouldn't know what to do with such a statement even if he made it.

Julia threw out the first line of defense that came to mind. "We never settled the issue of sex. I mean it when I say I'm not ready and you almost had me convinced you were okay with that. Zach, the kiss changes everything."

"Only if we let it, and we won't."

Zach advanced another step. She retreated until her back smacked flush against her car. "Stop. Please."

"Okay. I hear you." He held a hand up. "If us having sex is a stumbling block to doing what's right for the kids, then we'll do without. We'll go back to the way things

were last year other than sharing a house. I'll buy that daybed for the computer room first thing tomorrow.''

''Won't it seem strange to the children?'' What was she
trying to do? Convince him to say no to the marriage or
no to sleeping in another bed?

''I do not have to explain my sex life to my teenager.''
The eye tic flicked again. The tender comforter who had
lured Julia into considering his proposal slipped away.

''It's not that simple.''

''Sure it is.'' Military bearing starched right up his spine.
''If anyone else asks, I'm working late hours and don't
want to disturb the baby. Or the baby is waking up at night
and I sleep in there to keep from breaking crew rest. Whatever. It's no one's business where you and I sleep.''

Yeah, right. Like anything could stay secret in the fishbowl community of base housing. What a rumor-mill nightmare, as if there wouldn't already be enough gossip with
the commander's daughter and the base chaplain's son
caught together on the golf course. Not a chance would any
of their personal lives or sleeping arrangements stay secret.

She'd swallowed nearly a lifetime supply of pride over
Lance's affair. She wasn't sure she could sacrifice what
little she had left even to frivolous gossip. But what other
choice did she have?

Her legs folded and she sank back into her car.

''Julia?''

She jolted back to the present. ''What?''

''First thing tomorrow morning, I'll talk to the base
chaplain. Double duty since I have to speak with him about
his son and Shelby. With any luck, he can marry us before
the weekend.''

Julia bristled at his assumption. She wasn't one of his
men to be ordered around. ''Now wait just—''

''We should be able to get the license right after I meet
with Chaplain Murdoch.'' He pressed a thumb to his fore-

head. "No wait. I have a meeting after that. Count on one o'clock unless you hear otherwise from me."

He reached for the door, and she slid her legs inside without thinking. The door closed with a snap. When had she lost control?

With a curt nod, he thumped the roof of her car in a farewell salute and spun away on his boot heel.

Julia steamed. Damn his presumptuous orders and that fine butt sauntering up the steps. She flung open the car door to tell him exactly where he could go tomorrow at one o'clock and what he could do with his proposal when he got there.

Zach stopped.

He paused on the top stoop, his back to her. Shoulders as broad as the doorway dropped, his head falling forward. His hand fisted at his side, raising, halting then thudding against the doorframe. A shudder ripped through him and all those damning curses within Julia dried right up.

"Julia," he said, the single word whispering a need that had sent her running straight to his house barely twenty-four hours ago.

Her mouth closed. She waited. Wanted.

What she wanted, she didn't exactly know, but she stood on the edge of something scary. Life would change for her based on what she decided in the next few seconds. "What, Zach?"

"I guess I needed you more than I realized."

His soft-spoken words rumbled with more of that need, tipping her right over the edge. Come one o'clock, Julia knew she would stand beside him in hell itself if he asked.

Chapter 7

Zach leaned to tug open the bottom desk drawer without taking his eyes off the flight data in front of him. Fishing by feel, he sifted through. M&M's. Licorice. Some kind of snack bar, probably granola. All pitched aside. He settled on a pack of Pop-Tarts.

He flipped the pack in his hand. Blueberry frosted pilfered from Ivy's secret stash.

Not much of a lunch, but it would have to do. He had zero time in his schedule for picking up anything during his lunch break except a marriage license.

Married again.

He ripped open the wrapper, not quite ready to go there in his thoughts yet. If he started thinking about Julia, he wouldn't be able to review the files about Lance Sinclair with any objectivity. His role as commander precluded him from being a part of the investigation. But that didn't stop him from hoping to find evidence to exonerate Lance anyway.

Sounds wafted from the hall. Ringing phones. Jumbled

conversations. Muffled boot thuds on carpet. Minor distractions he could work around without shutting the door.

His open-door policy of commanding might chip away minutes from his day, but he believed it saved him far more time in the long run. Maintaining strong communication with his people made for a smoother-run squadron.

Why couldn't an open-door policy at home be as simple?

He bit off a quarter of the pastry. His empty stomach was snacking on itself. Of course, it had been five hours since his 6:00 a.m. breakfast with John's father. A widower, Chaplain Murdoch seemed as overwhelmed by the whole single parent deal as Zach.

Great.

Two Air Force officers, one in charge of national security and the other salvation, couldn't come up with much more than nailing their kids' bedroom windows shut.

Tipping back his chair with a slow creak, Zach studied the flag in the corner by his desk. The Stars and Stripes twined with the second flag, a squadron guidon made to resemble an old cavalry-days banner leading the charge. Guiding. Inspiring.

And not offering a single answer today.

Chewing his way though the second Pop-Tart, Zach drowned it with a cup of coffee. His fifth. He should have arranged for Julia to ride with him to apply for the license. At least they would have had time to talk in the car. He could use her input on his fruitless meeting with John's dad, and he didn't have a second to spare in his crammed schedule.

Echoes of past fights with Pam taunted him. Why not cancel a meeting? There were plenty of choices and the Air Force always came first.

Zach wadded the foil snack wrapper. Easy enough for her to say from Italy or whatever country she'd cooked her way through this week.

He finished the rest of his Pop-Tart and shoved aside

doubts. In twenty-four hours, he would have the problem settled. Just one other problem to tackle before meeting Julia.

Putting the military first again?

He slammed the file shut. Gut instinct told him Julia's presence in his house would have a calming effect on everyone and would make it that much tougher for Shelby to run rogue on him.

Damn it, marrying Julia was the right thing to do.

A cleared throat sounded just before a tap. Zach looked up to find Tanner Bennett in the hall.

"Got a minute, sir?"

Zach brought his chair upright and pitched personal thoughts aside as quickly as the wrapper. Bronco's meeting with the crash investigation team must have ended. "Come on in and shut the door so we can talk."

Zach closed the door so rarely, nothing short of a war would prompt anyone to interrupt.

Bronco stepped over the threshold and waited. Zach tucked Lance Sinclair's file into a stack and stepped from behind the mammoth wooden desk. He opted for the chair by the vinyl sofa, sitting so the junior officer could follow suit.

Curiosity flickered in Bronco's eyes before he masked it with military regimen. He must be wondering about the driveway scene, not that he would actually ask. Protocol and rank erected some boundaries no open door would override.

But Bronco would have a good idea from the phone patch, and Zach hadn't helped matters by making out in the driveway, for God's sake. Knowing that the coming interview concerned Julia's husband, would Bronco hold back?

The subject of Julia needed to be addressed before the interview began. Accident investigations could stretch into months, years even and he didn't need that kind of tension in his unit.

"Before we start this discussion, there's something you should know. The whole squadron will hear soon enough. But given it has some bearing on this meeting about Lance Sinclair, I want to clear it up now."

Bronco's face stayed diplomatically blank. "Sir?"

"Julia and I are getting married. This week."

Bronco's jaw went slack for three telling seconds before he snapped it shut. "Congratulations, sir."

"Thank you." Time to put the spin on it, one that would mesh with whatever Julia chose to say. Zach relaxed back in his chair, hooked his boot on his knee. "It probably surprised us more than it did you. We've been trying to help each other through a helluva year. And, well..." He shrugged.

"I'm happy for both of you." The big guy looked like he meant it, even if he didn't understand. "Kathleen will enjoy having Julia across the street, especially while she's on maternity leave."

Zach straightened, planting his boot back on the floor as he leaned forward. "Folks will all know by tomorrow, but I'm telling you now before we talk about the crash investigation interview so you have all the facts. And that's all that comes into play here. Facts. Nothing's changed as far as my role in this investigation. I was Lance Sinclair's commander, which already precluded me from offering anything more than data in his records. That said, what happened?"

Bronco's shoulders lifted and dropped with a hefty sigh. "Sir, unless we can come up with something new from those facts of yours to offer the investigation team, they're going to pin it on him."

Zach bit off a curse. He couldn't let that happen. He owed Lance Sinclair's memory better than that, owed Julia.

Owed a little boy who wouldn't have anything more than a picture and a few medals to remember his father by.

Zach's gaze slid to the flag and guidon, his focus steadying. He would just have to dig until he found whatever facts hadn't come to light. Because tomorrow, come hell or high water, Julia would be his bride and damned if he would be the one to put any more tears in her eyes.

"You may kiss the bride."

Standing in the chaplain's office, Julia stared into Zach's eyes, staunchly ignoring the drab government-issue furniture littering the cramped room.

She saw only Zach, her husband.

Commitment. Marriage. Something she'd never expected to do again, even on a temporary basis.

But it was real and official. Tanner and Kathleen Bennett bore witness. Beside them, Shelby held Patrick, the teen's disdainful slouch a real mood buster for an already tense day. Not that Ivy's crinkle-nosed smile weighed any lighter on Julia's conscience. What would they tell her when they split? Why hadn't she thought this through instead of impulsively jumping in with both size-ten feet?

Julia thrust doubts aside. They'd both done the best they could with the here and now. The "now" included getting through the next couple of seconds kissing Zach without completely losing control as she had in his driveway.

He cupped her face, thumbs brushing her cheekbones. Julia steeled her defenses and mind and every single nerve against a repeat of the sensory barrage from two days ago.

His head angled, but didn't move forward.

God, when had life gone into slow motion? Couldn't he move just a little faster? She rested her hands in the crooks of his elbows. Her fingers dug into the coarse fabric of his flight suit. She stared at his beard-stubbled chin and waited.

And waited.

Someone coughed. Heat stung her cheeks, from embarrassment, from his hands...and maybe from anticipation.

Julia looked from his chin up to his eyes. Intense brown eyes stared into her, waiting as well.

She hadn't thought of what the day would mean for him. His divorce had been messy. Julia wasn't one for gossip, but common-knowledge facts swirled even for those who didn't want to listen. Today had to be difficult for him, too.

His waiting let her know he would accept whatever she decided about the kiss, taking any hits to his own image for her. For once, he deserved to have someone put him first.

She smiled at Zach. And kissed him. Not some quick brush of the lips. No way. Julia flung her arms around his neck and laid a really full-out big one on him.

He didn't seem to mind in the least.

His hand slid to cradle the back of her head. An oh-so-quiet growl meant for her ears only rumbled through his chest against hers, vibrated beneath her hands flat against his shoulders.

Let people talk. She hoped they would, because Zach was a sexy, fascinating man who deserved to have a woman who wanted to marry him for real. For himself. Forever.

Since she couldn't give him that, she would give him this. She wouldn't be sharing any details of their marriage with anyone, not even her closest friends. She would show the world the perfect image of totally enamored, hot-for-each-other newlyweds, starting now.

And afterward?

He would transfer to another base after his commander tour ended. He would start his new assignment at Air War College in Alabama, a career opportunity of a lifetime only offered to five percent of his peers. He could leave the talk behind. Leave her behind.

Reality chilled her. Julia's hands slid from his shoulders, her mouth from his. Their eyes met, held, yearned.

An airplane roared overhead, breaking the silence.

Doubts clawed their way right back over her.

What had she done? With her thoughts slowing and bravado fading, the impact of delayed aftershocks rocked her all the way to her three-inch heels.

Sure, her impulsive nature led her into doing things she regretted later. This, however, wasn't the same as plowing through a whole bag of jellybeans in one sitting or road-tripping down the coast on a whim. She wanted to lose herself in another kiss, in his arms, in him. She'd done that once before with another man and had nearly lost herself in the process.

Then Zach smiled. And winked. Her friend was back, along with all the drab military furnishings and framed airplane prints.

It felt good to have Zach back in focus. She could trust his friendship. He'd said he would honor whatever she chose about sleeping arrangements. If nothing else, she knew she could trust this man to be honest with her.

Completely honest.

I haven't kissed you, Julia, not yet, but I still know I want you. Just you.

A shiver of desire danced down her spine.

"Congratulations, sir." Bronco charged forward to pump Zach's hand, the chaplain two steps behind as everyone offered over-bright good wishes.

Zach's arm slid around her shoulders, bringing more of those incredible shivers. She wouldn't have a bit of trouble convincing the world she wanted to jump all over Zach Dawson.

Julia gathered her baby into her arms, his sweet weight the best reminder of all of why she had to keep her head and hormones unmuddled. Patrick squirmed against her, his head turning as he rooted along the cream wool jacket for lunch.

Could this wedding get any more un-traditional?

Hitching him on her shoulder, she patted his back, whispering, "Hold on a few more minutes, hon."

She would have to nurse him soon, and hundreds more times over the next year. In Zach's house. At least they would have the older children as a buffer against any more awkward moments.

"Congratulations, Julia." Bronco wrapped her in a burly bear hug until Patrick squawked. Bronco stepped back. "You make the second-most beautiful bride I've ever seen."

Julia laughed. Finding something dressy to wear that fit had been a challenge and a half. She'd settled for mixing and matching a short, off-white pleated skirt with a long jacket. "Yeah right, almost seven weeks after delivery, I'm lucky I'm not wearing a potato sack." She patted his cheek. "But thanks all the same."

"You're welcome." He slung an arm around his wife. "Kathleen and I want the girls to stay over at our house tonight."

Buffer-loss alert! Julia opened her mouth to protest.

Bronco stopped her. "Uh-uh! Don't argue. We've already worked it out. They brought over everything they need for school in the morning. There's a wedding dinner from us already waiting on your table. It's not a Caribbean honeymoon cruise, but it's the best we could come up with on short notice."

They were all trying so hard, she felt like a fraud.

Zach's hand tightened on her waist. "Thanks, Bronco. That's mighty generous of you both."

Geez, why hadn't she thought to say thanks? Not even five minutes as the commander's wife and already she was blowing protocol. Not to mention simple courtesy. "Thank you."

Patrick wriggled, pumping his feet against Julia, each little huff an insistent reminder that she'd already pushed him a half hour past feeding time. She turned to whisper in Zach's ear. "I'll be right back, okay?"

One look at the baby, and Zach nodded. "Sure. I'll be waiting."

For her.

For just a second she allowed herself to imagine she could take him up on that offer for real. What an incredible rush to know this man who so dominated the room with just his towering presence wanted her. What would it feel like to have all that intensity focused on her?

A hypnotic possibility.

Time to run as fast as her heels would allow, even if only for the twenty minutes necessary to settle Patrick. Cowardly? Not a chance.

Plain smart.

Julia tucked into the hall and found a quiet corner in an empty conference room. She plunked the diaper bag on the lengthy table and sagged into a spinning chair.

She popped open the top buttons on her jacket, loosened the nursing bra. Patrick latched on with greedy appreciation. Julia settled back with a sigh. Much-needed peace flooded over her.

Twenty minutes to regain precious ground.

The door squeaked open, Kathleen pushing through with a determined stride. Uh-oh. This was a conversation she definitely didn't want to have yet.

Put on the good face for Zach. It wasn't anyone's business, no matter how much she desperately needed someone to pour out her fears to.

Kathleen twisted open a bottle of water before passing it to Julia. "I thought maybe you might want this."

Nursing did make her incredibly thirsty, but Julia recognized the drink for what it was. A convenient excuse to check up on her. "Thanks. You're a gem to think of this."

Kathleen lowered herself into a chair, hand pressed to her back, other hand grabbing the arm rest for balance.

"You'll be able to return the favor a hundred times over since you'll be living right across the street."

"Uh-huh." Julia grasped the out offered by Kathleen's pregnancy. "You really don't have to take on the girls for us. You should be home putting your feet up."

"Watching the girls is a lot less trouble than stitching up that pilot's foot this morning. Man, was he ever a baby about it."

Julia laughed with her stubborn, wonderful friend. "Promise me you won't overdo."

"Not a chance. Tanner has the evening all planned out." Kathleen smoothed a hand over Patrick's whispery white hair. "Sorry we can't keep the little guy overnight too, but he's still breastfeeding."

"You're already doing more than enough." *Too much.*

"I hope Tanner didn't overstep." She circled her hands along her stomach as the baby rolled visibly. "He can be like a Sherman tank when he locks in on an idea."

Julia couldn't halt the rogue rasp of envy for the serenity that warmed from the other woman. The contentment. The confidence that she was loved.

Pride shooed away any leanings toward confiding. "It's a beautiful, generous offer. Zach and I appreciate your thinking of us."

Kathleen's hands stilled, her eyes searching Julia's. "Just be careful. Be happy."

Julia met her eyes, no dodging. She wasn't fooling her practical buddy for a second. Julia settled for a neutral answer. "We know what we're doing." *Yeah, right.*

Kathleen nodded and let the subject drop. She arched her swollen body from the chair. "I'll go see if the girls want to order in or eat out while you finish up."

Julia watched Kathleen leave, her friend's contentment lingering long after she left, taunting Julia with how things could be.

Even as she listened to another airplane roar overhead,

she didn't doubt her decision to marry Zach or her resolve to put on a happy-couple face for the world. She did, however, question how the hell she would walk away without a few new bruises on her already battered heart.

Chapter 8

Zach cracked open a fortune cookie from the smorgasbord of Chinese food left by the Bennetts on his dining-room table. Popping both halves into his mouth, he read the slip of paper.

A beautiful woman has a message for you.

Scattered white candles and a dozen pink roses mocked him from the dining-room table with a festivity he should have thought to offer Julia. His fingers curled to crumple the fortune, then paused. He tucked the slip into the sleeve pocket of his flight suit.

Flight suit? He gave himself a mental thunk. Why hadn't he thought to change before the ceremony?

He'd been so damned pressed for time, he'd only just made it to the chapel after sprinting to the store for a ring for Julia. Buying one for himself too had been an impulsive last-minute decision.

The gold band felt alien on his hand. He clenched and unclenched his fist as if that might adjust the fit, as if that might make the whole thing more real.

Not that it could get any more real than having a woman in his bedroom putting her baby down in a crib by the queen-sized bed. Except he wouldn't be sharing a bed or anything else with her tonight.

And he wanted to.

He wasn't often surprised, but that kiss of hers had knocked him back a step. For half a second. Then he'd decided what the hell. Analyzing could come later. The stunned look on Bronco's face *had* been priceless. No one would question their marriage now.

Certainly the less talk, the easier on his kids.

Zach circled the ring on his finger around and around.

Julia's feet sounded in the hall just before she eased into the dining room. She'd ditched her stockings. Long legs stretched from that flirty white skirt of hers. Bare feet and legs. Elegant yet natural. Totally Julia and so enticing he wanted to drape her across the table in the middle of all those roses and candlelight and follow up on the promise of their wedding kiss. To hell with the repercussions.

And if the price were only his to pay…

Ivy's hopeful face drifted through his mind. The kid had already been through enough disappointment. He needed to keep things as uncomplicated as possible.

Set the tone now. "What do you want to do about the Christmas holidays for the kids?"

"Whatever the girls are used to is fine with me. I'm not set on a particular way to stuff the turkey or hang the icicles." She opened the red-and-white cartons of food one at a time, uncovering moo goo gai pan and shrimp fried rice.

"The girls won't mind if you want to pull in some traditions from your family."

"Traditions?" She laughed. "I grew up with a real mix of everything around the holidays. It wasn't a religious commune, so everyone brought something representative from their walk of life. Like any other neighborhood in some ways, just with all the doors open.'' She dropped into a chair across from him, tucking one foot under her. ''What about you? What do you and the girls do over the holidays?''

Candlelight cast warm shadows along her creamy skin. ''Zach?''

''Huh? Oh, uh, we do all the standard stuff, tree, presents, pageant at church, lots of food.'' He flipped a chair around and straddled it. He would eat later. A candlelit dinner made too tempting a scenario for his dwindling restraint.

''What about family?'' Her brows pinched together in a frown. ''I don't even know about your family.''

The less said the better. ''My mother died when I was fifteen. My father still lives in Texas, works the oil rigs along with my younger brother. We don't talk much.'' The holidays had been the one time his dad smiled, as if that made up for eleven other months. ''What was it like where you grew up?''

''It was more of a…I guess you could say back-to-basics kind of living, everything natural. Everyone pitching in. I know this may surprise you, but I wasn't on the cooking crew.''

They shared a smile as she spooned shrimp fried rice onto their plates. He hooked his arms along the back of the chair, rested his chin on his hands and allowed himself the pleasure of watching the candlelight play with the color of her hair.

''I never figured out if I'm a rotten cook because I didn't have the chance to learn or if I didn't cook because I was really rotten at it. Regardless, I always ended up on the building committee, Habitat for Humanity in its early form. By the time I left for college, I'd already been in on the construction of ten houses and a food kitchen.''

Her parents may have taught her all about helping others, but where were they now when their own daughter needed them? Either they hadn't noticed, or Julia hadn't wanted to ask them. She'd opted to marry him instead. The thought touched something inside him he wasn't sure he wanted to examine too closely.

She'd done so much for his girls during a year when most would have holed-up with their grief. She'd put him first today with that kiss of hers.

And what had he done for her?

He hadn't even changed out of his damned flight suit.

"Sorry there wasn't time to put together more of show for today's ceremony."

"No need to apologize. I had all of that first go-round." Julia twirled her fork through the food on her plate. "Actually, I prefer it this way. The fewer memories of the past the better."

"I can understand that." Yet he could see those memories misting through her eyes anyway and kicked himself for resurrecting them.

"At least with the children, you and I actually have more in common than Lance and I ever did." A grin teased at her lips. "He was my great rebellion."

"Run that one by me again?"

"I'd just finished college and was trying to figure out what I wanted to do with my life. Like most people starting out, I was convinced that whatever I chose, it would have to be the complete opposite of my parents." She paused waving a fork at him. "Now don't laugh, but believe it or not, I was ready to leave behind the Julia-Moonglow name from my childhood."

He smiled back, all the while thinking how the name fit.

"And into that coffee shop walked Lance with all his military bearing and conservatism at a time when I planned to be an architect and build the perfect house for myself. Man, were both of us in for a shock a couple years later when we realized what a mess we'd made."

She stared down at her rice until the faraway haze faded

from her eyes. With a sigh and smile, she shrugged off the past. "Maybe there's your answer with Shelby. Let your hair grow and join a heavy metal band so she'll do the opposite."

Her slightly wicked laughter skipped across the few inches separating them, enticing him to make this wedding night real. He cleared his throat and wished his thoughts were as easily controlled. "Do you think I'd look good with a mullet?"

"On second thought," she said, reaching to smooth back hair that never grew long enough to fall out of place. "Leave it just like it is. Shelby will eventually come to the same conclusion I did. My parents are people who did the very best they could and maybe I should learn a few things from them after all."

"They brought up a great daughter." Who spent her life making perfect doll houses for other people. Who'd taken on him and his daughters to make a home for them.

And he'd pulled her out of the first real house she'd ever had. But his job mandated he live on base. He didn't have a choice on this one if he wanted to keep paying his bills. "Your house will still be there for you at the end of the year."

She shook out a napkin. "I put away those home-and-hearth dreams a long time ago."

Gripping her wrist, he stopped her restless motion, wanting her to listen. The napkin draped from her fingers like a white flag of surrender.

"Julia, this was the right thing to do."

"I know." She gently tugged her arm free and nudged his plate toward him. "Quit thinking so hard and eat."

She savored a bite of an egg roll with a contented sigh, taking the typical Julia-Moonglow joy from every experience. A real sensualist.

He stifled an entirely different kind of moan.

It was going to be a long night.

For once, he was grateful for his killer schedule. He did *not* need time on his hands to think about how natural Julia looked sitting cross-legged in his dining room. And he absolutely did not need more nights alone in the house with Julia, a big bed and an attraction that didn't show any signs of letting up.

Zach shoved aside the persistent voice telling him for once he should have thought twice before launching into this plan of action.

"Measure twice, cut once, girls." Julia lined up the slim oak planks along the sawhorses under the carport in her makeshift workshop.

If only she could be as cautious in life as she was with her woodworking. The past four weeks of marriage had proven how perfect the solution could be for the children— and how frustrating as hell for the adults.

Julia gave herself a mental shake. She wouldn't let doubts ruin this beautiful afternoon and the rare opportunity to indulge her creative muse. By the end of the week, she would have Zach's Christmas gift complete. A glider for the screened-in porch, the latest in her string of never-ending attempts to teach the man to relax.

Would he understand the significance of her choosing a deck glider? Certainly not some high-tech winged glider for the air, but a lazy ground flight of sorts.

"Ivy, hon, bring your sandpaper over here and feel the edges of this one I've already finished."

"Sure would stink to get splinters in my bum, wouldn't it?" Ivy skipped up beside her. "Shelby, come help or it isn't a present from all of us."

"Sure." Shelby sat leaning against the house, headphones in place, music filtering free. "In a minute, Mouse."

How could she hear with those things on? Of course if

Zach had asked her to clean her room, Shelby would have been stone deaf to his request.

Shelby rocked to the beat, flipping pages in a magazine. So much for an attempt to draw both girls out with the joint project. At least Ivy appreciated the effort.

"Feel that?" Julia skimmed her hand over the two-inch wide board, her fingers naturally following the grain.

"Uh-huh. Okay, can I sand now? Please!"

Julia reassured herself that enthusiasm mattered more than perfection. "Go ahead."

Ivy scampered back to attack the wood with more frenzy than finesse, stirring a cloud of sawdust. A plane roared overhead in the ever-constant flow of air traffic that reminded Julia they lived within shouting distance of an active runway.

She flipped the strip and started the other side. For once the familiar textures and scents didn't bring the soothing effect she'd hoped for in suggesting this project to Ivy and Shelby.

Her eyes skittered to the backyard.

No doubt she could lay the blame for that disquiet solely on the broad shoulders of the man napping in the hammock. The Pawley's Island hammock had been first on her list of ideas for teaching him to relax, another languid ground flight.

And now *she* was wound tighter than the webbed weave of that roped sling strung between two trees, all because the simple sight stirred her hormones as well as her heart. Eyes closed, Zach sprawled, too tall for the length. One leg bent at the knee. The other draped over the side, his booted foot resting on the ground and nudging the hammock into a gentle sway.

Another plane rumbled in the distance. His military radio perched on the ground beside Zach, crackling a steady drone. But she wouldn't think about that radio and the planes. Not today when she desperately needed some peace.

His hand tapped a steady tattoo against Patrick's back as the baby snoozed away on Zach's chest. Tiny knees tucked up, her son rested securely against the broad chest.

Lucky kid.

If only it could be as simple as separate rooms. She'd forgotten the hundreds of other intimacies of sharing a home with a man, like sharing a bathroom, since Shelby and Ivy had commandeered the other one. Julia's hair mousse now rested beside his shaving gel, her lingerie slung over the shower curtain next to his towel.

Man, he looked great in a towel and nothing else. Just that morning she'd lounged in bed, sleep still lulling her, and watched through the part in the half-closed door while he shaved. Such a simple act and somehow intensely intimate.

His musky scent had clung to steam, permeating the air far beyond the bathroom walls, drifting into the bedroom until he invaded her senses without ever dropping his fine butt into her bed.

"Julia?"

"Yeah, hon?" Julia pitched aside the sandpaper and folded a new square for Ivy.

"I told my dance teacher how many tickets we'll need for the Christmas recital."

"Great. Have her let me know how much to make the check out for."

"The paper's inside with the prices." Ivy scrubbed an edge with exaggerated concentration. "Do the math for five tickets."

Five. Julia chose her words carefully. "And who are the extra two for?"

Please, please, please she hoped Ivy would say she wanted to have a holiday sleepover and bring along two friends.

"My mom and Edward." Ivy looked up with soulful

brown eyes so like Zach's. "It's Christmas. She's gotta come home for Christmas, right?"

Shelby cranked the volume on her portable CD player until Julia could discern words through the bleed-out.

"I'll write the check." And find a back-up for taking those tickets so Ivy wouldn't have to see empty seats if her mother didn't show.

A full-out smile wreathed Ivy's face, the complete version of Zach's half smile. "Thanks! You're the best." She dusted off her board. "So what color are we gonna make this?"

Julia stroked the length and envisioned a warm honey stain soaking into the grain.

"Purple." Shelby chewed her gum, never missing a beat in the tune.

"Cool!" Ivy chimed.

Julia struggled not to wince. "We'll make a trip to the hardware store and decide together."

She knelt at eye-level with the board. Pursing her lips, she blew sawdust into the breeze with a long exhale.

A tingle of awareness sprinkled over her, the sense of being watched. Her eyes flew straight to the hammock. Zach stared back with sleepy-lidded heat.

The man gave a whole new meaning to bedroom eyes.

Maybe she should buy him one of those electric razors for Christmas, the kind that worked in the shower so she wouldn't have to watch his broad back bent over the sink anymore.

Thank goodness for Christmas mayhem which left them all with little quiet time alone.

And after the holidays?

She would count on his kids and their hordes of friends to keep the house from ever being empty.

Chapter 9

The empty house echoed for the first time in the two months since she'd tied her life to Zach's. From the rocker in the corner, Julia snuggled Patrick and looked out at her bedroom that still held so many reminders of Zach.

His bed loomed so darn big and empty. If she'd balked at the idea of sleeping in a bed that had belonged to another woman, Shelby had cleared up any misgivings right away by assuring her Zach had donated their elaborate sleigh bed to charity the day after Pam walked out.

The simple wooden bed in its place had only held Zach. And now her.

"Come on, Patrick, sweetie," Julia crooned to her son resting on her knees. Holding his hands, she lifted him until he sat upright, working to strengthen his torso muscles for sitting later as she'd learned in his physical therapy sessions. "Don't you want to stay up and play with Mama?"

He stretched with a spine-arching yawn. Julia sank back into the rocker and gave up. She had to be the only mother on the planet who didn't want her child to go to sleep, but she needed something to occupy her, especially tonight.

Shelby was at a band retreat.

Ivy at a sleepover.

Zach not due home for hours, since his plane wouldn't even land until eleven.

Zach. Flying.

Don't think about it. Nothing's going to go wrong.

Julia tapped the rocker into motion, the creak of the chair and Patrick's huffing baby sighs the only sounds in the empty house. She glanced at the clock. *Five 'til nine.* Only two more hours until he would be safely on the ground.

A routine mission. Nothing to worry about, she reminded herself. He'd flown often enough during the past couple of months.

Every time, she had thrown herself into the kids' routine to keep from thinking. Tonight was different for more reasons than the empty house.

It was the anniversary of Lance's death.

Julia cradled Patrick closer and looked heavenward. "I'm trying, Lance, trying really hard not to be mad at you tonight."

Mad at him for dying, for lying.

Except she knew she would forgive him anything because he'd given her Patrick. Julia cradled her son up to her face and kissed his brow. "Okay, sweetie, I guess it's time for you to sleep."

She stood, cuddling Patrick to her chest as she turned to the crib nestled under the window. After covering him with a black-and-white cow blanket, Julia clicked on the monitor, closed the door and headed for the kitchen. Consolation food was a must tonight.

Why did Zach have to fly today of all days?

Julia dug deep into the cabinet for a bag of caramels. Ripping the bag open, she unwrapped two and popped them both in her mouth.

She'd tried to stay busy helping Bronco decorate his house with pink balloons and ribbons for Kathleen and baby Tara's homecoming. She was happy for them, truly, but the whole happy-family, new-baby celebration stabbed her at the worst time. Which made her feel even crummier for envying them.

Julia stuffed another caramel into her mouth and chewed, already tearing the wrapper off the next one. Lights swept across the window, an engine growling in the driveway.

Her eyes flew to the clock. *Nine-oh-three.*

Julia chewed slowly while looking back to the kitchen door. She couldn't see through the window with her sedan blocking the spot. Probably just a car turning around. Not that she could make herself look away from the window.

The car shut off. The bag dropped from her hand, thudded and spilled on the counter.

She wouldn't answer the door. She didn't care that it was probably just Kathleen on the other side. Or maybe Ivy coming home early. No way would she go anywhere near that damn door.

The hell of finding the ominous trio of chaplain, doctor and commander waiting on her porch a year ago washed over her again. Julia inched two steps to the side, just three inches until she could see…a red truck. Zach's truck.

Relief turned her knees to mulch.

For five unrestrained seconds, she devoured the sight of him so big and alive. Thick, dark hair gleamed in the porch light. Broad shoulders ducked out of the truck, his brown leather flight jacket zipped up a chest she desperately wanted to climb all over so she could listen to the steady reassurance of his heartbeat.

Julia squeezed her eyes closed and slumped against the counter. Slowly, she slid down. Okay, so he would find her sitting in the middle of the kitchen floor. Better that than having him find her knocked out on that same floor if she pitched over.

Frenzy and fear whipped within her. What if that hadn't been Zach pulling into the driveway? What if another routine mission went bad tomorrow or the next day? Stupid, torturous thoughts hammered her, images that didn't accomplish anything more than to start her shaking all over again.

She needed something to make the fear stop. Tomorrow, she would be strong for the children. Right now, she needed momentary relief from the pain of the past thirty seconds and from whatever insanity had grabbed hold of her the past months.

She needed to lose herself in a raging hot night of sex with her husband.

He had a raging headache.

Not surprising, since he no doubt suffered from a lethal case of deadly testosterone build-up months in the making.

Zach dropped his flight bag on his motorcycle seat and considered heading out for a long ride. Only around forty degrees and cloudless, it would make the perfect night for speeding under the stars. He could if he wanted, without worrying about the squadron since the last plane had landed.

He backed from the bike. Forget the ride, he would just lose himself in the kids as he'd done a hundred times the past two months to avoid looking at Julia. Talk about holiday mania.

The kids had enjoyed a blow-out Christmas.

He had a mind-blowing headache.

Zach eyed the kitchen door. With any luck, Shelby would have pierced her nose, or something equally as aggravating to keep his mind off Julia.

Marrying her was the smartest—and the most dumb-ass thing he'd ever done. Sure, the children were happy, but he was slowly losing his freaking mind.

Images bombarded him, so many accidental glimpses of

Julia that turned him inside out. Julia in his bed. Julia leaning over the bathroom sink wearing nothing but a sheer slip
so short it displayed miles of legs.

Other images no less torturous kicked over him. Julia
singing to Patrick. Sawdust glinting in her blond curls as
she taught Ivy to hammer nails. Julia wrangling a smile out
of Shelby at Christmas by doing nothing more than starting
kitchen wars with cans of whipped cream.

Home-life intimacy was killing him and there wasn't a
thing he could do about it. If only he hadn't just flown. At
least they would have their very own rugrat chaperones in
residence.

Zach yanked the kitchen door open. He flung his helmet
bag on the counter and turned toward the refrigerator.

Julia sat on the floor. Knees drawn to her chest, her back
against the wall. Her pale face glowed in the darkened
kitchen. What the hell was wrong? Something with the
kids? "Julia? Is everything okay?"

"Hi," her husky voice whispered, strangely hollow in
the silence. "You're home early."

He flipped on the lights. "The winds were too strong
once we returned to base, so we cancelled the touch-and-
go landings."

"Good."

Confused and more than a little worried, he crouched in
front of her. Was this some kind of delayed post-partum
depression thing? "Tough day with the kids?"

"Not at all. Shelby's at band camp, remember? Ivy's at
a sleepover, and Patrick's down for the night." She reached
to touch his jacket, tracing his nametag. "I was
just…thinking."

Beneath her fingers, his muscles twitched. He cleared his
throat. "Anything you want to talk about?"

Talk was good. Something to take his mind off those
elegant fingers gliding along his nametag.

"Not really." She tugged the jacket zipper down, link

by link, the rasp taunting him almost as much as her shower-fresh scent and low-riding pajama bottoms.

Zach shot to his feet. "All right, then. I'll just go change. Is there any supper left?"

Damn, but he was hungry.

"I'll warm something up before you get back."

If things got any hotter, the kitchen would combust.

Zach shucked his jacket and slung it over the coat tree on his way back down the hall. In the computer room, he yanked on a black T-shirt and jeans. Tying gym shoes, he tried not to think about how he did not want to spend another night in that single bed. His feet hung off the edge and it was cold.

His bed was right across the hall and belonged to a gorgeous woman—*his* wife—who spent her nights tangled in *his* sheets.

His wife. Who was upset about something. Time to shut down his libido—yeah, right—and take care of Julia.

He approached the kitchen as he would a loaded minefield. Fifteen years of marriage with Pam had taught him he had the unerring knack for stepping right on those land mines. Give him a plane to fly, a nation to feed and he was fine. Circumventing the female psyche in a snit, however, stumped him.

Standing at the kitchen counter, Julia spooned barbecue onto a bun, her drawstring pajama pants dipping to reveal an ivory patch of stomach. Her tank T-shirt outlined perfect breasts, small and high.

And unrestrained by a bra.

A land mine might make a welcome distraction.

She returned the plastic container of barbecue to the fridge, bumping the door closed with her hip. The door closed, the thump echoing in the silent house.

Silent house?

Hey, wait. He'd been so focused on Julia's pale face

earlier he hadn't really listened to her words. The kids were all gone or asleep.

He was alone. In the house. With Julia.

Hell and damnation.

Head pounding, Zach stalked into the kitchen. He jerked open the refrigerator and pulled out a beer bottle. He needed one. Or four.

He twisted the top. "So the house is empty until tomorrow."

"Pretty much." She passed him his sandwich like Eve handing over the forbidden fruit.

One bite and he would be toast. "On second thought, I think I'll save that for later. I'm going to unwind on the back porch."

He grabbed his leather jacket from the coat tree and bolted through the door to the screened-in porch. Dropping onto the glider, he tipped his beer back and gazed at the night sky through the long neck. Like that could help him escape her. Julia filled his whole damned life.

She'd even made the glider for him for Christmas with the girls' help. Why Shelby had opted for purple paint, he would never know. But of course Julia, being Julia, cared more about making his girls smile than clashing colors.

He knocked back another swallow, the yeasty glide down his throat doing little to mellow his need to get the hell out. The gold band weighed heavy on his finger. He needed space.

Now.

Julia bumped the door open with her bottom, two more beers in her hands. "Hope you don't mind if I join you."

"Nope." Liar.

The gentle sway of her hips nudged those pajama pants perilously low. The thin T-shirt provided pathetic little barrier against the night chill.

It was cold and her body knew it.

Zach knocked back the last swig of his beer and studied…a tree. Yeah, that tree needed trimming. He would take care of it this weekend, along with a hundred other things he would add to his to-do list until he worked himself into a dead sleep.

Julia passed him another beer and sat beside him. Not that she ever actually sat like other people. She wouldn't think twice about dropping to the floor. Or perching cross-legged in a chair. Or in this case sitting sideways, hugging her knees.

She wriggled her toes in the wooly socks. "My feet are cold. Do you mind?"

Mind what? "Sure. Whatever."

"Thanks." Julia slid her feet forward.

Tucking them under his thigh.

Those toes weren't cold at all. Heat seared straight from the back of his leg to a throbbing ache higher up. Didn't the woman have a clue how she was torturing him?

He studied her through narrowed eyes. "Julia?"

She smiled. "Much better. Thanks."

"Here." He shrugged out of his jacket, shuffling the bottle from hand to hand. "Put this on."

The cooling breeze helped him. Some. Not nearly enough.

Slowly, Julia slid one arm at a time into his coat. She tucked the collar tight under her chin with two hands and burrowed into the leather with a sensuous sigh. "Ahhh. It's still warm from you."

Where the hell had she put his second beer?

Oh, yeah. In his hand.

He picked hers up from the porch and passed it to her. "Here. You'll sleep better."

"Are you having trouble sleeping, Zach?"

Hell, yes. "No."

"Well, I am." She wasn't smiling anymore. The Eve look slid away and left Julia. Open. Honest. And straightforward as always. "Kiss me."

The woman was giving him whiplash. "What?"

"Kiss me. Because it's a beautiful night and we're all alone on our porch."

If it sounded too good to be true, it was, and this sounded beyond too good. "Julia, there's no need to put on a show. Sure somebody might stroll by, but this little domestic scene will say enough to satisfy the gossip hounds."

"Zach, you make me crazy sometimes."

"The feeling's a hundred-percent mutual."

"Good." She rose up on her knees, pressing her body flush against him.

His arm locked around her waist to keep her from pitching off the glider.

"Kiss me because I want you to," she whispered the caramel-tinged invitation against his mouth. "You told me all I had to do was let you know, and you wouldn't turn me away." She slipped a finger into the waistband of his jeans, inching his T-shirt up and out.

He gripped her hand, his stomach going taut against the soft temptation of her fingers. If he could keep her talking, maybe he could stop himself from making a Texas-sized mistake. "I'm not turning you down, Jules. Just wondering about the big turnaround."

"No turnaround at all. I've always wanted you. I wasn't ready then and now I am. We could go inside and I'll prove it to you." She shook her hand free and tunneled under his shirt, fingernails scoring lightly against his stomach. "Or I can show you over there in the playhouse."

Her words blasted away the last of his restraints. Forget questioning what had changed her mind. He would dodge those land mines later. For now, he would take her to bed and do his determined best to show her how un-freakin'-believable he knew it could be between them.

Zach scooped Julia up and headed for the door.

Julia locked her arms around Zach's neck and eyed the door. Only three more steps to the total forgetfulness she knew Zach would give her.

She didn't doubt for a minute that he could deliver. The intensity of his gaze told her flat-out. She would be the lucky recipient of Zach Dawson's meticulous, determined, totally intense attention. He toed the door open, tucking sideways before kicking it shut.

Julia secured her hold on his shoulders. "I should tell you to put me down before you hurt yourself."

"You're kidding, right?" he answered, never breaking stride. "You don't weigh half as much as Bronco."

"Bronco? Thanks, I think." She laughed and loved the sound. She needed this, fun and Zach. "You carried Bronco?"

Zach charged down the hall, stopping outside the computer room. She wasn't about to question the locale. The daybed might be small, but there wasn't a baby in there.

He bent to grab the doorknob. "Fireman's carry during an emergency exercise. Fire drill from a plane."

Fire drill? Her heart thumped a nauseating pace. Don't think. She stuffed thoughts of fire drills and crash preparations deep into the mental trash where they belonged. Julia drew Zach's head back down to her as he strode into the room, kissing him, drinking the heady mixture of Zach and the lingering taste of his beer.

He stopped at the foot of the narrow daybed. "Are you sure this is what you want?"

She traced his ear with the tip of her tongue. "I haven't made love with you, Zach, not yet," she whispered an altered echo of his words to her from two months ago. "But I still know I want you."

He growled his appreciation against her mouth, reaching down to swipe aside a pile of pillows.

One knee on the edge of the bed, he lowered her. She inched up the fluffy comforter, urgency pulsing through her as she extended her arms for him to join her. Zach's solid weight pressed her into the downy softness.

Three mind-numbing kisses later, he seared a path down her neck with gentle nips that sent her arching up, frenzied for more. He worked his way down with the methodical attention to detail she'd known he would shower over her. Her shoulder, the hollow of her neck, already her breasts tingled in anticipation, strained, yearned. His mouth closed over her, leaving a damp circle on her T-shirt before he lingered along her stomach.

He gently snapped the waist of her pajama pants with his teeth. "You ready for more?"

"Yes," she gasped, tearing at his shirt. Damn it, she wasn't thinking warm and gentle, not tonight. She burned with a do-me-baby desperation born of a need to forget the hurt.

Zach tugged her pajama pants down and off, flinging them away, leaving her in nothing more than her white T-shirt and tangerine panties. He devoured her with his eyes, melting every inch of her with heat, desire and a crooked smile. "That scrap of orange has haunted my dreams for months."

"The real thing's always better than dreams," she whispered, all the while longing to shout for him to hurry. She raised up on her elbows, lifted her foot to trail her toes down his chest.

He caught her foot before her path dipped lower and pressed a kiss to her ankle. "Do you know how crazy you've been making me for months? How much I've wanted to do this." Strong hands with callused fingers rasped a path from her calf, up further, dipping behind her knee, then along her thigh to travel further still. "No one should be allowed to have legs this long."

His husky growl slid over her with a heat equal only to that of his body stretching on top of her. The power of Zach, the words, his warmth pulled her into the moment as she'd hoped. She tugged at him, draped her legs over his and locked him to her, showing him just what those legs could do for them both.

He edged to the side, cool air wafting over her, too cool after the heat and musk of his body blanketing her.

"Don't stop." She clutched his shoulders. "Even for a minute." *Make me forget.*

"Just bringing some birth control into the equation."

"In a minute. We haven't even finished undressing." Something she planned to change.

He clasped her hands to stop their restless motion and pinned them over her head. Linking her wrists overhead with one hand, he slid his fingers under the edge of her shirt. "Slow down. We have all night."

"So glad you came home early."

"Me, too."

"But you're here. And you're warm. Really warm." On fire like the coil of need unfurling in her belly and spreading through her.

Her hands trekked a frantic path into his jeans. "You scared me at first, though."

His fingers paused just shy of her breast. "What?"

She tightened her legs around him, needing to bring him closer so she would stop babbling things that brought questions. Geez, what was she trying to do, sabotage this before they even started? "Let's back up. Forget I said anything and keep doing exactly what you were doing two seconds ago."

He released her hands. "When did I scare you?"

Zach wasn't going to let it go. One slip threatened to ruin everything, something that promised to be so very perfect, something they both deserved so much.

Her head fell to the side. "I asked you not to stop."

"When, Julia," he insisted, "when did I scare you?"

"It's nothing now. Okay? I wasn't thinking clearly a few

seconds ago. It was kind of tough to form rational thoughts when you had your hand shoved up my shirt.''

He hooked a finger under her chin. ''If it's nothing, then why won't you tell me?''

She threaded her fingers through his tousled hair, desperate to return to the promise of forgetfulness, already knowing the ever-honorable Zach would pull away when he heard, damn him. ''Just a stupid minute earlier when you pulled into the driveway. You weren't due home yet, and I didn't know who was out there. I thought it might be... I thought something had gone wrong on the flight.'' She stared at his throat. ''Like before, with Lance a year ago.''

Julia's words sluiced over Zach like ice water. Actually, ice water would have shocked less.

How could he have missed the date? He'd seen it stamped all over accident files a hundred times during the past year.

Because he hadn't wanted to remember. Not now.

And now he couldn't forget.

Zach rolled off her and sat on the edge of the bed. Not that turning away kept his mind from seeing the imprint of her breasts straining against the T-shirt. Straining toward his mouth.

Julia scrambled to her knees behind him. She looped her arms around him, her cheek against his ear, her breasts too perfect against his back. ''I was scared, okay? Scared something had happened to you. So sue me. Or better yet, get back here and finish this. Prove to me you're totally all right.''

Her warm breath caressed him with a promise hotter than her words just before she nuzzled his neck.

He shoved to his feet. ''I don't think so.''

''What?''

Being honorable blew, but he wasn't crawling back in that bed with Julia and a ghost. ''This isn't right for you.''

She leapt to her feet, eyes blazing. "Who made you the god of deciding what I can and can't do with my life? Last time I checked, I was a consenting adult and I want us back on that bed."

"Not tonight. You're not ready for this."

"Oh, now you're a mind reader too? The great commander can take care of everything before we even think it." Julia closed the last inches between them. She linked her hands behind his neck, her body grazing his in a sinuous stretch that brought her mouth a whisper from his. "So tell me, Colonel, what am I thinking right now?"

He couldn't stop his body's reaction, and she wouldn't miss it. But he could control what he did about it.

"You want to forget that one year ago today I stood on your front porch to tell you your husband was dead." The words fell from him harsher than he'd intended, but then he wasn't feeling particularly pleasant.

She froze against him.

He loosened her hands from his shoulders and put much-needed distance between himself and the powder keg of pain radiating from Julia, ready to detonate. He wanted to pound a wall and maybe Lance Sinclair as well.

Zach gentled his hold on her wrist, trying to gentle his tone as well. "I won't be a stand-in for another man."

"I never said you were a substitute for anyone." Even pain-filled, her eyes didn't waver from him.

He almost believed her. Except when it came to relationships, he'd blown it too big in the past to trust his instincts now when the fall-out could be so bad for her. "No, Julia. Not now. You need time to think."

Her eyes flared again. "Why do you get to tell—"

"I need time to think," he said because he knew it would sway her, and because damned if it wasn't half true. "We need distance from this day before we make any decisions. Time apart would probably help too. I was going to tell you tomorrow, but I'll be leaving Monday to go TDY for a few weeks.''

As if accepting the inevitable, she shoved the strap to her tank top back up her shoulder, only to have it slide defiantly down again. ''Where are you going?''

He didn't answer, couldn't answer because of security, a reality of his job that had shredded his first marriage.

She dropped to the edge of the bed. ''Please, don't say it's one of those 'can't tell ya, babe' kind of TDYs. Not tonight.''

His silence said it all anyway. His job had been hard enough on Pam. Why hadn't he realized how much tougher moments like this would be for Julia? Sure, she didn't love him, but marriage and friendship had drawn her into his world, a world that had already dealt her the worst blow.

Julia traced a toe along the seam in the wood floor. ''Can you tell me when you'll be back?''

That much he could share. ''I should be home in a month, a few days before the squadron Valentine's Day party.''

She nodded, her toe making inroads along the wood grain. ''Okay, then.''

Zach scratched his unshaven face and searched for a way to fix the mess he'd landed them in. He could feed her a few details of the mission without breaking security, enough to reassure her.

He sat beside her, his eyes fixed on his hands between his knees. Zach circled the wedding band round and round his finger. ''I'm taking a couple of crews to assist the Secretary of State on some diplomacy visits for the next few weeks.'' By necessity he omitted the location. ''We're hauling supplies for the Secret Service detachment. Their surveillance equipment, SUVs. That kind of thing.''

She didn't need to know about the boundary dispute heating in South America, or that he'd volunteered his unit for this mission so he could dig into control tower data linked to Lance Sinclair's crash.

Beyond what he owed Lance, Patrick and Julia, three other crew members had died that day. He needed answers.

"It's safe." He hoped. "But I can't promise you it will be next time. Julia, the last thing I want is to check out and leave my kids behind, but this is what I do. On any given day, war or peacetime, the US military has troops deployed in *seventy* countries. That's just the average. Humanitarian relief, drug intervention patrols, peace-keeping forces. War or no war, we're out there doing our job and it's not always going to be safe."

Julia stared at the floor. Did she even know her hands shook?

Skimming her drooping tank strap back up onto her shoulder, he wanted to hold her until she quit shaking. "I want you, no question about it. I've always been upfront about that, and turning you away right now is the hardest damned thing I've ever done."

He allowed his thumb to explore her fragile collarbone, a reward for holding strong. "Think it through while I'm gone and see if my job is something you can handle before we go any further."

She looked up, direct with no wavering. Her hands might be trembling, but her gaze was rock-steady. "You missed out on something incredible tonight."

The soft skin beneath his callused thumb, and her eyes so passionate about everything affirmed that fact even more than her words. "I know."

His hand fell away and he stood. He swiped his T-shirt off the floor. "I'm going up to the office and clear out some paperwork before I leave."

Run a few hundred laps on the way.

He opened the door.

"Zach."

He glanced over his shoulder. "Yeah, Julia?"

"Could you go the extra mile in reassuring me while you're gone? A call when you land. Let me know what you can so my imagination doesn't go crazy. The more I know, the less I'll worry. It's the things I don't know about that drive me nuts."

The weight of his half truths landed square on his shoulders, but damn it, this was different than the lies Lance had shoveled her way over an affair. This was about his job and giving what honor he could to Lance Sinclair for Patrick, a child he found himself thinking of as a son.

Telling Julia that Lance's reputation was even in question could only hurt her, likely for nothing. He was protecting her. No need to tell her anything more until after the investigation was complete.

Zach nodded. "I'll call."

As he walked away from Julia, he knew that even a month apart wasn't going to stop the inevitable. He would end up in her bed. It would be incredible. And it would be the first step toward a first-class crash-and-burn, because those half truths insisted he didn't stand a chance in hell of being any better a husband this go-round.

Chapter 10

Julia wiggled her toes in the foam separators while Ivy painted each nail. The girl's brow furrowed as she slicked on Five Alarm Red, a fitting color for Julia's night at a Valentine's Ball.

And, she hoped a red-hot night with Zach.

He'd been right to insist on a month's distance from the anniversary of Lance's death, but now, she was ready. No more waiting. Well, she would have to wait another hour until he landed from his TDY and dashed home to change. Then she planned to tear up one very sexy Lieutenant Colonel.

Uncomplicated passion. Just what they both needed as a haven from the stresses in their lives.

Julia shivered in anticipation.

Shelby's reflection in the mirror smiled back at Julia. "Hold still! Only a few more curls to go."

"Thanks, hon." Julia reached over her shoulder to pat Shelby's arm, grateful for her stepdaughter's smile more than her help.

The teen wielded the curling iron in a flurry of twists and spins, the thin wand creating a halo of spirals around Julia's face. Patrick squealed from his swing, feet pumping as he tracked all the activity with his eyes. Life felt good for the first time in over a year, longer than that actually, since she and Lance had been going through such rocky times.

God, she was more than ready to experience life again.

Zach had been scheduled to arrive home two days ago, but a faulty indicator light had delayed his takeoff. Now, she would have to endure the whole evening and their mandatory appearance at the Valentine's Dining-Out formal before she could have him all to herself.

True to his word, he'd called her every couple of days. No lengthy conversations, just the steady reassurance of his deep voice rumbling across the phone lines. *Great mission today, Jules. But we're wasted. Need to hit the rack and sleep. Give the kids a hug for me.*

Sometimes those connections crackled with so much static she didn't even want to speculate where the call originated. So she didn't. Instead, she'd thrown herself into putting Lance's death behind her and making a life for herself and her child, spreading some of that healing to Zach's children as well.

"All done." Shelby untwirled the last curl. "So, Paddy-my-pal, what do you think of your mama?"

Patrick cooed his approval with a gummy grin. Julia halted the swing to kiss his head. "Thanks, sweetie. You're a prince." She twisted toward Shelby. "And thanks to you, too."

"It's *so* not a big deal. Now glue those curls in place before they fall." Shelby passed a can of hairspray to Julia, then plopped down to sit by Patrick. "Hey there, little buddy! Wanna go for a walk? Me, you and Aggie can make it around the block twice before it gets dark. Huh? Whatcha think?"

Shelby tickled his tummy and gabbed nonstop, her face uncharacteristically open whenever she played with Patrick. She'd surprised them all by asking to take a Red Cross baby-sitting course so she could watch Patrick. She'd even begun attending his family-support meetings with Julia. Who would have thought an infant could make more headway with maturing Shelby than a house full of adults?

Ivy plugged in the blow-dryer and waggled it over Julia's wet toenails. "I need some money for recital tickets. Could you write it out tonight in case we're in a hurry in the morning?"

"I thought I already sent that in."

"I, uh, told my teacher to save two more."

Patrick's swing creaked and swooshed in the silence.

How many times would Julia have to pass off the unclaimed tickets to the Bennetts so Ivy wouldn't be faced with those empty seats? God love him, Bronco had been a real trooper about sitting through two hours of Nutcracker excerpts and *Santa's Elves Go Broadway* last Christmas. "I'll leave the check on the table."

Ivy's grin crinkled her nose. "Thanks."

Shelby chucked Patrick's chin and puffed in his face until he giggled. "Well, Patrick, I sure hope the Bennetts like *Swan Lake*."

Julia swatted the air behind her chair to wave Shelby quiet. "Thanks for all the pampering, girls. Why don't you call for the pizza while I finish dressing? I'll come out for a fashion show in a minute."

The door closed behind them, muffling arguments about pepperoni versus sausage. Julia tossed aside the toe separators, grateful for the modern miracle of quick-drying nail polish. She stepped into the bathroom and shrugged out of her robe.

She unhooked the dress off the back of the door, basic black velvet to the floor, but with a surprise slit up the leg, well past the knee. Zach liked her legs and she planned to

drive the man as crazy with need as he'd made her a month
ago. She eased into the dress, gliding it up her body and
imagining how it would feel sliding down later.

As much as she wanted time alone with him, she was
actually looking forward to the evening out, for more than
just the chance to torment him a bit. Her circle of friends
had widened into a community she'd never realized existed
beyond the handful of crew members she'd known through
Lance—like the families she'd met in the new base support
group led by Rena Price, a loadmaster's wife.

Unfurling sheer black stockings, Julia rolled them over
her legs. Her life was back on track. She'd made her peace
with Lance's death, or as much as she believed she ever
could. She intended to make the most of what life had to
offer her now with Zach. For however long they were together.

Seize the moment.

And Zach.

Yeah, she definitely had plans for seizing Zach.

The doorbell pealed through the house. Julia glanced at
the clock. Zach should be landing right about now. Her
heart stuttered once. Most crashes occurred during takeoffs
and landings.

No. She wouldn't go there. The twinge of fear was just
that, only a twinge. She would probably never completely
eradicate the fear of losing someone she…cared about. But
she wouldn't let fear rob her of anything more. She'd faced
the worst and survived. Whatever else was waiting for her
behind that door, she could handle.

Julia scooped Patrick onto her hip and walked with sure
steps to the hall just as Ivy jerked open the front door.
Silhouetted in the entryway stood the last person Julia expected to see and the very person guaranteed to threaten
what little peace they'd all found over the past months.

Pam.

The woman's perfume preceded her.

Sleek black hair swinging forward, the mother of Zach's children threw her arms wide. A Godiva bag dangled from her wrist as she gathered Ivy close. "Hey, sugar baby. Mama's home for your recital."

Almost home.

The C-17 landing gear skimmed the runway just as the sun dipped into the horizon. Zach nailed the brakes, two days late and suffering from a near-lethal case of get-home-itis.

"Charleston control," he clipped into the headset mike, "Reach two-three-five-six is on the deck at fourteen past the hour. Duration, eight point nine. Fuel on board twelve thousand. Aircraft's code one." Nothing broken, not even another damned indicator light. The maintenance debrief would be a speedy ten minutes in and out before he could sprint home to change for the squadron Valentine's function.

And to see his wife.

Anticipation fired through him.

Park the plane first, pal.

He guided the aircraft from the runway to the hammerhead and idled the engines. "Tower, Reach two-three-five-six is clear of the active runway. Switching to ground control."

Zach nodded for the pilot sitting behind him in the instructor's seat to run the final checklist clean-up. Follow procedure. Keep everything reined in.

Captain Nola Seabrook behind him and Lieutenant Darcy Renshaw in the copilot's seat beside him exchanged the checklist call and response.

Multitasking was a must for any commander, and this TDY had offered the chance to address three concerns along with completing the core mission. He'd finished the re-qualification for veteran pilot Seabrook, ensuring she was back up to speed after her lengthy medical leave.

Then came the problem with Renshaw. Something was eating the young lieutenant, and she was too set on proving herself to the rest of the squadron to share. He hoped Renshaw would find a mentor in the unflappable Seabrook.

And he'd come close to accomplishing his most important task the past month—retracing the steps of Lance Sinclair's fatal flight. Zach knew in his gut something had gone wrong in the South American control tower.

With luck, the flight next week would prove just that, with the help of those who knew Lance Sinclair's flying habits best, those he crewed with most often—Tanner Bennett and Jim Price. Even Gray Clark had flown in with his family from Washington the night before to crew on the upcoming mission.

Only a week more and Zach could finally close that file once and for all.

Seabrook snapped the checklist shut and tucked it in her oversized black flight bag. "All clear."

"Roger, Captain." Zach nodded. "Renshaw, how about taking over and calling us into the parking area."

Thirty minutes later, he climbed into his truck. The past month, the sound of Julia's voice on the phone had left him so damned hard, no way would he torture himself with long-distance discussions of sex. They'd kept conversations superficial.

Until that last call when she'd ended with, *I'm ready now.*

She'd disconnected before he could answer, and he hadn't called back before takeoff. He needed to see her face to know she meant those words. Things would be complicated enough when they ended the marriage without adding another halted encounter to the mix.

Another divorce.

He stifled a curse.

One day at a time. And tonight, he had plans for his wife.

Zach pulled into the driveway, frowning over the strange car parked behind Julia's. The pizza guy maybe? If so, the pizza joint was paying big these days since the sedan looked new.

Zach sprinted for the steps, no detour to check out his bike. He wanted to see Julia. Shoving open the door, he called, "Hey, gang, I'm home."

The kitchen gaped empty.

Where were the kids?

Julia stepped into view. "Hello, Zach."

Any other thoughts flew straight out of his head. Holy hell, the woman looked awesome. Black velvet draped over her all the way to the floor and down long sleeves, in a regal way totally contradicted by the drop-dead-incredible flash of leg showing through the side slit.

Damned if beads of sweat didn't pop out on his forehead.

Her hair fluffed around her face in a mass of blond curls. Already he could imagine those spirals tousled from his hands plunging through while he made love to her.

Zach started toward her. "Jules, you look incredible."

Her stark expression stopped him before he finished his step or sentence. She cut her eyes toward the family room. He followed her gaze through the connecting dining area all the way to the sofa where Ivy sat with…

Her mother.

Anger simmered, roiled, threatened to fire free in a need to lash out before this woman hurt his children again. Her timing couldn't have sucked more, just when his girls finally had some stability.

One breath at a time, Zach regained control. His kids did not need to live with the memory of a scene. Rein it in and start the damage control. He wouldn't think about the past. And he definitely couldn't think about the woman standing beside him looking so hot she threatened to distract him from the mess in the making waiting on his couch.

Resolutely, he shut down everything inside him as fast as those engines on the runway. "Hello, Pam."

Shelby glared at her mother sitting on the sofa gushing all over Ivy about their sleepover plans. Couldn't the woman give it a rest? She hadn't shut up since the Colonel had come home fifteen minutes ago.

Flopping on the floor, Shelby snapped for Aggie to join her. Julia and her father stood all stiff and uptight by the patio door, her father holding Patrick. His smile earlier when he'd come home had lasted all of four seconds, right up until he'd seen the witch sitting on the sofa. He'd gone totally tense, even worse than the time she'd cut school to go to the beach.

Her dad scowled. Julia picked at one of her curls.

One big happy extended family.

Not.

Her dad was pissed. Sure, he didn't say anything, just held Patrick and stayed silent while Julia hovered beside him looking so pretty. Shelby had hoped maybe her dad would notice.

But Germany, France, Italy had shown up.

Shelby wanted to scream. Throw things. Pierce a path up her body that would make everybody stand at attention and notice. *I exist. What you do hurts me. Why couldn't you stay gone?*

Why didn't you come back sooner?

"Shellie, sugar." Her mother leaned forward. "Are you sure you don't want to come along with Ivy for the night? Edward and I would love to have both of you stay."

Fat chance, Denmark.

Shelby looped an arm over Aggie and tucked closer to her dog's furry body. "I promised I would watch Patrick."

Julia released the curl to spring against her head. "I can find someone else or not go. You don't need to miss out on my account."

''No, I *want* to watch Patrick,'' Shelby said through gritted teeth, pleading with her eyes, *Please don't make me go.* She even included her dad in the look, not that the iceman commander seemed to notice. What a nimrod.

Begging didn't come easy, but this was extreme. She was not spending the weekend with Sweden and Eddie.

Julia cocked her head to the side, then gave Shelby a tiny nod of understanding. ''Okay, hon, thanks.'' She turned to the other woman. ''Shelby does have a band competition in the morning. It's probably simpler if she stays here.''

Thank you, Julia. ''Yeah, it's not like we can just drop everything because you decided to stop by. But then, if you stick around for, like, longer than a week this time, maybe I can fit you in.''

The room echoed with the ticking clock and Aggie panting. Shelby clamped her mouth shut. Why had she said that? She absolutely did not want to give that woman the satisfaction of knowing she'd hurt her kids.

Her mother pulled a smile, making nice like always. ''Okay, Shellie, later then. I'll just enjoy some special time with my baby girl tonight. How about a hug before I go?''

Her mother reached. Shelby ducked away, pretending to tighten Aggie's flea collar, but she could still smell her mother's perfume, just like when her mom used to read her bedtime stories. Shelby stuffed away those thoughts that didn't mean a thing since her mother had left.

Her mother's smile tightened, and she patted Shelby's cheek instead. ''I'll call you and we can schedule something. Maybe a trip to the mall.''

''Sure. Whatever.'' Not in this lifetime. No way could that woman stroll back in with her chocolate and mall bribes. Geez, she couldn't buy them off with candy like some child.

Like Ivy.

Sucker.

Poor kid.

Ivy was gonna get her feelings stomped again. *But not me.* Not this time.

Shelby picked rug fuzz and listened to her mother's shoes click out the door.

"Zach," Julia's soft voice filled the room, "do you want to cancel going out tonight?"

Her dad shook his head. "We have to show, and we're barely going to make it on time as it is. I can't not put in an appearance at the Dining-Out. It's my squadron."

Shelby held back a laugh. She should have known. Nothing would stop the commander from doing his duty, not even a surprise fly-by from the Wicked Bitch of the West.

Light footsteps trod across the room. Julia's stockinged feet stopped in Shelby's line of sight, the black velvet dress swaying to a stop. "Shelby, I could stay. We'll stuff our faces with popcorn and watch a movie."

"No thanks." She forced a smile and looked up. "Patrick will be asleep soon and I can veg on the sofa with Aggie. Go. Please. I just want to kinda like, be by myself."

Julia frowned but relented. "If you're sure." She turned to pull Patrick from Zach's arms. "I'll put him down early while you change."

Her dad watched Julia leave the room, that commander mask of his slipping a little. One good thing out of the whole rotten day.

Had he noticed how pretty Julia looked? Shelby had thought Julia and her dad would finally get around to doing it tonight. Like they really thought she bought their lame story about why he slept in the spare room.

They just had to do it soon so Julia would stay. Even thinking about her maybe leaving, Patrick too, made Shelby's chest go tight, like running an extra lap in gym class.

Sure, life wasn't great, but it was a helluva lot better

now than before. It wasn't fair that *Mother* had to screw up everything.

Her dad crouched in front of her on one knee. "You sure you're okay with what happened tonight with your mother coming home?"

Duh, of course she wasn't. Tears stung. She blinked them back. Wouldn't want him to be even later for his stupid party.

"Yeah, sure, *Colonel.* I'm fine." She poured on the sarcasm so he would leave before she did something lame, like ask him to hug her. "But if you're really worried, you can always program some time into your palm pilot for us to talk about it. What do ya say? Let's do lunch, next month maybe?"

Pushing to his feet, he sighed the whole way up. "Love you too, Shel."

She'd wanted him to leave, right?

Shelby hugged Aggie closer, burying her face against the dog's neck. She absolutely did not want to cry. They couldn't hurt her anymore. She was only mad. Totally pissed.

They all had a life, well, so did she.

Shelby shot to her feet. She grabbed the cordless phone and punched in the numbers. Ducking out to the screened-in porch, she waited for an answer. "Hey, John. It's me.... My folks are going out tonight, Ivy, too. The baby's almost asleep. Can you come over? We'll have the whole house to ourselves...."

She ignored the pinch of guilt at having John over while she watched Patrick, something she'd never done before. But the baby would be asleep, so what did it matter? Right?

Everything would be fine in an hour when John showed up. He knew she existed.

Chapter 11

Julia nudged her half-eaten dessert away. Sitting at the long head table, she allowed herself the luxury of watching Zach, more satisfying by far than any chocolate-cherry cheesecake. She devoured every inch of his lean body in the deep-blue uniform as he strode across the Magnolia Ballroom toward the stage festooned with red satin hearts.

She couldn't wait to get him all to herself. Julia glanced at her pearl watch to find three hours that felt like three years had passed. The evening had been a surreal bubble in time. They'd danced and dined with each other and friends, like Grayson and Lori Clark who'd flown in from their Washington base for a family vacation.

Valentine's romanticism blended with patriotic pageantry in a haze of red, white and blue. Silver candelabras spiraled in the middle of every table. Red roses rested above each place setting.

Julia twirled a rose between two fingers and resolved to enjoy the Valentine's holiday. Worries from home would intrude soon enough. Surrounded by friends, she wanted to pretend that this moment could last.

From across the room, Bronco cupped his hands to his mouth. "Wolf! Wolf!"

The shout spread. "Wolf! Wolf! Wolf!"

In one of the quirky rules of the Dining-Out, no one was allowed to applaud. Spoons banged the table in a rattling din of approval like a medieval banquet of clanging utensils.

Vaulting on to the dais, Zach commanded attention for more reasons than his height and the impressive rows of medals across his chest. He carried that indefinable something within him that inspired the unwavering loyalty echoing from the room full of men and woman he led.

The calls of "Wolf" boomed. Fists pounded the tables along with the clanking silverware, all a part of the formal military Dining-Out custom that traced its roots to antiquity. Roman legions, Viking warlords, King Arthur's knights—for centuries, warriors thrived on gatherings to celebrate their victories and achievements.

Although Viking warlords had probably done so with a few less lace-paper doilies.

More than just friendship radiated from these people. Julia recognized a deeper sense of belonging that she hadn't witnessed since her childhood.

Zach swiped the microphone from its stand. "Thanks everyone. Thank you." He let loose a piercing whistle into the mike, silencing the shouts. "Thank you. I appreciate all of you coming to our little Valentine's soiree tonight. Just want to say how great it is to have the whole squadron together stateside for a change."

A cheer roared through the room.

Zach absently patted a rhythm on his pants leg until the clamor waned. "It's my duty now to call an end to the official part of this Dining-Out."

Groans rippled like a wave from table to table. Fliers partied almost as hard as they fought.

"Hey, now," Zach groused with a grin. "Some of us have to pay off baby-sitters. But for those of you who want to hang around, I've already written a check for the band to stay on until two."

The shouts doubled. "Wolf! Wolf! Wolf!"

Zach's smile never wavered while he waited them out, his rhythmic tapping resuming. Julia's fingers slowed along the rose. How many times had he done that throughout the evening? She looked closer. The brace of his shoulders wasn't nearly as relaxed as his smile implied.

She listened more closely to his words as he rallied his squadron. When had she become so in-tune to his inflections that she could detect even a hint of tightness to his tones?

"That said, nobody do anything stupid tonight," Zach continued. "If you've been sent to the grog bowl for protocol infractions a few too many times and don't have a designated driver lined up, check with Bronco over there. He's volunteered his chauffeuring services since he's not getting much sleep anyway with a newborn in the house."

Laughter rumbled through the room, Zach joining in. Julia wasn't fooled anymore. For a man who displayed so little of his emotions, those small gestures bellowed louder than the squadron shouts. He was distracted, agitated even.

Her mind raced to the obvious. Pam's return.

Jealousy pinched Julia. Hard.

Zach raised his hand, shooting a thumbs-up to the crowd. "I declare this Dining-Out officially concluded. Carry on."

Then he shifted his attention to her. Fully. A tingle rippled through Julia like a near-miss with an electrical socket.

His eyes never leaving her, he marched down the steps toward the head table with long determined strides, his fingers still drumming along his thigh. Seeing Pam again wouldn't have this much power over him unless he still harbored unresolved feelings.

Close on the heels of jealousy followed a wash of loss. How damned tragic that just when she'd moved past losing Lance she realized Zach might not be over Pam.

Julia's hopes for the evening faded. He'd been strong for her a month ago. He'd given her time to come to terms with Lance's death and helped her heal. How could she do any less for him?

Chandeliers glowed, glinting off Zach's coal-black hair and casting shadows along the bold angles of his face. God, he was beyond handsome. With a sigh of regret, she bid farewell to her late-night plans for peeling that uniform off every muscled inch of his body.

Less than a half hour left until he could peel that velvet dress off Julia's sleek body.

Zach strode straight toward his wife. Julia.

He shut out thoughts of his first wife. Pam's return wouldn't change a thing, even if she bothered to stick around this time. Any feelings for her had died a brutal death years ago, long before they'd filed for divorce. Now, he only wanted to protect his daughters from having their hearts trounced again. Zach absently patted the side of his leg, impatient to leave.

Pam had no bearing on his relationship with Julia.

A relationship he intended to deepen very soon.

Zach cupped a possessive hand on her shoulder. His thumb worked a slow caress along her back, away from prying eyes. The crushed velvet didn't come close to rivaling the incredible satin of her skin.

The head table rose for the official recessional. Once they were out in the hall, others thronged around them, but he kept his eyes firmly set on the door. No need to sweat leaving now. The party was well underway, Bronco making an effective bouncer/keeper-of-order with his linebacker-sized bulk.

The band started their next set, Major Grayson "Cutter" Clark commandeering the microphone to growl out a tune. Zach threaded through the crowd toward the coat room, Cutter's Eagles revamp filling the hall.

Finally free, Zach guided Julia toward the coat check. The low scoop of her dress in back showcased the graceful curve of her spine. An enticing view and he intended to see more soon.

He draped an insubstantial red gauzy wrap over her shoulders, leaning closer until the sweep of her curls caressed his cheek. "Have I told you how incredible you look?"

"Your girls deserve the credit. Left up to me, I'd have probably worn silk overalls and high tops."

"Either way, you'd look as gorgeous."

"I'm not so sure the general's wife would have agreed." Julia twirled the flower between two fingers, her laugh too high, too thin.

But he'd take care of that soon enough. The wait had strung them both tight. Time to get her alone.

Zach swung open the front door and followed her along the brick walkway to Julia's sedan. Street lights hummed, illuminating a path to their car. The inky sky glinted with a partial moon and the occasional airliner in flight, but it held none of his planes tonight. He had hours left before he turned on that radio again, and he intended to make full use of every minute.

Holding the door open for Julia, he tracked the mesmerizing glide of her legs as she slid them into the car. She dropped the flower on her lap. On her thighs. In ten more minutes, he'd be grazing her bare skin with those soft petals.

Zach shut the door and beat a path around the hood.

Behind the wheel, he looked over his shoulder to back out of the parking lot. Almost in the clear.

Julia pleated her red wrap between her fingers for three stop signs before she broke the silence. "I called home again at ten, and Shelby sounded okay."

"Good thinking." The fifteen mile-an-hour speed limit through base housing had his foot twitching. With any luck his daughter would be asleep by the time they hit the driveway.

"Shelby checked on Patrick for me while we talked, and he was sleeping soundly. She even put the cordless phone up to his face so I could hear his sweet little baby breaths. Isn't it funny how I can recognize my child just by the way he breathes?"

"Parenthood has a way of changing the way we see things." Damn but he wished he could figure out how to fix things with Shelby, but an ice cream cone and trip to the park didn't cut it anymore.

"The parenthood thing still feels so new to me. I second-guess all those instincts. I had a great time tonight, but I couldn't stop thinking about the children. What do you plan to say to Shelby about Pam?"

Say to Shelby? He'd already tried, for all the good it had done. "I'll talk to her tomorrow after band."

He pulled into the driveway behind his truck. Three minutes to take-off. Zach reached for the door.

Julia stopped him with a hand on his arm. "Pam showing up out of the blue like that was tough for both the girls." She traced the silver band circling the wrist of his uniform jacket. "How are you?"

Sexually frustrated as hell. "How am I what?"

"About Pam coming back."

The muscles along his arm flexed beneath her touch. "It doesn't affect me in any way other than how it affects my children. Pam and I were over a long time ago. The divorce was only a formality."

He didn't want to discuss Pam, especially now. Zach fingered one of those spiraling curls. "Jules, let's talk about something else."

"We can't pretend she's not back."

"I'm not saying we should." The three-minute wait suddenly promised to stretch into at least an hour.

Okay, so Julia would need a slower pace to relax, thanks to Pam's surprise return. He could handle that, even found the revised plan for seducing Julia had definite merits. Through the windshield, his tarp-covered Harley loomed, offering the perfect way to romance his free-spirited wife.

Zach bolted from the car, calling over the roof to Julia. "Wait right there. Don't go inside yet."

He unlocked the kitchen door, ducking into the darkened kitchen. The television droned from the next room. "Shel," he called, tugging his leather jacket off the coat tree by the door, "everything going okay?"

A rustling sounded from the family room just before Shelby shuffled into the kitchen. Rumpled and bleary-eyed, she shoved a hand through her mussed dark hair.

"Everything's cool, Colonel. Patrick took a bottle at about nine, but went right back to sleep." She pulled the nursery monitor from her pocket, Patrick's steady sighs filled the silent kitchen. "Hear?"

"Good. Julia and I will be gone for another couple of hours," *at least,* "if you've got everything under control here."

"No rush."

He started to back out the door, then hesitated. "How about after I pick you up from practice tomorrow, we grab a burger? Just you and me."

When she didn't respond, he stepped farther into the kitchen.

"Sure," Shelby answered quickly. "A burger is cool. Now go have fun with Julia. She deserves a break."

Maybe the stability of the past few months had steadied

Shelby enough to withstand her mother's return after all. God, he hoped so.

"Thanks, Shel." Zach pulled the door shut again and faced Julia.

Sweet Jesus, she looked good silhouetted by the moonlight. He loped down the steps to his shrouded motorcycle without taking his eyes off Julia for a second.

One tug and he swept the black tarp from the Harley Electra Glide, unveiling the bike like a lover. "Wanna go for a ride?"

Julia was tempted—by more than the bike. And the lean, gleaming lines of the motorcycle were pretty darn enticing.

Her respect for Zach's restraint a month ago upped another notch. Saying no when her body so very much wanted to scream yes could well drive her nuts. How had her plan to start him talking gone so astray? But convincing him to open up wouldn't be any easier inside with Shelby still awake.

Maybe a ride on the Harley wasn't such a bad idea after all. Shelby would be asleep by the time they returned. They could sit outside on the glider, away from the temptation of an inviting bed.

Meanwhile, she could indulge herself in an hour on that incredible motorcycle with her arms wrapped around Zach's even more incredible chest. "Give me five minutes to run inside and change."

"Uh-uh. Stay just like you are." He dangled the leather jacket from one finger. "Put this on."

The unconventional image of the two of them in formal clothes on the motorcycle appealed to every boundary-pushing bone in her body. "You do know how to roll out the Texas-sized enticement, Colonel."

He held open the jacket while she slid her arms inside, even though she didn't need it on the temperate Southern night. February could bring temps ranging from the twenties to the fifties. Lucky for her, tonight the fifties had won. The jacket and Zach's back would lend more than enough warmth.

Zach pulled on a helmet and passed her another. He straddled the bike and brought it roaring to life. The man sure could stoke her fantasies. For the rest of her life, she would carry the memory of him on that vintage Harley— sharp creased uniform, gleaming medals and a hundred percent man, all on display for her eyes only.

She perched on the bike behind him, adjusting and tucking her dress around her legs, her arms around his chest. Enveloped in leather and the lingering musk of Zach's scent, she swallowed, twice, and still her mouth dried right up.

Zach kicked up the stand and guided the motorcycle through military housing, into main base, past the clinic while holding to a sedate speed.

Until he cruised through the front security gate.

The Harley leapt to life, accelerating along the curving access road, faster. He leaned, urging the motorcycle farther, hugging the road in a heart-thumping turn that would have had her screaming if anyone other than Zach had been in control. He wouldn't risk hurting her. Zach would know just how far to push that bike and the boundaries to bring her the maximum thrill.

Pine trees blurred into a haze of green on one side. On the other, the length of runway behind a fence whipped past. A short ride on the highway led them up onto the interstate, raised roads and bridges so much a part of the water-locked Charleston way of life.

Wind churned beneath, over and around them. Overhead, street lights illuminated the lanes with nothing but black swirling below them, sky above. City lights sprinkled too far away to touch. The bike hummed along the bridge, the stretch of road seeming suspended in midair flying a path into infinity.

A totally different scream built within her, a shout of exultation as everything else fell away and she plunged into the sensations of hurtling into that void with Zach. Julia closed her eyes, pressing herself to his back, certain she could feel his heart thudding through his uniform and leather. If only life could be this simple—feel and fly forever.

Eventually the wind-tunneling roar faded, slowed, stopped.

Julia blinked, momentarily disoriented until she realized they were back on base outside Zach's squadron. Residual excitement still buzzed through her as she leapt from the motorcycle.

She whipped off the helmet and shook her curls loose. "Wow! I have absolutely got to get myself one of these."

Zach swung a leg over the seat. Grinning, he unsnapped his helmet. "I thought that might appeal to you."

"Thank you."

"You're welcome."

As far as a Valentine's memory, it definitely beat some moonlit carriage ride. Zach's choice showed how well he knew her and that touched her most of all.

And it was the only Valentine's season they would celebrate together, the ride likely to be the only excitement they could share.

The night air chilled.

Back to the reality of Pam's return and what it would mean for the fragile peace they'd built. "Why are we stopping here?"

"I need something before we go home." Palm flat against her back, he ushered her toward the door.

Couldn't the man put work on hold for even a few hours? Her heels clicked double-time along asphalt. "Slow down, will you? These heels are tough to run in for a girl used to sandals and gym shoes."

How could he be in such a hurry to reach his office when

all she could think about was the great sex they could have been having?

"Sorry." He punched in a code and stepped into the squadron, flipping on a hall light.

She hugged the coat tighter around her in the nippy corridor and followed him into his office. Fluorescent lights flickered.

The lock clicked.

Before Julia could think, much less protest, Zach twirled her by the arm. He flattened her back against the door. He kissed her, hard, fast and full. Reasonable thoughts fell away as fast as the leather jacket he tugged from her arms and flung to the floor.

"I swear, Jules," he mumbled against her mouth, her cheek, her neck. "That was the longest damned party of my life."

Hers too. Heat poured from his lips over her skin, pulsing through her veins into a pool of longing, low and needy. Saying no was tougher than she'd expected. Why hadn't she pressed him to talk more in the car so they could move past Pam's return?

"Zach, wait." Gripping the lapels of his uniform, she scrambled for control. "I thought you needed to get something before we go home."

"No. I said I needed something. You. Now. Where no one will interrupt us."

His mouth returned to hers with a mind-drugging draw that threatened to steal her focus. Much more and she wouldn't stand a chance of stopping him. Or herself. "Zach. Zach! Please. I need to say something."

His forehead thunked to the door. "You've changed your mind."

"No! Yes. Not really." She rubbed her cheek against his shoulder. Her eyes swept the room as she grounded herself with visions of concrete objects, a looming wooden desk, flags tucked in the corner, framed certificates and photos of planes filling the walls. "I know what I said earlier on the phone, but—"

Zach pushed away from the door, away from Julia, and walked to his desk. Keeping his back to her, he straightened a stack of files. "Indecision is the same as a no, Jules."

"I'm not saying no for me. I'm saying it for you."

"For me?" He shot an incredulous look over his shoulder, then turned to sit on the edge of his desk. "Want to explain that one? Because I'm certain I want us both already naked."

His words hummed through her, not unlike the hydroplaning sensation of the bridge ride. Gathering her thoughts proved tougher than she expected with Zach's piercing gaze probing her as she walked.

She paused by the flags, fingering the coarse canvas. Tucked away in a closet, she'd saved a folded flag just like this one for Patrick, the flag that had draped his father's coffin before being presented to her. Still, she could hear the roar of the planes flying a missing man formation overhead, the reverberation of a twenty-one-gun salute.

For the first time in over a year, she allowed those funeral memories to march through her mind and found she could face them now without falling apart. Thanks to Zach. "A month ago, you told me you wouldn't share your bed with a ghost. Well, I'm telling you the same thing. You need to sort through your feelings for Pam first."

Never again would she share her husband with another woman.

"Pam?" His arms folded over his chest. "In case it escaped your attention, neither of us died. She and I are divorced."

She and Lance had nearly divorced. Her life had been thrown into such turmoil over his affair, she'd wondered if she would ever recover from the betrayal and learn to trust again. "A divorce doesn't necessarily erase all the feelings."

"In this case it sure as hell did." Hard and steady, his eyes met hers. "I do not harbor any lingering feelings for Pam. Our marriage was over long before she left. We stayed together for the kids."

Hope teased her, too much so. It shouldn't be so important that he convince her. But it was. "Then why did seeing her upset you? Don't even try to tell me otherwise."

He pushed away from the desk. "Geez, Jules, I'm scared as hell she's gonna rip my kids' hearts out again."

"Oh."

"Yeah, oh."

Julia sank to the sofa.

He dropped down beside her. "We got married so young, while I was still at Texas A & M. She didn't have a clue what kind of life we would have in the military. We went through four trial separations, even gave marriage counseling a shot before she walked for good."

An unwanted flash of sympathy stirred for Pam. Not that it excused how the woman had treated her children, but her difficulty handling military stresses somehow made Pam more human, and Julia didn't want the confusion that brought.

Hands between his knees, Zach twisted his wedding band around and around. "She couldn't take the Air Force way of life, the TDYs, the moving. The combat. During Desert Storm, Pam received one of those front-porch visits from the commander letting her know I was MIA."

Julia forced herself not to wince at the stab of pain his words inflicted. She'd wanted Zach to talk and she wouldn't let her own agenda interfere with what he needed.

"Her next visit from the commander wasn't too much better. They'd located me. I was a *guest* of the Iraqi people."

Horror prickled over her in icy shards. "You were a POW?"

"For two weeks until the war ended."

''How did I never hear about this?'' Why hadn't he told her? ''Do the girls know?''

''No, and I'd rather they don't know until they're older. I flew the A-10 back then, took some anti-aircraft fire and ejected over Iraq.'' He scrubbed a hand along his jaw. ''Once they brought me in, my face was such a mess no way would they put me on television to use for propaganda purposes. I wouldn't have made much of a convincing poster boy for their cause if it looked like they'd forced me to talk.''

A dark chuckle rumbled from him, but Julia didn't find anything in the least amusing. She blinked fast, searching his face. She traced one finger along his mouth, up into the one-sided curve of his smile, then to the other side.

His quirky half smile. *Ohmigod.* ''Zach?''

''There's some residual nerve damage on the left side,'' he recited, his voice as calm as if relaying facts from one of those files on his desk. ''Nothing extensive, just a half-asleep feeling.''

Her throat clogged, her mind swirling with images of what he must have endured, all the details he'd left out of his sparse retelling. Her jaw worked, but she simply couldn't find words for this one. She caressed his cheek as if that might somehow heal the loss.

He gripped her wrist, turned his face to kiss her palm, then drew her hand away. ''It's over, and only a two-week sampling of what guys in 'Nam survived for years.''

''One day is too much.''

He didn't answer, just stared at their linked hands. ''When I came home, Pam had already left. Packed up Shelby and gone to her mother's. It took us over a month to put things back together.''

All sympathy for Pam incinerated. Zach deserved better than that, and Julia couldn't escape the fear that she might not be any better for him if put to the test.

Zach hooked an elbow along the back of the vinyl sofa

and angled toward her. "I'm only telling you so you'll understand how far back my marriage started falling apart. Every conflict after that, Somalia, Kosovo, Afghanistan, made it worse. When trouble started brewing in Sentavo, I knew it was over and we filed for divorce. She stayed with the girls until I finished my rotation overseas, but that was it for her. Believe me, when Pam and I signed those divorce papers, we didn't feel anything other than relief."

Heaven help her, she believed him.

She couldn't do anything about how Pam had failed him all those years ago, and she couldn't promise she wouldn't disappoint him in the end. But right now, she could be there for him the way he deserved. She could soothe a wound he seemed unwilling to acknowledge, but one that needed healing all the same.

She would give Zach the hero's welcome home he deserved.

Chapter 12

Julia stayed silent so long Zach looked up and found tears in her eyes. Ah, damn. What the hell had he been thinking? He'd only meant to convince her that he and Pam were over. He hadn't meant to spill so much.

She glided up to her knees on the brown vinyl sofa. She leaned across and pressed a kiss to the left corner of his mouth, then rested her cheek against the numbed side of his face.

Ah, damn again. He definitely should have kept his yap shut and just seduced her. He could have done it so easily. Instead he'd launched into a morbid story guaranteed to send an Air Force widow running.

He palmed her back, her skin warm and soft under his hand, her tears hot on his face. "Hey, Jules, it's all right. It was a long time ago. I shouldn't have told you."

She swiped away tears with the back of her wrist. "Of course you should tell me. You lived it. The least I can do is listen. When does somebody get to do something for you? Yeah, hearing what happened to you hurts me. It should hurt, but it hurts so much more knowing you were by yourself." Determination fired through her tears. "Now close your eyes."

"What?" Following Julia's train of thought rivaled the challenge of flying without radar.

Her hand trailed from his brow over his eyes. "Shut them."

Darkness enveloped him, like flying through an inky night sky by instincts. All other senses heightened, the feel of her velvet dress warm against his hand. The lingering rosy scent clung to her, drifting up to permeate the still office air.

"Zach?"

And sounds. The way she said his name twisted him into knots as tight as the first time she'd whispered it nearly five months ago. "Yeah, Jules?"

"I want you to imagine you're on the plane again coming home from Iraq."

Huh? Where the hell was she going with this? Not that he intended to stop her since she'd quit crying.

Because it seemed important to her, Zach traveled back through his memories to that day on the plane—the longest ride of his life. He hadn't expected Pam to be the supportive wife of the year, but he'd been pretty damned sure she would be on the runway waiting for him.

She wasn't.

Julia's soft voice slid over the memory. "This time when you land, I'm there waiting for you. We're all there—me, Shelby, Ivy and Patrick. Okay, I know technically the younger two weren't born yet, but I'm the one building this fantasy and I want them there."

The image settled in his mind so damned right his chest tightened.

She linked their fingers. "We're standing with the rest of the families. Ivy's holding a poster she drew for you, and I have a bottle of champagne ready to pour over your head the minute you reach the bottom step. Shelby's pretending to be mad because I made the kids all wear Welcome Home Dad shirts and she vows they're lame. But I know she's kept a picture of you on her dresser the whole time you were gone.''

Zach squeezed her hand, knowing that image only stood a chance of ever coming true because of Julia.

''Then you're right there in the middle of us and we're all hugging and laughing and crying a little, too.'' She brought their clasped hands up to her face and skimmed away fresh dampness with the back of his wrist. ''But that's okay because tears are a part of a hero's welcome home. You deserve them for what you've been through.''

Those tears soaked into his skin clear to his soul, soothing a raw place he hadn't even known existed. He'd lived through those two weeks of captivity. Survived it. Dealt with it.

But afterward? He'd been too busy working to salvage his marriage to do anything but move forward. Discussing those two weeks with Pam was never an option.

''When we get home, there's a gourmet dinner waiting that I cooked just for you.'' She tapped his lips. ''Shh. Remember it's my fantasy, okay?''

A laugh rumbled, rolling free and joining hers. Leave it to Julia to know he needed to laugh.

He opened his eyes. ''Thanks, Jules.''

''Not yet.'' Her hand skimmed over his eyes again. ''This is my fantasy, and I'm not done with you.''

Her voice shifted from soothing to sultry, upping the temperature by at least twenty degrees.

''Finally, we tuck our children in bed and we're alone.'' She canted closer, velvety-encased warmth molding to his side. ''I'm more than ready to give you the rest of a hero's welcome home, the best part.''

His heart rate kicked into mach speed. ''The best part?''

''Very best.'' Her breath caressed his neck. ''I kiss you,

or maybe you kiss me. Who can tell? We're both so hungry for each other we're stumbling down the hall to our room. I've missed you so damned much. Waiting all through dinner has me ready to jump out of my skin and finally I have you to myself.''

The past blended with the present in her words, in her touch.

''I've been scared and confused, but it's okay because you're here and we're going to put everything else aside. We need each other and somehow that's all that matters right now. We deserve this moment. Just us.''

She tugged his tie until it came free. He forced himself to listen when he really wanted to flip her onto her back and plunge into her.

Her fingers walked along his collar, dipping to stroke his neck. ''You shut the door, and we can't even make it to the bed. You flatten me against the door, and you feel so good and warm and hard.'' She grasped his wrist and slid it inside the slit of her dress to rest on her knee. ''You touch me and I want to touch you, but I'm not sure I can move because you have me so hot for you I'm shaking.''

She urged his hand up her stocking-clad leg until he reached…ah, hell.

The snap of a garter hooked along the top of her stocking.

Julia inched his hand farther to the bare skin of her thigh. ''I lean into you and whisper my little secret that I've carried with me all night long.'' Her mouth brushed his ear, her words breathy and full of promise. ''I don't have on any underwear.''

Inching back to stare into Zach's narrowed eyes, Julia waited for his reaction to a declaration she still couldn't believe she'd made. She didn't have to wait long.

One broad hand palmed her back, the other lay still warm against her bare upper thigh as he flipped her onto her back.

The air wooshing from her lungs had nothing to do with the fluid change of position and everything to do with the mesmerizing man looming over her. Her night of fantasies promised to reach new heights that far outstripped the Harley ride or her dream seduction.

And speaking of outstripped… Julia reached for the silver chain holding his uniform jacket together.

Zach's hands closed over hers. "No, ma'am. It's my turn now."

His husky Texas drawl slid over her skin and along her every heightened nerve.

"Your turn to do what?" She invited him with a slow arch of the back, a gentle glide of her foot along his calf.

His hand snaked down to stop her progress, then tunneled inside her dress again and up the slit to stroke her leg. "You've had your way with me, and I intend to return the favor. I have some ideas of my own about how I want to play out this homecoming."

Bold, callused fingers snagged along her stockinged leg, higher, rasping along her bare hip. Julia shivered, waited, yearned. "Please, haven't we waited long enough?"

"Too long, and that's why we're not rushing."

His arrogant assumption of control might have irritated her if she hadn't been so very certain he would make the agonizing wait worth her while. "I'm all yours, then."

His eyes never once leaving her face, he continued, "All the way across the ocean, I thought of doing this."

Zach cradled the back of her neck and lifted slightly, baring her throat for his mouth.

"And all through dinner, I imagined doing this." His words warmed skin already on fire, his fingers finding the top of her zipper.

She bowed to accommodate him, her breasts pressing against the solid wall of his chest. He tugged the zipper down bit by excruciating bit until the sofa warmed her back.

Zach drew the black velvet from her shoulders, slipping it free from her arms, so methodical and slow. She spied the passion beneath all that control, glinting white-hot flecks in his darkened eyes. She felt his need pressing insistently against her just before he stood to unveil the rest of her body.

With a bra built into the dress, she truly didn't have any underwear between all that velvet and her skin, just a garter belt and stockings. And for tonight, she didn't intend to allow anything from the past to slide between them either.

Imprinting the vision of Julia in his memory, Zach let her dress slither from his fingers to the floor. If he lived to be a hundred and ten, he would never forget the image of her draped across his office couch wearing nothing but a black lace garter belt, spike heels and a come-and-get-me smile.

Control snapped. Forget fantasies. The reality sprawled in front of him in a long-legged display beat any fantasy, hands down. "You're right. No more waiting. We'll do slow later."

"And later again." Julia swung her legs off the sofa, gliding up to stand in front of him.

Zach whipped off his jacket and shoved down the suspenders. Her frantic hands double-timed opening the studs along his starched white shirt.

"Birth control." Zach eased away. "Just let me get my wallet." He reached for his jacket, but she stopped him, hands gripping his hips.

"No need. I went on the pill the day you left on TDY." Rambling breathlessly, she struggled to loosen the top button of his pants. "Doc said I could take the progesterone kind until Patrick finishes weaning, just not the estrogen ones, and oh, Zach, what are you doing to me that I can hardly string together rational thoughts or—"

He silenced her with his mouth, or maybe it was his hand sliding up a silken thigh, between her legs and finding her so warm, wet and ready for him. Definitely no need to wait now. They weren't limited to once. They could have slow, fast and whatever else they wanted tonight.

With trembling fingers, she eased his zipper down, her hands sliding inside to wrap around him. A shudder ripped through him. Enough. He'd gone too long without, too long without *her* to hold on to control another minute.

His arm dipped low, under her bottom as he lifted her up and against the locked door, ready to play out every inch of her fantasy. Julia's long legs locked around his waist in a magnificent sweep that almost sent him over the edge. Slowly, he slid inside her, up, deeper until she encased him in velvet heat that taunted, enticing him far more than the sexy velvet dress of hers had.

Then he couldn't think beyond moving inside her, kissing her, holding her and holding back for as long as he could. Praying she would find release soon because he wasn't going there without her and the need to finish roared through him like engines at full throttle.

His mouth caressed along her shoulder, his free hand cradling the gentle curve of her breasts just before his mouth found one perfect peak. A moan vibrated through her chest, against his mouth, building to a gasping cry of release until her head fell back on the door.

Finally, he allowed himself to plunge one last time, deeper and harder, his hoarse shout of completion muffled into the soft curve of her neck as he flew full-out into the clouds and Julia.

Sprawled over Zach on the sofa two hours later, Julia listened to the steady thud of his heart against her ear. No doubt hers raced at double the speed.

She wished she could attribute the pattering pace to his hands massaging along her back. Or the scent of musky sweat and sex linking their bodies. Or the memory of their mind-tingling encounter against the door.

But she knew better.

Her heart hammered out of fear. So many emotions pulsed through her, confusing yearnings to cuddle with Zach through the night, to wait until he fell asleep and shed a few more tears over his battered, beautiful face.

She hadn't expected to feel so much. Wasn't sex just a physiological need? She hadn't been with anyone other than Lance for comparison. Their sex life may have been physically satisfying, but it was nothing like this.

Being with Zach had gone beyond fulfilling some basic urge, transporting her into a wild, unknown territory. Like flying over those bridges with him on his motorcycle, there was nothing below or above them, just the two of them holding onto each other as they hurtled into the night.

No safety net.

While she had reconciled her past with Lance, that didn't mean she planned to risk entrusting all her tomorrows to another man. She and Lance might have patched their marriage, but the price had been so very high to her heart.

She was scared. Already, Zach stirred more within her than Lance ever had.

Damn it, Zach was supposed to have been her friend and friend-sex should be warm and fun, not this tumultuous turning her mind and body inside out with feelings. She didn't want the desperate need to do it all over again while wondering if there would ever be enough. She could lose herself in this feeling, and she'd vowed to never lose herself in a man ever again.

She needed space and time to regroup. She couldn't think with his hands on her skin and his heart beneath her ear. What would happen to her emotions if they shared a bed, so much more intimate than what they'd done together against that door?

On the floor.

On the couch.

Oh damn, she was a mess. Julia listened to the steady

thrum of his heart and couldn't make herself roll off him. She would just be honest with Zach. They'd always had that between them.

He dropped a kiss to her shoulder. "Well, Jules, we can't camp out here forever."

"Not unless we raid the snack bar," she answered absently.

"I have a desk drawer full of junk food, but I think you'd grow tired of Little Debbie cakes after a while." His gravelly voice rumbled against her, enticing her to avoid the world a while longer. "Are you about ready for us to find our clothes and go home?"

"I guess so." For five seconds she actually considered telling him she wanted to stay the whole night in his office, indulging in each other and that box of Little Debbie cakes.

Not a chance would he understand why she was too terrified to share a bed with him. How could he when she didn't understand herself?

She only knew one thing for certain. Wild, escapism fantasy was easy. Facing the reality awaiting her at home scared her all the way down to her do-me-flyboy heels.

Zach cruised the Harley to a stop under the carport, Julia's arms loosely looped around his waist. They both needed a few solid hours of sleep, but then he had plans for her. Already his body stirred through the exhaustion.

Being with Julia had been like one of his Harley rides, the closest thing to flying on the ground. Better. He couldn't imagine how he would ever get enough, but he intended to spend the next few months trying.

They had their life back on track. He'd been right about sharing their children and friendship. Now they also shared a jet-engine-hot attraction beyond even what he'd imagined.

And his imagination had been mighty damned active lately.

Zach parked and covered his motorcycle while Julia unlocked the door without speaking. Her silence boded well, in his estimation. No need to hash through all the implications of what they'd done back in his office.

Definitely a good sign.

He and Julia weren't going to put each other through the emotional wringer they'd both gone through in their first marriages. This was about being practical, not about feelings.

Zach ignored the persistent voice that told him he'd been *feeling* anything but *practical* when he'd plastered Julia against his office door.

He followed her up the steps and into the dark house. The television still echoed from the family room, but all was quiet otherwise. Helping her slip out of the leather jacket, he skimmed his fingers along her arm. "I need to pick up a few things from the spare room first," he whispered low so as not to risk waking Shelby or Patrick.

Julia ducked free of the coat, backing toward the dining room. "I should turn off the television."

She disappeared around the corner, into the den. A gasp sounded, just before a thump.

Frowning, Zach slung the jacket on the coat tree. Shelby must have left some kind of mess.

The realities of life with kids. He strode through the dining room, stopping behind Julia and looking over her shoulder. Disbelief quickly shifted gears into anger.

Reality sprawled glaringly across the sofa in the form of Shelby, her boyfriend and a tangled mess of half-clad arms and legs.

Chapter 13

Zach stared at the teens on the sofa through a red haze of fury. Shelby and John gaped back with wide, deer-in-the-headlights eyes.

Chaplain Murdoch's delinquent, about-to-be-dead son bolted to his feet, open shirttails flapping. John raked back his long hair into a band. "Sorry, sir. We fell asleep."

Damn it, why did it have to make him feel a hundred years old to think no kid with hair down to his shoulders could have good intentions toward his daughter?

Zach fought his way through the anger and brushed past Julia. "Damned well doesn't look like you're sleeping to me."

Shelby closed the last button on her purple silk shirt, rhinestones blaring Princess across a pocket. "Cool your jets, Colonel. We weren't doing anything."

Zach pinned her with a glare.

"Anything much." Shelby flung her black hair over her shoulder with a surly twitch.

He knew too well how much could be accomplished on

a sofa in a couple of hours, and his daughter better not have been doing even half of it.

Julia swept past him. "Where's Patrick?"

Shelby winced, looking guilty for the first time. "He's asleep." She snatched the monitor from the coffee table and held it up in defense. "I kept this on the whole time. I wouldn't let anything happen to him."

Julia took the monitor from Shelby, lips tight as if holding back the very accusations Zach longed to hurl at his daughter. A shuddering sigh later, Julia hurried past and down the hall.

John ambled forward, baggy clothes rippling with each step. "Sir, this is my fault. I shouldn't have been here."

"That's right. You shouldn't." Zach kept his voice level, a near-impossible task, reminding himself John was just a kid.

A kid who'd had his hands all over Shelby a few short minutes ago.

The red haze threatened to blaze over him again. "It's time for you to leave. No detours, I'll call your house to make sure someone's up waiting."

"I'm not going until I'm sure Shelby's okay."

Restraint edged further away. "Want to run that by me again, boy?"

"I'm not leaving yet."

He might have admired the kid's courage, if it weren't so damned stupid given the circumstances. "Keep this up and I can guarantee your father will be volunteering for an assignment in Nairobi." Zach stepped toe-to-toe with the kid and allowed the quiet heat of his anger to seep into his words. He wanted this boy scared and running. "Good luck finding a girl to sweet-talk into *falling asleep* with you there when everyone's speaking Swahili."

Shelby slid between them. "Stop, Colonel. Okay? This is so lame." She turned to John. "Go home, really, it'll be better if you leave. He's not gonna hurt me. He'll just ground me again, but I'll see you at school Monday anyway.''

John hesitated, then nodded. Shelby followed him to the screened porch while Zach waited, piecing together control and what the hell he would say to his daughter.

He pressed a thumb between his eyes, right above the throbbing headache with Shelby's name tattooed all over it. Honest to God, he was going to have a stroke before the girl graduated high school.

What would Julia say? He steadied himself with thoughts of her calm voice.

The door snapped closed and Zach opened his eyes to confront his daughter. ''Well, Shelby Lynn, what do you have to say for yourself?''

''Nothing. Not one thing.'' She spun on her heel, flouncing out of the room.

''Think again.''

Shelby sighed a lengthy beleaguered teenage exhale that had long ago lost any impact due to overuse. She pivoted back around and stared at some point over his head with pretended boredom. He wished he could just lose his temper and have it out with her as he had done with John. Except, control became more elusive with this daughter of his who meant so much more to him.

Zach clenched and unclenched his fists and knew he would never use them on his children the way his father had. But he also knew angry words thrown like punches could leave other bruises. He tried to think as a reasonable parent or even a logical commander, not just an enraged father who'd found his kid a second away from screwing on the sofa while she should have been watching her little brother.

Brother?

Zach pinched the bridge of his nose. ''Shelby, we trusted you to watch Patrick tonight.''

''I *was* watching him,'' she insisted, swiping a strand of

her rumpled dark hair out of her eyes. "I could hear him on the monitor. I checked him every twenty minutes."

"You knew there wasn't a chance I would agree to John being here alone with you."

"I needed to be with him tonight."

Shelby blinked back tears, which would have moved him if it hadn't been for that damned hickey on her neck. Zach wanted to pound a wall. "Sex without commitment is wrong."

She rolled her eyes. "Like you're really committed to Julia. It doesn't take a rocket scientist to figure out you two just married because of your kids. And it's no great leap either to guess that you didn't spend all this time on your motorcycle."

True, but none of her business. His daughter needed to remember who was the adult. "Shelby, don't push me."

She hooked her hands on the hips of her low-slung jeans, attitude and anger radiating from her. "You can ground me now and ground me again, even pitch my phone in the trash, but you can't control what I'm thinking. Another year and half and I'll be old enough to leave if I want."

Her words stopped him cold. Of course he knew her age, but somehow he couldn't erase the image of her at nine years old climbing a tree to save a nest of baby birds.

But she was sixteen, almost seventeen. He and Pam hadn't been more than eighteen months older when they'd started "just sleeping" together. The past sure had a way of biting a man on the ass when he least expected it. He needed Julia's help keeping track of Shelby now more than ever.

Zach scrubbed a hand over his unshaven face, up to his bleary eyes, suddenly so damned tired beyond what the flight, party and unbelievable hours with Julia should have drained from him.

Bottom line, he couldn't post round the clock guards on

his daughter, although the idea had merit. "At least promise me you'll protect yourself. Don't count on the guy to—"

"Why won't you ever stop being such a nimrod and listen to me?" Stomping forward, she shouted in his face, big fat frustrated tears in her eyes. "I told you already. We weren't doing anything. But if I'm going to be accused of the crime, I might as well go ahead and enjoy myself, don'tcha think?"

She spun away and ran down the hall to her room. The slam rattled windows three rooms over.

A baby squawk sounded, echoed and built as Patrick cried. Aggie barked, scratching at Shelby's door, woofs turning to whines when she ignored her.

Zach reached down to scratch the dog's head on his way past. "Well, that went well, didn't it?"

Patrick's wails picked up speed and velocity. Man, the little fella was breaking a few sound barriers. Zach strode into the bedroom, Aggie dashing past to leap on the bed. The golden retriever burrowed her head under quilted pillows, Julia's additions to his room.

Julia lifted Patrick from the crib, her white terrycloth robe twirling around her bare legs. "It's okay, sweetie, everything's okay."

"Want me to take him?"

Patrick wailed, his face tomato-red.

She shook her head. "Now that he's awake, he knows he's hungry."

"Of course." Zach leaned against the dresser, nudging the rainbow assortment of nail polish scattered along the wooden surface. When Patrick's cries didn't stop, Zach glanced up.

Julia was still standing by the rocker.

Her gaze skittered away from his and he could have sworn she seemed… Embarrassed?

He'd seen her feed Patrick hundreds of times the past months. They'd long ago moved past any awkwardness, and tonight should have cemented that. Why the sudden attack of nerves now?

He must be misreading her. Who could think anyway with the baby screaming? Patrick paused for a breath, then shifted the wails into high gear.

Surrendering to the inevitable, Julia sank into the oak rocker, slipping down one side of the robe to nurse him. The baby squirmed and kicked, hiccupping sobs between gulps.

Zach set aside a bottle of Passion Flower Pink polish and crouched beside her, stroking a hand over the baby's soft white hair. A surge of protectiveness rushed through him. "Is he okay?"

She nodded. "I think so. The noise probably just startled him, and babies sense tension."

Plenty of that to go around. "I'm sorry Shel let you down."

Julia didn't answer, just rocked and cradled her son.

Zach dropped to the floor, leaning against the foot of the bed. His head fell back. "God, Jules, I don't know what to say to her anymore."

"From in here, it sounded like you told her all the right things. She's right about one thing though. We can't control her thoughts. We just have to hope she listened, and if she didn't, pray she'll be careful."

Not the reassurance he was looking for. "Sometimes it's all I can do not to lose it with her. She knows how to push my buttons until I want to shout it all out there."

"Maybe that wouldn't be such a bad thing."

"Now there's a new chapter for all those parenting books on my shelves."

"Put the books away for a minute. Maybe yelling at each other would be better than not talking at all."

He stared at his hands, shaking his head. "Not a chance. I lived that way growing up. My dad opted for the 'spare the rod, spoil the child' school of parenting. I swore I wouldn't go that route with my kids.''

The creaking of the chair slowed, but he didn't want to look at her, not until he could be sure the memories wouldn't show in his eyes.

''You're not your father. You would never hurt your children.''

''I know that,'' he said automatically, rather than risk any more discussion on a subject he'd rather shut down.

The day was already ending on a bad enough note with the baby awake, teenager bawling her eyes out and dog in his bed. Of course the day might have had a crummy end, but it sure had been great before he'd parked the Harley under the carport.

He shrugged out of his jacket, draped it on the edge of the bed by her velvet gown and started on the shirt studs. He would salvage what was left of the night. Julia could make him forget. He worked a cufflink free.

''Uh, Zach?''

''Yeah, Jules?'' He pulled his shirt off.

She cradled her son closer, chewing her bottom lip with that self-conscious air again. ''I know this may sound crazy after what we did tonight, but I'm not sure I'm ready for you to sleep in here.''

A cuff link dropped, bounced off his shoe and rolled along the hardwood floor. Slowly, he looked up.

''Why?'' he asked and hoped like hell she would roll out some explanation about how the cranky baby might bother him and he would reassure her he didn't give a damn. He wanted to crawl into that bed with her and sleep for twelve hours.

''I just don't think I'm ready to take that step yet. I heard what you said to Shelby, and you were right. Sex without a commitment is wrong. That demeans it, turning it into something less than it should be.'' The rub of red along her neck from the scratch of his beard mocked him from across the room.

"For God's sake, Julia." He stood, draping his shirt over a hanger, a shirt that still carried the scent of roses and Julia. "We're married. You can't get much more committed than that."

"Commitment is about more than a piece of paper." Her soft-spoken words didn't dilute the power of the punch. "We both know this isn't a committed marriage beyond the summer when you leave for Alabama."

"Do you want it to be?"

What the hell had he said?

Shock leveled him like a SCUD missile.

Once the shock faded, the idea shifted around in his mind. Why impose a deadline that would end a good thing? A better-than-he'd-ever-imagined thing, judging by the scratches Julia's nails had left on his back tonight.

They'd started this for the kids, and his girls needed a unified front now more than ever. And damn it, he'd grown attached to the little bruiser. He wanted to be there for those first steps.

Yeah, he'd been a rotten husband for Pam, but he and Julia were going at this from a different angle, as friends. Hadn't they both learned their lesson about romanticized views of marriage? Real life meant getting through a day at a time and that's just what he and Julia should do.

First he had to work past that stunned glaze in her eyes. "Well? Do you want to give it a shot past the summer?" He took her silence as permission to persuade. "We're not doing too bad here. Why not give it a chance? We have the kids, friendship and incredible sex in common. That's more than a lot of people ever have."

"You aren't in love with me, Zach."

What was he supposed to say to that? "You aren't in love with me either, Jules. What's your point?"

"Without love, this isn't going to last. If we go beyond

the summer, eventually one of us is going to break it off. Someone will get hurt, most likely the children, and the longer we're a couple, the worse it will be for them if they grow more attached to us being together.''

Zach sifted through her words, searching for the best way around her defenses. Aggie nudged his hand with her nose. He reached behind him to scratch the dog's head while he strategized.

''Zach? I'm serious.''

''I hear you.'' Even if he didn't agree. But he would wait to push it later when she didn't have that stubborn set to her jaw.

''That's it? You're okay with this?''

''I'm not happy about it, but you made your point.''

She slumped back in the chair. Was that a hint of disappointment on her face or wishful thinking on his part?

Standing, Julia shifted the sleeping baby to her shoulder and tightened her robe. She stopped in front of Zach, holding her son to her like a shield between them. ''Just so you know, I don't regret what we did tonight.''

Before he could answer, she pressed her fingers to his lips. ''But I will regret it if we weaken again without thinking it through first. We owe it to ourselves and the children to be honest with each other and hold steady to our plan. We let our hormones mess with our minds tonight. We lost our focus and that can't happen anymore.''

He knew her too well to miss the ache in her eyes. Her arm cradled Patrick so protectively, but her fingers against Zach's face trembled. She was torn, and he could play on that now.

Except he would lose her trust. He needed to think beyond the moment.

Her hand fell away. He tracked her as she put Patrick in his crib. Time for a temporary retreat to rearm for the next advance.

Julia was dead wrong about losing focus on the kids.

Hell, he was a master at multitasking. He'd made a successful career of juggling fifty agendas at once.

They didn't need some fairy-tale version of love to build a relationship. Pam had vowed to heaven and back that she'd loved him even as she'd walked out the door. No way did he need any more of that in his life.

Julia's "welcome home" image had been a near replica of what he'd planned for himself all those years ago back in his father's one-bedroom trailer. He'd wanted a life and family different from the one he'd grown up with. Now that he finally had it, he wouldn't let it fall apart.

He hadn't risen through the Air Force ranks by admitting defeat at the first sign of opposition. Against what should have been insurmountable odds, he'd convinced Julia to marry him.

Now, he just had to convince her to stay.

"You don't have to stay, Shel." Julia folded her legs under her on the blue exercise mat. Shelby sat across from her, holding Patrick's hand while he balanced on his tummy on top of an over large ball. Maternal warmth filled Julia's heart as her son squealed in delight over his favorite of all physical therapy games.

"The weather sucks too bad for me to walk back to the house." Rain pounded the roof, slicking the lone window in the small room in back of the base recreation center. "I'll get soaked."

"I can give you a quick ride home before the break's over." Julia edged out of the way of another child lying over a ball, one who didn't seem quite so taken with the exercise.

"I want to be here when they talk about your blueprints for the new playhouse." Her eyes pleaded for forgiveness. If only she would look at her father that way.

"Okay, then." The kid really was trying, and Julia didn't want to be late for the presentation. "Thanks for realizing how important this is to me.'' In time for summer, she would finish her model playhouse, complete with modifications for the special needs of the children in their group.

Now they just needed a space large enough to hold it.

Eleven children and their parents filled every inch of floor in the overcrowded room, the only place available for the newly founded group led by Rena Price, a civilian counselor from Family Advocacy at the base clinic.

This meeting differed from the Down syndrome support group she attended bimonthly downtown. Rena had designed it as a catchall meeting for any base family with a special needs child. Along with laughter, tears and support, they shared information to alleviate the specific stresses families constantly on the move faced—plugging in with new doctors and facilities, not to mention the insurance nightmares. All these challenges were often met by one parent alone, given that an active-duty spouse averaged fifty percent of the year TDY.

Of course she wouldn't be a military wife much longer. She'd spent so long resenting the Air Force, the flash of regret surprised her.

Do you want to give it a shot past the summer?

Did she? Even thinking about it brought back the teeth-chattering panic she'd felt in Zach's office after they'd made love. Zach had been doing his determined best to convince her to stay without ever laying a finger on her. He'd made it all too clear he didn't intend to have sex with her again without an invitation into her bed.

And oh man, but he was wearing her down with a full-frontal attack that showed just how well he understood her.

This guy didn't romance her with a dozen roses that died by the week's end. No, sir. He'd surprised her with a rechargeable drill, complete with an extra battery pack.

Just yesterday, she'd dashed home late after picking up Ivy from ballet practice, already irritable as hell from walking the floors with a cranky baby all day. Zach had expanded his cooking repertoire from chili-mac to a bubbling Crock-Pot of beef stew. All done to convince her he meant business about giving their practical marriage of convenience a chance.

What more could she want?

You aren't in love with me, Zach.

You aren't in love with me either, Jules. What's your point?

A beach ball whizzed past, just before another thunked Julia on the back of the head.

Grateful for the distraction, she scooped it up and tossed it to the six-year-old twins behind her, one of whom had cerebral palsy.

"Julia?" Shelby nudged Julia's knee. "Could you talk to my dad for me?"

Dad? Had Shelby actually referred to him as something other than Colonel for the first time in as long as Julia could remember? A promising sign and she intended to push it further. "I'm sorry, but no. I can't be your go-between. Whatever you need to work out with him won't mean anything unless it comes from you."

Shelby held Patrick's tiny hands and rolled him gently along the top of the ball, his giggle spilling free. "I'm sorry about, well, you know, when I was supposed to be watching Patrick."

"I know you are, hon."

"But you still won't let me baby-sit him."

Julia hugged her knees to her chest. "Trust is a strange thing, Shelby. It only takes a minute to break it, but it can take so much longer to rebuild." Had she and Lance ever repaired that trust? Not really.

"Like with my mother."

Dangerous territory there. Commenting at all would make for a no-win situation. Only time and Pam could mend that one. Meanwhile, Shelby needed her father, especially if Julia left.

If?

Thunder reverberated outside, rattling the window, jarring Julia back to the present. "Think about having a little faith in your dad. Give him a chance. He may not always say what you want to hear, but you can trust he's going to be there for you."

Shelby snorted. "When he's not thirty thousand feet in the air."

The whirring of an electric wheelchair cut off Julia's reply. Fourteen-year-old Nathan zipped past, circling with a devilish twinkle in his killer baby-blues.

"Hey, Shel-by," he exhaled the last of her name with the ventilator whoosh. The flexible tracheotomy tube trailed from his throat to the back of his wheelchair into a ventilator the size of a laptop computer.

Such a small machine, but without it Nathan couldn't breathe. Bronchopulmonary dysplasia, BPD, had left him with chronic respiratory problems after he'd inhaled meconium at birth.

The kid also had a razor-sharp mind—and a wicked wit. "What do ya say we blow this place, Shel-by? Me and you? Hop on and I'll drive you around the base."

He sounded so much like Zach angling for a Harley ride Julia couldn't suppress a smile.

Shelby winked at Nathan and slapped a hand to her chest. "Ah, Nathan, you'd just dump me when somebody new came along."

"Prob'ly right." He winked back. "There's this hot new babe in my rehab class. Can't keep her eyes off me."

"Go get her, big guy." Shelby hefted Patrick off the ball, placing him on the mat while she continued talking to Nathan. "Help me set up the snacks?"

"Only if you show me," exhale, "that belly-button ring of yours."

Shelby swatted his arm with her overlong sweater sleeve. "You are *so* bad."

Julia rested her chin on her knees and watched the two teens move to the refreshment table. She loved moments like these best in the meetings, times when the universality of human nature transcended disabilities and birth defects. The way she wanted it always to be for her son.

The door swung open, rain sheeting inside and startling Patrick. She patted his tummy and wished someone would close the door soon. Zach sprinted through, slamming the door shut.

Zach? What was he doing here? He'd attended Patrick's doctor and therapy appointments when in town, but he'd never gone to the family support groups.

Until now.

He must be trying to tell her again how he wasn't giving up in his quest to build a family together. Heaven help her, he was making progress.

Zach whipped his hat off and swiped water from his flight suit while he looked around the room.

Finding her.

How could he make her body come alive with just the sweep of his eyes?

Zach paused to speak with Rena, before stepping around the playing children on his way to Julia. "Sorry I'm late, Jules. Mission planning ran long."

He scooped Patrick from the mat and held him high overhead. Patrick squealed, then chortled through his wide-open smile.

"Howdy, Bruiser. What did you do today? Huh? Win a bottle-chug contest with your pals over there? Play a little ball? Watch some cartoons?"

As Zach rambled on with nonsensical chitchat to Patrick, realization seeped into her. Genuine affection for Patrick shone from Zach's eyes. Pure adulation radiated back from Patrick's smile. There was a bond between the two of them that had nothing to do with her.

Julia's throat closed as the meaning of that simple, so

beautiful shared smile swept over her. Zach hadn't come to the meeting for her at all. He'd come for Patrick, and the spontaneous gesture proved far more tempting than a calculated buy-out of a hardware store.

If only she could follow her own advice to Shelby about trusting that Zach would always be there for her.

If only she could be content with nothing more from him than friendship and awesome sex.

If only she didn't love him.

Chapter 14

God, he loved flying.

But today's mission wasn't about flying.

The crew bus jarred along the South American runway. Zach scanned the horizon, morning sun cradled between two mountains. He would take to the skies soon. Today, come hell or high water, he would find answers to Lance Sinclair's crash.

As the Squadron Commander, Zach accepted he would live with the weight of that crew's death on his shoulders for the rest of his life. But through this flight he hoped to find a sort of closure, lay Lance Sinclair's ghost to rest in his own mind so he could claim Julia as his own.

Nothing from the past between them.

Rows separated each member of his crew as they spread throughout the bus. No normal pre-flight banter or laughs rang through the tin can of a bus rattling along the asphalt.

The runway stretched ahead of them alongside a string of mountains, control tower perched to the left. Lush green peaks characteristic of the tropical landscape made flying through this airspace challenging—and potentially deadly.

Silence echoed. A funeral-like solemnity fogged through the compartment.

Grayson ''Cutter'' Clark, co-pilot for the mission, sprawled sideways in his seat, back against the window. The renegade flight surgeon, one of the few who flew as well as healed, had packed away his do-rag and CDs. No practical jokes or impromptu concerts today.

In the middle of the last row, normally chatty Bronco Bennett sat, looming stone-silent, boots planted, hands on knees and staring straight ahead. With his prior experience as a C-130 navigator, he would plot a detailed longitude-latitude log. Forget relying solely on computerized data.

And finally the loadmaster, Jim Price, senior in service years, but still an enigma around the squadron when it came to anything other than work. The man lived for the Air Force and would go to any lengths to protect military honor.

Zach could identify with that.

Flipping his headset over in his lap, he bent and twisted the ear cups to adjust the fit, steadying himself in pre-flight routine. Damn things never stayed set right. He tossed them aside restlessly.

The gray aircraft loomed ahead of them, tip to tail one hundred and seventy-four feet long and nearly that long across in wingspan. Two days ago, they'd flown in medical supplies for a local village, then spent the next day mission-planning for the flight out when they would refly Sinclair's doomed mission.

Retracing the route was a common investigative technique in accident inquiries and had already been utilized. Twice. With the same conclusion. Pilot error—for lack of a better answer.

Pilot error. The epitaph every flyer dreaded.

Every man on the bus knew that accident report could

have held his name. Their wives and children could have been the recipients of the front-porch visit from the commander. Military spouses deserved the assurance that the Air Force would do whatever it took to retrieve the fallen body or honor of a comrade in arms. They'd all pulled combat time with Lance, trusted him with their lives as he'd entrusted his to them.

They wouldn't fail him now.

Zach grabbed his headset from the seat again, tweaking the fit. Julia would understand his silence about the mission once he explained. He'd worked like hell for five months to find something that would clear the accident report. Yeah, he'd kept quiet about more details than security required. But after a year where Julia was already juggling a new baby with special needs and coming to terms with widowhood, he couldn't see that she needed to hear about him flying her dead husband's final flight.

Zach shoved aside niggling reservations. Now wasn't the time to question himself, not when doubts could shake his focus.

Had Lance allowed home-life concerns to rock his concentration?

No. Once they closed the hatch, training and instincts from thousands of hours in that seat assumed command. The flyer became one with the machine. Zach had to believe that or he was going to be in a helluva mess once he took to the skies.

The bus jerked to a stop beside the aircraft.

Mission time. Today, he would erase that "pilot error" blot. Today, for this crew, the outcome would be different from the results of the investigative team, because for these men, it was personal.

And for Zach, it couldn't get any more personal than the woman waiting at home for him. "Okay, crew, let's roll."

"You sure did roll in late last Friday night." From the picnic table, Kathleen pinned Julia with a curious stare and mischievous gleam that promised a lengthy girl-chat to pump for information.

Strolling to the tire swing, Julia looked to Lori Clark by Patrick's swing for help and found nothing more than a second set of inquisitive eyes peering back. She reminded herself that the friends surrounding her in her backyard were a blessing.

A nosy blessing.

Julia pushed the tire swing dangling from the tree, launching squeals from the Clarks' little girl and Ivy. "Nothing wrong with staying out late on a Friday night."

"Late?" Lori's brow puckered as she tapped a mani-cured nail to her lips. "I thought you two left the party early."

Kathleen reached into the infant seat on the picnic table and adjusted the lightweight blanket around her daughter. "Rumor has it, Julia didn't even finish her chocolate cherry cheesecake."

"Criminal." Lori pressed a hand to her lightly rounded stomach, pregnancy hormones obviously protesting the blasphemy of neglected chocolate. "Well, it's more than a rumor from where I was standing. Since you were home with little Tara, you missed the decided spring in the com-mander's step as he hustled Julia out of the Valentine's Dining-Out."

Kathleen hugged her sweat-suit-clad knees to her chest. "Tanner's a dead man for leaving that part out."

Every word of the good-natured teasing dinged Julia like a staple gun attacking her tattered emotions. She reminded herself they meant well. It wasn't their fault she was so damned confused. If only she had someone to confide in, but her best friend was the problem, so she couldn't exactly turn to him for help on this one.

Lori fingered her braid with a dreamy sigh. "So? Where did you go? A late-night romantic make-out at Patriot's

Point? Or a lovers' stroll along the Battery Park with water crashing against the harbor wall?''

All those beautiful images didn't come close to the perfection of their windswept motorcycle ride. Except love hadn't played any part in Zach's plans. Hadn't he flat-out said as much?

She'd seen well how shaky a marriage could be without love. Lance hadn't loved her either, not like he'd loved the other woman. He'd stayed in his marriage out of duty. Sure, Zach had shown her all the logical reasons why they should stay together. But for once, she wanted to be more than someone's duty. She wanted to fill a man's life and every thought, totally.

A ridiculously romantic dream for a practical woman who preferred power tools for presents over perfumed roses.

Kathleen canted forward like Mata Hari. ''Did I forget to mention they came home on the motorcycle?''

''Motorcycle?'' Lori pivoted to Julia, braid swishing with the quick turn. ''Ohhh, girlfriend, you *have* to talk now.''

No doubt the Air Force had a first-class interrogator in Major Kathleen Bennett, and she wasn't walking away without her information. Of course she had an inside scoop since she'd scrawled out the prescription for Julia's birth-control pills.

Julia offered a token nugget. ''Zach took me for a ride on his Harley after the party.''

Kathleen tapped her watch. ''You didn't get home until after two. Where did you go? California?''

''Geez, Kathleen.'' Julia laughed rather than cry. ''Do you and Tanner never sleep?''

''I was feeding the endlessly ravenous Tara.''

Lori gave snoozing Patrick a final push before advancing toward Julia with a determined gleam. ''Spill it. We want details.''

Julia surrendered. Why not enjoy the memories and the sisterhood of sharing new romantic confidences without going into the deeper details of her marriage to Zach? Her months with him had taught her to look past the military regimen of pruned lawns and identical houses to see a communal spirit of support she hadn't experienced since childhood.

She might need that support soon.

Hugging her sweater tighter around herself, Julia dodged a tree root and plopped down beside Kathleen on the redwood bench. She waited until Lori's daughter Magda and Ivy scampered into the playhouse before continuing, "We took advantage of the time away from the children and stopped by his office."

"His office?" Lori frowned, then gasped, sitting across from Kathleen. "He'd just flown. You know how they can be after a flight."

"Ahhh, of course." Kathleen's sage nod said it all. "And the poor guy had to wait through that party? No wonder he checked out early."

Lori rested her chin on her hands, a faraway look in her eyes as she gazed up at the sky. "This one time, Gray landed early and rather than going home to wait for me to finish at work, he abducted me right out of a Feed-the-World strategy session I was conducting with two interns." A satisfied smile slid across her face. "I would have felt guilty, but those college kids brainstormed their hearts out to impress me while I was gone…uh, taking inventory…in the supply closet."

Kathleen leaned back, her elbows on the picnic table. "If Tanner so much as looks at an airplane, forget waiting to make it home."

"Ohmigod," Julia said. "You two didn't…"

Kathleen shrugged.

"In a plane?"

Kathleen straightened, a blush creeping up her redhead's complexion. "Well, it *was* parked in a deserted hangar."

Julia slapped a hand over her eyes. "There's not a chance I'm going to be able to look at either of them with a straight face if they come by here to meet up with you after they land."

She welcomed the laughs and the relief they brought from worries that dogged her with increasing persistence. Friendship brewed, comforting her like the gentle swirl of the breeze through the evergreens. Ivy flung the playhouse shutters wide and crawled through, Magda tumbling after her as both girls giggled in a tangled heap on the ground.

Julia tucked a leg under her, until that moment not realizing how tense she'd been about Zach's flight after all. "Thanks for making me laugh. I needed to smile today."

Lori reached across the table to pat her hand. "That's what friends are for."

Julia wrapped her arms around herself, more to ward off the memories than the wind. She checked her son, still snoozing away in the gently swaying swing. She'd wanted to fill his first year with joy, but all that joy was tearing her heart out. "I never used to worry about the flights before, not beyond some vague sort of concern. Lance didn't share much about his work, so I had no idea how many times he'd flown in harm's way. Now, sometimes my imagination runs crazy with awful scenarios." She held up a hand to stop any sympathetic outpourings that would drag her down deeper. "But I'm doing better."

Kathleen's nod offered a blend of compassionate doctor and steely military will. "You deserve to be happy."

Julia wanted to fall further into the comfort of friendship and ask for their advice. Could she turn Zach's friendship into something deeper? She didn't know which would be worse: staying only to find out she couldn't win his love, or walking away now, knowing she would always think of him, worry about him and wonder if he'd found someone else to entice that beautiful half smile of his.

The mere thought of another woman in his life turned her green from the inside out. She wanted to be the one who brought all his defenses crashing down.

The phone reverberated from inside, jarring her before she made a weak mistake in spilling all. "I'll be right back."

She swung her leg over the bench seat. Just as she reached the screen door, Shelby sprinted from the house, cordless phone in hand. "It's Command Post, asking for the Colonel."

"Thanks, Shel." Julia took the phone from her.

"Ma'am, this is Airman Vance from Command Post. I'm looking for Colonel Dawson."

"He's TDY." Julia tucked the phone under her chin and scooped Patrick from the swing. "But he'll be home tonight. Can I take a message?"

"No message, ma'am. We're just initiating a pyramid recall exercise. Only a practice. I should have checked the board first." The squeak of a spinning chair eased over the airwaves. "Now I see he's on his way back from South America. Sorry for bothering you. I'll just go to the next on the list. Have a nice evening, ma'am."

The dial tone buzzed in her ear.

South America?

Surprise mingled with dread. He'd said he would be in Florida. Either he'd lied or he'd fudged the truth by calling a stopover in Florida their final destination because the mention of a South American mission would bring memories of Lance's crash.

She wanted to let it go at that, but so many things tickled her sixth sense. Lori and Kathleen both showing up uninvited to keep her company while the guys flew. Wonderful, but why today?

Lori's stiff-shouldered stance took on a whole new complexion that had nothing to do with simple back strain from pregnancy. Why was Gray flying with them on a TDY mission when he'd come to South Carolina on vacation? "South America."

Both women sat up straighter. Not even a hint of surprise flickered across their faces. Just concern.

"Kathleen, why are they in South America?" Julia tucked Patrick closer, stealing comfort in his solid baby weight against her hip. "Lori?"

Neither answered.

Insidious panic nibbled at her insides. Kathleen would be privy to military secrets, but if Lori knew too then Zach had withheld information he could have shared.

Julia strode across the yard, kicking a ball aside. "Talk or I'm going right up to that flight line and causing a scene like nobody's ever seen. Believe me. I'll do it."

The two women exchanged glances before Kathleen forged ahead. "They flew down to South America to clear up some unanswered questions about Lance's crash."

Julia's stomach lurched. "Unanswered questions?"

"The accident review board never found a conclusive reason for the crash. Sometimes that happens and we never know, so they just blame it on pilot error. The Colonel isn't satisfied with that answer."

How like Zach to carry his responsibility to his men all the way to the grave. She had to admire him for it even while she longed to slug him for closing her out. "Why all the secrecy?"

"Maybe he didn't want to dredge everything up for you until he closes the case conclusively. Who knows how men's minds work?"

Too many memories paraded through her head of another husband who'd evaded the truth, using extended TDYs and the "can't tell you where I am, babe" excuse to cover an affair. She couldn't handle that game-playing again. Even while she had to believe Zach wouldn't actually cheat on her, she still hated the sick feeling all the lies brought roiling through her.

"Why the secrecy about today's flight?" Julia didn't intend to quit without an answer.

Lori avoided her by jumping up to check on her daughter behind the playhouse.

Unease shifted to something darker, something all the more frightening because of the unknown. "Kathleen? You'd better tell me, because it can't be any worse than what I'm imagining."

Kathleen stared back as two cars rumbled past before resolution settled over her face. "It's a common practice to retrace a route when there's been a crash to try and identify what went wrong."

Realization trickled over Julia one icy drop at a time. Zach was in the air, now, reflying the exact route that had killed Lance. Nausea nailed her. She swallowed it back one breath at a time.

Lori stopped beside Julia, carefully prying Patrick from her trembling arms. "He was trying to protect you."

Kathleen managed a half smile. "Men can be pretty pig-headed about the whole over-protection thing. But you don't have anything to worry about. Yes, they're retracing the route, but during the day. Not at night as Lance flew it. They're being careful."

Anger slowly dulled the edge of her fear, or maybe only masked it. She didn't care or intend to waste time analyzing.

She'd thought at least in their friendship they'd been partners, but this news made even that partnership a lie. She might call him Zach, but he was still the Colonel. He might as well still be rotating her tires and cleaning leaves from her gutters, taking care of the poor widow woman. Damn him again for bringing all that fear slamming into her double force.

Lori and Kathleen could tell her all day long it was a

safe, daytime mission and it wouldn't stop her from fearing the worst. She couldn't sit around watching for him to come striding through the door. Or not. Waiting on the runway would shave away a few of those excruciating minutes.

"Lori, I need you to watch Patrick. The girls' mother is picking them up in about an hour." Julia's fingers made fast work of her sweater buttons in spite of the shaking. The runway would be chilly and her wait could well be long. "Patrick eats at five. There's expressed milk in the freezer. Bottles in the cabinet."

"Hang on." Kathleen grabbed her arm. "The SPs will arrest you if you blast onto the runway like this."

"So?"

"Then you won't be there when the Colonel lands."

Julia's hands fisted at her sides. "Just let them try to stop me."

"Whoa. Wait five minutes and I'll take you. I need to run home for my flight-line badge first." All order and efficiency, Kathleen pivoted on her heel, military bearing starching through her. "We'll still be there long before they land. Renshaw's slated with Supervisor of Flying duties tonight. You can wait in the truck on the runway with her. Lori, can you watch the kids until I get back?"

"Uh, Julia?" Shelby called, still on the bottom porch step. "I'll baby-sit."

While Shelby's offer seemed the easiest route, Julia hesitated. Zach had finally convinced the teen to meet with her mother today. They couldn't lose critical ground now just because Julia's life was splintering. "No need, hon. Go ahead to Pam's. I don't know how late I'll be."

Given the scene she already knew was inevitable, the security police might well arrest her anyway. Not that she cared. What more could she lose? She would never be uppermost in his mind. For a man like Zach, the job would always come first and this secretive stunt proved her needs would always take a back seat to the needs of his troops.

Even if Zach skimmed to that runway unscathed, she'd already lost another husband.

"Shit! Climb!" Zach yanked back the stick, pushed up the throttle. Adrenaline pulsed. Blood pounded through his veins as the plane shot through the haze.

All the while, his spider-tingle instinct screamed they were off course.

Which meant he didn't know where the hell they were.

Or where those mountains peaked.

Clouds whipped past his windscreen. The visible reality of rattling full-power speed had nothing to do with flying games and everything to do with staying alive. Of making sure Julia didn't face the hell of another front-porch visit.

Climb, damn it. He urged the plane as if his force of will could shoulder it higher, faster.

A part of Zach shouted for him to savor images of Julia if they were going to be his last. But he couldn't afford the distraction.

Focus. Fly. Get the plane above MSA, minimum safe altitude, only used in an emergency when the plotted flight plan went all to hell.

That spider tingle told him this qualified.

Seconds later, he nosed out of the haze.

A mountaintop crested through the clouds.

Realization gripped him in an arctic fist. The spider tingle had been dead-on. Sure death loomed, shrouded in the haze below if they hadn't pulled up.

Zach continued to climb, banking away from the mountain range below. Adrenaline blasted through his veins. More visions of Julia spun through his mind. Sure he'd known there would be risks involved in this flight, but he'd never expected to cut it so close.

"Colonel," Bronco barked over the interphone, "confirm we're on three-two-zero radial."

Zach checked the dial. "Confirmed. Cutter?"

''Three-two-zero checks on mine as well.'' The copilot swiped an arm over his sweaty brow.

''Bronco, pull up the MFD.'' The multifunction display screens would provide additional navigational information for instances when normal radio-based air navigational systems failed. Which was next to never. Ground stations were supposed to be internationally standardized, damn it. ''Then plot out our course the old-fashioned way.''

Other than the mix of steady, overly controlled breaths, silence hummed over the airwaves. Later, he would let the reality of what could have happened roll over him. Later, after he'd held Julia, after he'd lost himself in her smile, in her softness, in her body.

Bronco's soft whistle of surprise cut the silence. ''Well, I'll be damned. We don't appear to be plotting on our planned track line.''

The answer to why hovered in Zach's mind, just within reach. Answers for Julia. He kept his hand steady on the stick, mind on the job. ''Are we diverging at a regular rate?''

''Confirmed.''

A mental visual of the chart played out in his head, complete with a widening divergence from the route due to what he now suspected had to be a ground radio navigation system error.

Zach's grip on the stick tightened, any thrill over solving the cause of the crash killed by a primal anger. Lives had been lost, not by accident, but because of a screw-up. ''Gentleman, anyone recall the sixty-to-one rule?''

''Of course.'' Bronco thumped his head. ''Sixty-to-one. Every one degree of error on the navigation aid heading translates into three miles off course from this distance.''

Radio navigation required daily re-calibration to stay true to heading. Even one missed day could make that subtle one-degree difference.

Cutter slumped back in his seat with a lengthy sigh.

''Enough error for a controlled flight smack into a mountain, especially during a night flight. How the hell did the investigation team miss it? They flew this same route twice.''

''After the crash, someone at the tower likely fixed the error.'' Zach tossed out his gut guess. ''Now that time's passed, they probably slacked off again.''

And if Zach and his crew hadn't caught the error, another crew would have likely rolled into a turn, crashing into the same mountain range.

They could have smacked a mountain.

Silence reigned supreme over the interphone. Zach knew too well all those steady gazes held images of what each man could have lost. More than ever, the need to fix things with Julia burned within him.

Damn it, they were on their way to building something solid together and he wasn't going to let her throw it away. She'd been hard as hell to resist before their night together, but now he could barely look at her without remembering the way her legs felt wrapped around his waist.

Keep it focused. He would be home soon, Julia waiting for him on that purple glider with her soft smile and incredible legs.

Six hours later, Zach skimmed the plane to the Charleston runway, centered neatly between the parallel lights illuminating the darkened stretch of asphalt. He turned onto the hammerhead. ''Reach three-two-four-five, clear of the active runway.''

''Roger, clear of the runway.''

Gut-twisting relief still pulsed through the cockpit, restrained but palpable. Ten more minutes to park the plane and then they could let emotions steamroll free.

He guided the plane behind the truck with the big Follow Me sign on back. The crew would report for an in-depth debrief in the morning to document their data and file their findings with the accident investigation board.

Waiting in the parking area, the blue SUV for the Supervisor of Flying chugged exhaust into the chilly night air. Lieutenant Renshaw stepped from the truck, no surprise to find the eager-to-achieve lieutenant pulling SOF yet again. The young pilot was hell-bent on proving she received no favors for being General Renshaw's daughter.

Zach tracked the two glowing orange flashlights in an airman's hands as he guided the plane. The orange lights circled, then the airman gestured one across his throat.

Run 'em up. Shut 'em down.

Silence hummed with a final goodbye to Lance Sinclair as the last page closed on the mission.

Zach nodded. "Well done, crew."

Bronco fist-punched the air. "Hell, yeah!"

Laughter rumbled through the interphone. Order and honor restored to the unit. The crew whipped off headsets and unstrapped.

Amid the echoes of cheers and self-congratulatory backslaps, Zach loped down the narrow stairwell, through the hatch into the biting wind. A haze of fluorescent lights illuminated his path down the metal stairs.

Twenty yards away, the passenger door on the SUV flung open and Zach found he would be fixing things with Julia sooner than he'd anticipated. Her long legs slid out of the vehicle. He didn't have to see the rest to recognize her. He would know those mile-long legs and pink high tops anywhere.

For a flash of time, Julia's homecoming fantasy hit him, full force and full of the promise for a hundred more like it throughout the years. Then her head cleared the truck and he saw her stony expression.

She knew. He didn't question how she'd found out, but somehow she already knew about the day's mission to trace her dead husband's final flight and she didn't plan to thank him for it.

Julia stormed across the tarmac. Gusting wind plastered

her jean skirt to her legs, stirring her curls into a tangled frenzy around her face.

Footsteps behind him on the stairs slowed. Bronco, Cutter and Tag fanned around him, stopping still and wary as they looked from Zach to Julia and back again. Renshaw didn't budge from her perch beside the truck, her arms braced on the door as she watched.

Zach stood and waited while Julia closed the last few feet between them.

Her hand shot out. Palm flat, she swacked his shoulder. "Damn you."

He planted his feet and prepared to wait out the storm. Unlike Pam's no-show on the flight line, at least Julia cared enough about him to shout her concerns to his face.

She thumped him again. "Damn you. Damn you. Damn you!" The wind flung her shouts across the flight line. "I trusted you, damn it. You made me trust you."

She shoved again and again with surprising strength from a woman already unquestionably strong in so many ways, which made her meltdown all the worse for Zach. He reached to pull her to him. "Julia, I know you're upset."

She knocked his arm away. "You don't know a damned thing about me if you didn't realize how betrayed I would feel hearing you'd kept this flight secret."

A security cop advanced. Zach held up a hand to stop him without taking his eyes off Julia. "This isn't the place."

"I don't care." Her arms flailed the air, wind filling and puffing her sweater.

"Well, I do."

Bronco stepped forward. "Julia, let's all just take a deep br—"

"You back off!" Fearless in her fury, she jabbed a finger at him, before returning the full power of her anger to Zach. "You had to know I would find out eventually."

Tears filled her eyes, hovered, spilled free to be carried

away in the tearing wind. She swiped her arm across her face, her chest heaving. She stared at him, waiting for him to answer, but he only stared back. There wasn't a thing he could say to make this easier for her.

"Why the hell did I even bother?" She backed away, one stumbling step at a time. "I've seen for myself that you didn't hit a mountain today and that's all I came for anyway."

Julia spun on her heel.

Three strides and he caught her by the arm. "Julia—"

"Let me go." She jerked in his grip.

"No." He held firm. The woman was so out of control no telling what could happen to her.

He didn't let himself think of his own emotions, boiling and threatening to break free after a beyond-tense day, the culmination of months of frustrating uncertainty.

She pulled harder, kicked at his shin. "Damn it, let me go."

Zach caught her other flailing arm and yanked her close, chest to chest, their hearts hammering against each other. Heat and spark, anger and need pulsed between them. "We *will* talk. Just not here."

She stiffened against him, and he backed her toward the truck. The tension trembling through her broadcast she was five seconds from exploding and those itchy SPs standing twenty feet away wouldn't hesitate to haul her off.

"Julia," he said through clenched teeth. "Flight line security is nothing to play around with. There are military cops with guns standing all around you. I don't want to sling you over my shoulder and carry you out of here, but I'll have to in about three seconds if you don't come with me quietly."

The fight in her eyes cooled to a simmer. Warily, he relaxed his hold. Julia drew back her shoulders. She was the only woman he'd ever known who could make pink high tops and denim look regal.

Regal yes, but also looking so mad she could spit nails as she slid inside the truck again.

Stopping beside Renshaw, Zach extended his hand. "Keys please, Lieutenant."

"Sure, Colonel." Renshaw dropped them in his palm with a clink and edged backward. "I'll just—uh—snag a ride back in the crew bus so you two can—uh—talk."

Zach gave Renshaw a tight nod and settled behind the wheel. Julia slammed her arms over her chest and stared forward. Her eyes glinted with anger and tears, and somehow he'd put it all there.

The past had bitten him on the ass in more ways than one in a few short days. He'd screwed up another marriage, and still he couldn't see his way through to a way he would have handled things differently.

One look at her clenched fists told him hearing that wouldn't put a dent in her fury.

The impending showdown in his office promised to have a different, helluva lot less satisfying outcome than the last time he'd locked them both behind those doors.

Chapter 15

The lock click echoed in Zach's office.

Julia stood in the middle of the carpeted floor, fury and fear still battling for dominance inside her. If she had her way, fury would win hands down. She'd made the mistake of holding back with Lance, and by God, she wasn't repeating that mistake again.

But the battle would take place with her on her feet.

She certainly wasn't sitting on the sofa with all those memories of tangled bodies, sweat-slicked skin and an out-of-control need she wouldn't let have its way with her this time.

Zach turned to face her. "I'm sorry."

That threw her. For half a second. Then the disillusionment came swelling back up to clog her throat. "For what? For lying to me? Or just that I found out you lied?"

He hooked his hands on his hips, one boot forward as if formulating the most effective tactical approach. Damn it, she wasn't some strategic campaign. "How do you think it made me feel finding out you'd lied? That's the one thing I can't take, having a husband lie to me again.''

Zach reached.

She backed.

He held up his hands, flight suit stretching across his broad chest. ''I'm sorry Lance hurt you then, and I'm sorry you're hurting today. But you know there are things I can't talk about in my job and it's damned unfair to call that lying.''

How dare he turn this all around on her? ''Life isn't that clear-cut-and-dried. You could have told me *something* instead of making some commander-like unilateral decision for me. I hoped from those calls during your TDY that maybe we'd begun to work as partners somewhere other than with the children and in bed.''

Or on the office sofa.

Julia kept her eyes firmly fixed on his face, no wandering to tempting brown vinyl. ''You couldn't tell me anything to prepare me? Can you even imagine how scared I was having this drop out of nowhere?''

''You'd just had a baby.'' Scratching his jaw, he paced in front of her like a stalking wolf. ''How the hell was I supposed to tell you then? You already had enough on you without hearing the Inspector General had reopened the investigation into Lance's crash.''

The betrayal went deeper than she'd thought. ''You've known since Patrick was born?''

He stopped. His eyes narrowed, hardened. ''How does it feel to be kept on the outside, Julia?''

Confusion put a temporary hold on her anger. ''What?''

''You didn't tell me about Patrick having Down syndrome until after he was born. Hell, you didn't even tell me then. You left me to figure it out on my own.''

Guilt seeped through her. She couldn't dodge her own culpability. She'd hurt him with that omission and he'd been carrying that around for months, perhaps an unacknowledged pain like the one Pam had dealt him, but lingering all the same. "You're right. I should have told you when the test results came back."

"Were you hoping I would say or do something wrong that day in your hospital room?" He sauntered toward her, muscles rippling beneath his flight suit with each muffled thud of his boots. "Then you would have all the more reason to push me away. You could say, 'What an insensitive ass' and throw me out of your life so you wouldn't have to face whatever the hell it is we have between us."

"That's not true at all." Or was it?

"When have you ever stopped searching for reasons to shut me down?"

Julia started to apologize again, then paused. How had he sidetracked her? Maybe he'd been right to hold back initially, but later he should have told her. "When have you ever stopped trying to control everything around you?"

He stopped in his tracks. "Run that one by me one more time."

His totally clueless look stirred the embers of her anger. How could he understand so little about her and still expect her stay with him? "If you want me to call you something besides Colonel, then quit treating me like one of your troops."

His eyes heated from brown to molten gold as they swept over her. "Believe me, Julia, I've never wanted to do to anyone under my command the things I want to do with you under me."

The fire within her combusted into a blaze.

Julia trembled from the effort to hold herself back. Although she would gladly trade the confusing swirl of emotions for something she understood perfectly.

Lust.

Zach advanced a step, the hungry wolf aura returning. All those memories rose from the sofa and taunted her with everything she was giving up by pushing him away. She backed from the couch until her legs bumped the edge of his desk, all the while knowing she was lying to herself. She wanted Zach Dawson any way she could have him.

And right now she wanted him in at least fifteen different ways.

He closed the last inches between them, flattening his palms to the desk until his arms bracketed her. One lean, muscled thigh insinuated between her legs, his face only inches away. "What the hell do you want from me, Julia?"

"Everything," she blurted the truth she couldn't hide from herself any more than from him. "I want a man who's honest with me even when it hurts. I need a man who'll give me everything of himself and expect the same from me."

But for now, she would settle for what she could have.

Julia grabbed the front of his flight suit and jerked him to her. Not that he needed much coercion. Apparently his intention to hold out for an invitation to her bed had combusted in the moment. His mouth sealed over hers, open and needy, tongue thrusting while his hands slid low to cup her bottom, lifting, molding her against him.

No gentle meeting or mating, she gripped at his shoulders, crushed herself to him. She explored the moist heat of his mouth with her tongue, battling for dominance with a man who never relinquished control.

She couldn't win. She understood that all too well. The best she could hope for was some kind of equality here in this moment, a victory in knowing he became as mindless as she whenever this desperate craving between them ignited.

Control spiraled elusively away, and Julia grappled for some stronghold to steady her long enough to drag Zach into abandon with her. She skimmed down his broad shoulders, over the muscles rippling along his back. Sliding a hand between them, Julia scored a nail down his chest, along the links of the zipper on his flight suit, a zipper perfectly designed for her intents since it opened from the bottom as well as the top.

No slow sensual glide, she yanked it halfway up his chest and dipped her hand into his boxers, finding him hard and hot and so ready for her.

Groaning, he stumbled. Not much, just a slight lurch before he braced a hand on the desk. A thrill of feminine victory trilled through her.

Then he scooped and lifted her to the edge of the desk and she lost serious ground in the battle for control. Zach burrowed a hand under her sweater, palming her breast, his thumb stroking, tantalizing until she groaned into his mouth. Without raising his lips from hers, Zach swept open her wrap-around jean skirt, tore her panties down and off.

His chest heaving against hers, he paused to kiss her eyes, her ear. "If this isn't what you want, you'd better say something now."

"I only want you to finish what you've started." How could he even talk? Forming words or coherent thoughts proved almost impossible. "I just want…"

She let her body speak for her as she kissed him, her fingers encircling him, guiding him forward. One bold thrust and he was inside her, then she couldn't have spoken even if she'd wanted to.

And she definitely didn't want to talk.

Her legs locked around him, heels digging in to hold him closer, safe and alive, oh so alive, against her, inside her, all around her.

So very alive when she could have lost him.

She could have still been standing on the runway, waiting for a plane that would never land and that scenario made her long to grab what she could from life and this man. Faced with the possibility of losing him, the sense of what it would be like never to have any of him ever again, made her wonder if she could settle for less than everything.

Although, right now he was giving her everything she could handle and more.

Forget control. She collapsed onto her elbows. Her head flung back as she met each thrust, surrendering to the sensation of Zach moving within her. Maybe she could live without his love if they never had to talk, if they just plunged into this desire for each other until it consumed them both.

In her heart and even in her mind, she knew better. But that didn't stop her from wanting to be unwise and reckless, taking what she could from a life that had already taken so much from her.

She fought to hold on to Zach and this stolen pocket of time until the need for release clawed at her with painful intensity. She arched up, flinging herself against his chest, clinging, moving, straining toward…

Zach.

His mouth muffled her scream. Or had she taken his shout into hers? She couldn't pull together enough thoughts for more than melting into the moment and against him as wave after wave of completion crashed over her.

Trembling in the aftermath, Julia cradled his head in the curve of her neck and savored each caress of his heated breath over her skin. He filled her body and heart so completely. Why couldn't she be content with that? Instead, she could only mourn that she would never fill his heart as fully.

Zach held Julia against him until they both stopped shaking.

And until he could be certain his legs would hold him if he backed away from the desk.

Just the scent of her drifting over him stole what little control he had left. He wondered if he'd ever find stable ground again. Or if he would even be given the time to try.

All his progress in convincing her to stay had been blown away in a day. In one flight.

Who the hell was he kidding?

The flight had been months in the making. He'd screwed up bit by bit in a hundred ways and still didn't know what he could do differently. The need to serve, defend and protect went beyond a simple occupation. Compromise too often involved life-and-death decisions. How could he reconcile his duty to his job with what Julia and his family seemed to want from him?

He didn't have a clue. Like flying through a storm with his instruments shot to hell and back, he could see the crash coming, yet couldn't formulate any plan for avoiding it.

But that wouldn't stop him from trying all the way to ground.

Sliding his hands beneath Julia, he lifted her from the desk. She mumbled a weak protest against his shoulder, but held on as he walked across the office carrying her. He lowered them both to the sofa, Julia in his lap.

Zach rested his cheek against her hair until her warmth seeped past the numbness into his skin. "Do you think we'll ever make it to the bedroom?"

He wanted to know in more than some passing sort of way. Letting him into her bed and making that room theirs implied a commitment Julia didn't seem ready to make. If ever. And time was running out with the ground screaming toward his windscreen at mach speed.

"Well, Jules?"

Slowly, she stirred against his chest. Her fingers circled a light dance along the back of his neck. "After what happened today, I just don't know."

Even predicting her answer didn't stop the stab of disappointment. "I meant it when I said I was sorry. Today's flight was about more than fulfilling some job obligation or even trying to reconcile in my own mind what happened on my watch." His gaze gravitated toward the flags with unerring navigation. "It wasn't his fault, Jules. They tried to pin it on him, but damn it, I couldn't let that happen. A control tower down in South America screwed up and gave him the wrong headings. He probably never even saw that mountain coming—"

"Stop." She tensed against him. "Enough, Zach."

He rested his cheek on her hair, inhaling the mix of strawberry shampoo, fresh night air and Julia. "I flew today for Patrick so he could be proud of his father, so he could hold onto those hero's medals from a father he would never know."

Zach clutched her to him, his fingers digging deeper into her arms than he intended, but he couldn't make himself be gentle. He couldn't make himself let go when he could feel her slipping away. "Julia, I did it for you."

She lifted her head from his shoulder, her bottom lip quivering. "Oh you big, dense man. I don't need another dead hero. I need you. Alive."

Searching her eyes, he finally understood the full implications of her anger. She'd made it clear she was furious with him for keeping her out of the equation, but he hadn't thought beyond that.

Her anger and *pain* were all for him. She wasn't hurt because Lance's memory might have been dishonored. Knowing would have upset her over the past months, but not in any devastating way. Dead was dead as far as Julia was concerned.

She'd been afraid for *him*, Zach.

And even in her fear she hadn't shied away from that runway as Pam had. It hadn't been a champagne-showered homecoming, but Julia had been there waiting for *him*.

In a flash of her tear-tinged green eyes, Zach saw everything he and Julia could have had together. He saw everything he'd thrown away.

From his desk, a muffled ringing sounded. From Julia's purse. A phone.

In increments, Zach's world widened beyond the woman in his lap. Julia stood, sweeping her jean skirt back in place.

He grabbed her wrist. The minute she answered that phone, he knew the moment and any chance to work through this would be lost. He would lose her. "Let it ring."

She squeezed his hand. "I can't. It could be one of the children."

Damn, where was his mind that he could have forgotten that? Zach adjusted his clothes, zipping his flight suit while Julia grabbed the cell phone from her purse.

"Hello?" She tucked the phone under her chin as she re-tied her skirt. Her face blanched. Zach's hand paused in straightening his flight scarf.

"We'll start looking." Her hands hurried to tug her sweater down. "Call us on the cell phone if you hear anything."

Julia disconnected. Concern and shock strained her face, launching Zach's every parental instinct on full alert. She touched his chest, just a small comforting gesture that had him ready to bolt out of his skin with uneasiness. Which kid?

"That was Pam. Shelby's missing. She left a note saying she and John have run off together."

Zach spun away, spitting out a curse. His whole damned world was crashing down around his ears at once. "I'll take you home before I head out to find her."

He just prayed he could track Shelby before she threw away her life.

Julia tucked around him in front of the door. "You're never going to get it, are you?"

Impatience pumped through him. "Later, Julia, and I do mean later. Now isn't the time for us to finish this."

"Stop and listen." Tender comforter long gone, Julia jabbed a finger in the middle of his chest. "I'm not the wilting flower type. I don't need you to protect me. I don't want you to shove me behind you when things go—''

Her teeth gritted back a frustrated shout. "Forget it. You're right. This isn't the time. There may never be enough time to make you understand. We have to look for Shelby. And I do mean *we,* Colonel. Now get moving. We have to find your daughter before she proves she's as thick-headed as her father.''

Zach shifted gears on his motorcycle and shot up the asphalt shoulder to avoid the jam-up of rush hour. Julia had insisted the bike would be faster and easier to navigate through traffic, well worth the slight delay it had taken to stop by the house for her to change and for him to fire up the Harley.

If—when—they found Shelby, he would decide how to get her home. For now, speed was essential. Time equated miles of distance between him and his child.

Julia's arms locked around him, Zach whipped down another exit ramp, tearing through the parking lot of a cheap hotel, the twentieth in forty-two minutes. He cruised past the small square pool with a tarp stretched over it for winter. A lone umbrella table listed to the side.

No sign of John's car.

Zach sped back onto the access road to the next hotel. Orange letters blared Vacancy with the *y* blinking as a light struggled to burn out. A string of rooms lined the lot, sagging eaves shading the walkway to an ice machine. The lot gaped empty except for...

A solitary car parked at the far corner, the blue compact car the same make and model as John's, with a military ID decal on the windshield. Julia's arms tightened around Zach's waist.

Anger churned as he drove closer.

The collection of bumper stickers proclaimed school pride and a local rock station, all stickers identical to the

ones on John's car. Straight ahead, lights shone through the
curtains of one room.

Zach cut the engine.

Julia leaned into him. "Take a few deep breaths first,
Colonel."

Screw deep breaths.

He jammed down the kickstand and flung himself off the
bike. The slit in the curtain parted before fluttering closed
again.

"Zach, wait," Julia called after him.

Like hell. He pounded the door, each thud slamming
through him, hammering home frustration and a determination to regain control of his world. "Damn it, Shelby.
Open up or I'm calling the police."

The door swung wide, John Murdoch defiantly blocking
the entrance. "Hello, Colonel."

"I'm taking Shelby home." Zach advanced a step.

John didn't budge.

"You'd better step aside." Zach towered over the teen,
and still he didn't move.

Man, the kid had more guts than brains.

Julia's hand fell to rest on his shoulder. He shrugged it
off.

"Shelby, come outside. Now." He looked over the boy's
shoulder. Shelby stood hovering between a television and
a bed with rumpled covers.

Her brown eyes red and puffy from crying.

Overlong jersey rippling above her bare legs.

All the bottled frustrations of the day, hell, the past two
years, detonated. Rage a lifetime in the making roared
within him—at Lance Sinclair for hurting Julia, at Pam for
hurting their children, at Julia for shutting him out.

And most of all at himself.

The restraints on his anger snapped a half second before
his hand shot up to catch John by the shirt collar. Zach
slammed the teen up against the door. "What the hell did
you do to my daughter?"

Chapter 16

Shelby's scream bounced off paper-thin walls.

"Zach. Wait." Julia struggled to keep her voice steady and low, hoping some of that calm might leech into the wild-eyed trio before blood started spouting.

Shelby lurched forward. "Stop it!" she shrieked. "Put him down." She pummeled her father's shoulders.

Like a fly battering a bull.

Zach didn't budge. His stare bored into the teen he'd flattened against the door.

Julia sidled between Zach and Shelby. With firm hands, she edged Shelby away. "Take a deep breath." Or ten. "And I'll handle this. You'll only make it worse."

Could it get any worse? Zach never lost control.

She called upon every seasoned diplomatic skill honed from living in the commune for years. She knew well how to defuse tensions of people from all walks of life confined in small spaces.

Julia rested a light hand on his arm. "Put John down and let's talk."

"Back up, Julia." Muscles flexed under her touch.

"You know I can't do that." Time to set aside her own needs and deal with the mess at hand before Zach irreparably damaged his relationship with his daughter. "You may want to hurt John now—"

"Damn straight," he barked, his chest pumping with primitive rage. His flight suit strained against his back with each labored breath.

"It won't solve anything." What a turnaround. Now she would be the one to halt a scene guaranteed to bring the police. She didn't always manage her own temper, but she knew countless techniques for coping with other people's. Time to put every one of those techniques to work. "The desk clerk will call the cops if you keep this up. Stop. Think."

Traffic growled past in waves while she waited. Tension hummed through the room, more palpable than the gusting from the ancient heater. The air filled with Shelby's sniffles, echoed with ragged breathing, from her, Zach, John.

John's eyes flickered with ill-disguised fear. His baggy clothes hung from his body like multiple sweatshirts and jeans on a hanger. A pulse throbbed in Zach's neck.

She didn't recognize this man, but suspected those who'd followed him into war would. "Fighting won't solve anything here, Zach. Let's hear what they have to say. You can even shout all you want." Desperation clawed at emotions already raw. "This isn't like you. Please, just put him down."

Zach's fingers flexed, then relaxed as he lowered John. Julia allowed a sigh of relief to shudder through her for one self-indulgent second before she stiffened her shoulders and resolve.

"Okay, everybody listen up. We need ground rules here. No one talks without permission." She pointed to Shelby before shifting her gaze to John. "Everyone gets a chance to be heard.'' She saved the last for Zach. ''And no one gets physical. Understand?''

A car swooshed by in the disgruntled silence.

''Good.'' Julia nodded. ''I'll take that as a yes.''

The teen backed, flicking a strand of hair from his face. ''Sir, I know it looks bad, but nothing happened.''

Zach loomed forward a step. ''Can't you come up with something better than that?''

''Zach,'' she warned, her arm shooting between them. It sounded like a stretch to her too, but no need to toss gasoline on the fire. ''They do have some clothes on. We probably arrived just in time.''

What would have happened if she hadn't insisted on searching with him? Horror nipped at her. She saw one last chance to help Zach and his daughters, a way to heal the rifts in their family. ''Shelby? What's going on, hon?''

''John's telling the truth. We didn't do anything.'' The silver stud in her brow winked above a defiant glare. ''But I wanted to. He's the one who stopped.''

Zach's brows slammed down into an even darker scowl. *Whoosh.* Direct hit of kerosene on those embers.

''Okay, Shelby, you win.'' Julia charged past Zach into the hotel room, forcing the teens to back deeper inside. Putting distance between them and Zach.

Confusion momentarily replaced defiance on Shelby's pale face. ''What?''

''You win.'' Julia pinned her with a give-no-quarter stare. ''You hurt your dad. Isn't that what this is all about? Hurting him?''

Shelby tugged the hem of her overlong jersey, her brown eyes gleaming with a battlefield fervor she'd no doubt inherited from her father. ''You're all ganging up on me.'' She swung an accusing finger toward John. ''First him telling me I'm not ready for sex. Now you telling me what I'm thinking too. I'm so tired of everybody deciding my life for me.''

Zach stepped further into the room, his eyes hardening as they scanned the rumpled bedspread, then shifted back to Shelby. "Nothing happened?"

John skimmed a finger inside the neck of his sweatshirt. "No, sir."

A sigh heaved through Zach. "Okay, then. Shelby, put on some…" He waved toward her crumpled jeans on the floor. "Put something on and let's go."

The commander had spoken.

No wonder Shelby was pulling her hair out to get her father's attention. Just leave? Julia wanted to scream. How like a man to think this was only about sex, Zach and John both, when nothing had been solved. She knew too well sex only complicated life all the more.

Shelby yanked on her jeans, muttering as if already planning her next great escape. She grabbed a brush off the bathroom counter and yanked it through her tangled hair with brutal swipes.

No way were they leaving until Zach and Shelby battled this out once and for all. Julia shut the door and plunked down in a chair.

He frowned. "Julia?"

She ignored his question and plowed ahead. "Shelby, what's really going on here?"

Shelby hurled her brush into the sink. "John and I were running away to get married."

"Like hell." Zach moved in front of the door, boots braced apart, the officer standing sentinel.

Why couldn't they see past what the other said to the real meaning? "You had to know we'd find you before then."

Shelby charged across the room and pitched a half-eaten pizza in the trash. "At least I'd get a few hours away. Then maybe he—" she paused in the midst of shoving the left-over six-pack of sodas into her suitcase to shoot a glare at her father, "—would understand that John and I are in love."

Zach's low snort sparked defiance in Shelby's eyes. She shot an exasperated eye-roll Julia's way. "See what I have to put up with?" She flung a handful of T-shirts on top of the sodas. "John's the only one who understands."

Julia leaned forward, hoping to defuse the tension by enticing them all to relax their toe-to-toe battle stances. "Understands what, Shelby?"

"What it's like living in a gypsy caravan on high speed. Pulling into some Podunk town just long enough to make friends you'll miss forever when you have to haul ass to another hole in the wall for your father's I-Must-Save-the-Planet freaking job."

Shelby stopped in front of her father, fists jammed on her hips. "Most of all, I hate living with everybody always watching me."

Julia nudged Zach's boot with her foot. Twice.

Finally, he uncrossed his arms, working the back of his neck with his hand. "That's what parents are supposed to do. Watch their kids."

Shelby's shoulders raised and lowered with a beleaguered sigh, which carried some weight for once when coupled with her trembling jaw.

Her frenzied ranting tempered to restless pacing. "I don't mean all that parent garbage." She flicked the trailing edge of the spread up onto the bed. "I mean *everybody*. I can't go anywhere without people knowing who I am, watching everything I do and telling you about it. Being a military brat is like living in some kind of fishbowl." She waved a hand to encompass her father's flight suit. "Except everybody wears green."

Zach stepped closer, head dipping as he listened. "Go on."

Knee bumping the bed, Shelby picked at the polyester spread, flicking aside one fuzzy pill at a time, an endless task on the cheap coverlet. "I don't get a say in anything. Ever. Nothing stays the same. You're already making plans to haul us all to another state this summer. Just when I get to liking it somewhere, we move. You change jobs. You change wives.''

Julia kept her eyes fixed on Shelby. The weight of Zach's insistence that they give the marriage a try whittled away at her already shaky and weary resistance.

Shelby tugged at the hem of her jersey. ''It's like I don't count. John understands.'' She angled a wobbly smile his way. ''I mean, geez, it's even worse for him. He's a military brat *and* a preacher's kid.''

Julia waited and wondered if Zach would pull it together. She willed him to be the father she knew he could be.

Slowly, he closed the distance between himself and his daughter, absently circling his wedding band round and round. ''Your mother and I started seeing each other when we weren't much older than you two.''

''Oh, great.'' Sarcasm dripped from Shelby's words like water condensing on the ice bucket. Flopping on the edge of the bed, she swept up a pillow and clutched it to her stomach. ''Thanks for the big, fat endorsement, Colonel.''

''Remember what Julia said, Shel. Everyone gets a turn. So hush up and listen to mine for a minute.'' Zach pulled the pillow from her and tossed it aside. ''You think you're the only teenager to pull a tough road? Your mother had to deal with bringing up four younger brothers and sisters while her mom supported them.''

His jaw tensed, and Julia could almost see him working to draw the words from inside himself.

''By the time I was fifteen, I'd moved twice as much as you have now. We followed my father from rig to rig because that's how he put food on the table. Then my mother died.'' He scrubbed a hand over his face, but couldn't swipe away the exhaustion from his eyes. ''After that, life was…not good. We weren't exactly living the American Dream, kiddo.''

Julia's joy seeped from her.

His spare-the-rod-spoil-the-child father.

Zach always understated his own disappointments and pain. For him to share this much, his teenage years must have been beyond bad. She didn't need tender yearnings to be the one to soothe his hurts. Not now when there was still so much unresolved between them. They were even farther than ever from establishing a true partnership.

"Just like you, Shel," Zach continued, pacing a relentless path in the threadbare carpet. "I planned to take control of my own world. For me, your mother and the military were my ticket out for making a real life. I won't ever regret marrying her because I have you and Ivy. But what we see for our lives at sixteen or even eighteen may only be about fifty percent on target, if you're lucky. Keep that in mind when you're making decisions."

Silently, Shelby jabbed her toe through a quarter-sized hole in the carpet.

"This is who I am, Shel." Zach thumped his chest right over his military nametag. He dropped onto the edge of the bed beside her. "I wish I could promise you things will be different at home. All I can say is I'll try."

"Yeah, yeah, I know. Somebody's gotta pay the bills."

Zach tucked a knuckle under her chin, tipping her face up. "If it was just about paying the bills, I'd be flying for the airlines. But it isn't. I've had a fair glimpse of what it's like to lose control of your life. And there are people out there in the world who are feeling that a helluva lot worse than you or I ever will. I can't just say it's not my problem and turn away."

The words may have been meant for Shelby, but Julia heard the deeper implications for her relationship with Zach. She knew first-hand how he took on the troubles of others, and she couldn't help but admire and love him for turning his life around even as she wished for more from him.

He slung an arm around his daughter's shoulders. "Shel,

if you want me to respect where you're coming from, you're going to have to do the same for me.''

While Shelby didn't return the embrace, she didn't pull away either. Her head fell to rest on his chest, nothing overt like some Ivy hug, but Julia saw the tears Shelby wouldn't show her father.

They'd made a start in reconnecting as father and daughter, transcending into a new stage of the parent-child relationship as Shelby left behind Ivy-days of unquestioning acceptance. Julia blinked back her own tears, touched.

Then it hit her. They didn't need her anymore. She sat on the outskirts, much as John slumped against the wall, both of them unnecessary now.

Pam had returned and from all appearances planned to stay. Both girls had bonded with their father. Patrick was thriving, and Julia had a solid support system in place now to maintain that progress.

And she was a stronger woman than she'd been a year ago, or even five months ago when Zach had sauntered into her hospital room. She'd learned from him how to strengthen her dreams with a solid focus.

They'd accomplished their goals in marrying in half the time they'd thought they needed, which should be cause for rejoicing. Except now, there wasn't anything holding them together. No more crises to solve or major single-parenting hardships to wade through.

Now, there wasn't anything to stop her from leaving.

''You're leaving, aren't you?'' Zach said quietly over his shoulder to Julia without taking his eyes off Patrick asleep in the crib. Exhaustion pumped through him after his longest day on record since he'd walked into Julia's hospital room.

Her light tread sounded along the hardwood floors, then muffled on the rug as she eased closer. Stopping beside him, she didn't answer, just stared down at the sleeping baby with him.

While he wanted to hope she would disagree, he knew better. He might have salvaged something with Shelby, thanks to Julia's intervention, but he'd blown it with Julia by losing his temper in the hotel room. By the whole damned way he'd handled the flight. If only he could have kept control, thought through his words to fix the fact that he should have been straight with her about Lance's crash. But damn it, Julia stirred emotions that weren't calm or even rational.

Her scent swirled around him, strawberry shampoo and fresh air. "We've accomplished what we set out to do with the children. They're back on track."

He noticed she didn't flat-out state she planned to leave. He pushed that advantage to the wall. "Why tear that apart now?"

He'd reclaimed his daughter, but would he lose a wife again? And this time, he would lose a child too if his marriage ended. Patrick might not be his biological son, but the boy couldn't be any more his if he'd fathered him.

"If I stay any longer, it will only be worse when I leave. Shelby expects me to go now. Ivy's excited about having her mother home so this won't hit her as hard."

"You're deluding yourself on that one, Jules."

She didn't answer, just patted her son's back. Zach tucked the blanket around Patrick's feet, using the familiar ritual to steady himself while he thought through ways to convince her, something he could do to make her stay. "What about Patrick?"

"I'll miss being with him all day, but I'm stronger now, more confident in myself and the support system I have in place."

"That's not what I meant." Stirrings of residual anger edged past his exhaustion. "Don't you think Patrick will miss me? Or that I'll miss him?"

Her grip on the edge of the crib whitened. "It will be harder for him the longer he has to grow attached to you."

Zach grasped her shoulders and turned her toward him, finding her face as pale as that tight-knuckled grip. "If you're so much stronger now, then give us a chance."

Patrick stirred, snuffled, then stilled with a sigh.

Julia's eyes slid back to Zach. "Do you think this is easy for me?" she whispered, her words laced with frustration. "I want to do what's best for the children."

"Bull."

"What? I can't believe you said that to me."

She tried to inch back but he held firm.

"Hell, Jules, I'll say it again if it will make you listen." He could see she was three seconds away from packing her high tops and swiping all those bottles of polish right off his dresser, into her bag and out of his world. "You won't stay because you're too scared to try. Fantasies are easy. Real life is hard. At least be honest."

"You want honest? Yes, I'm scared." She met him toe-to-toe, pain and pride stamped on her pale face. "So reassure me with a reason to stick around that has nothing to do with the children."

His hands fell away. A trick question? Regardless, he knew if he answered wrong, those polish bottles would be clanking their way into her suitcase within minutes. "I've given you solid reasons to stay."

"Not the one I want."

Okay, so she needed a reason to stay. The bottles received clemency for a few minutes longer. If he just knew what it was she wanted him to say. "Help me out here, Jules. I want to get this right, but I'm stumbling around in the dark."

"If I have to tell you, it doesn't count."

Ah, hell. He was screwed. Zach jammed the heels of his hands to his forehead. "Women!"

The baby stirred. Zach grasped Julia's elbow to drag her

across the hall into the study. Shutting the door behind them, he spun her to face him. "Julia, I'm just a man, as clueless as the rest of them when it comes to understanding how a woman's mind works."

Exhaustion be damned, he would keep at this all night if that's what it took to make her understand.

She darted a pointed stare at his hand on her elbow. "Let go of me, please. I can't think straight when you touch me."

An endorsement for putting his hands all over her if ever he'd heard one, but he respected Julia too much to play that game, even if every fiber in him shouted to use any weapon to keep her.

He raised his hands, palms up.

"You want direction for this conversation? Fine then. Here it is, Colonel."

Sparks showered from her eyes. Zach prepped for anything.

"I love you."

Anything except that.

Just when he thought she'd thrown her last surprise at him, Julia flipped his world again, this time in a good way. Relief chugged through him. She loved him. He wanted to pump a fist through the air, shout...until he saw the defeated slump of her shoulders.

Zach reached to gather her close. "Ah, Jules—"

She batted his arms away. "Do *not* touch me! I may love you, but that doesn't change anything. It doesn't change the fact that, hell yes, I'm scared this won't work. I'm scared of being hurt again." Her voice cracked on the last word.

"Jules, you know I would never cheat on you."

"That's not what I'm talking about." She backed, her hand between them. "Yes, Lance cheated on me. Not just once. Over and over again he lied about where he was, who he was with. But he didn't just cheat with his body. He cheated with his heart. He loved someone else. He *loved* her, the kind of woman he should have married. Sure, we patched it up, but I'm not so certain anymore that it would have lasted. I want it all this time. I want to be everything to a man, to be his first thought in the morning, the reason he smiles in the middle of some important meeting."

Julia looked at him waiting, but he didn't know what the hell to say to reassure her.

"Zach, you asked me to help you with the answer, so here it is. I wasn't first in Lance's heart. Ever. I can't live that way again. I need you to love me as much as I love you."

She stared at him with such wary hope he wondered why couldn't he just make himself say the words. Time was running out and he knew they were seconds from smacking the mountain that would end it all. "I've shown you in a hundred different ways how much I want you to stay, and that's what counts. What we do. Not what we say. Lance's actions proved that."

She winced, but he wouldn't stop now. He had a point, damn it, even if it hurt. He needed to make her understand how much she meant to him. "Explain to me, Julia, how a bunch of insubstantial words makes a commitment."

Frustration knotted his gut. Forget playing fair.

He pulled her close, chest to chest, legs tucking between each other by instinct, and let the inevitable heat, sparks and need sear them together. "Pam spouted to heaven and back how much she loved me as she walked out that door. My father pounded us one minute and said he loved us the next."

Everything went still inside him.

What the hell had he just said? Apparently Julia had heard every word. Tears streaked down her face, just like the ones she'd shed in his office over his POW days.

No way did he want her staying out of pity.

Her hand drifted up. He clasped her wrist before she

could touch his face. Emotions revved within him like an engine drone, faster, harder, without any hope that a simple flip of a switch would shut it all down.

He could feel every ounce of Julia's compassion pulsing through her. She was weakening. He could take advantage of that weakness, press, convince her to stay a little longer as he'd done for years with Pam.

But damn it, Julia wasn't settling? Well, neither was he. He'd thought she was the one person he didn't need to jump through hoops for, the one person who didn't need him to put on a commander show.

He tightened his grip on her wrist. "If you want to prove all that *love* you say you have for me, then have the guts to stay."

Zach dropped her hand.

He pivoted away and out the door, needing to put as much distance as he could between himself and her soft touch tempting him to throw away defenses a lifetime in the making.

Chapter 17

Stunned by Zach's harsh words, so full of hurt, still hanging in the air, Julia stared at the half-open door. His wounds and lack of trust ran so much deeper than even she'd known.

The front door opened and closed. Softly. Zach wasn't a door slammer, no surprise, but the solid thud echoed with finality.

Oh God, she couldn't let him leave. Not like this.

Julia sprinted into the hall just as his motorcycle growled to life. She slumped against the wall, the sense of failure turning her legs to sawdust.

He'd needed her, just as he'd needed Pam, but Julia hadn't been able to pull it together and be there for him. She'd spouted all about love and being stronger, but hadn't come through for him when it counted.

Across the hall, Shelby's door opened and she slouched against the frame. An overlong T-shirt grazed her knees, one of Julia's pilfered from the laundry. The shirt declared in board-like letters Woodworkers Kick Ash. Julia knew she certainly hadn't lived up to the motto tonight.

Shelby scratched her ankle with her toes. "Men can be such nimrods."

Julia welcomed the laugh, even a watery one. Comfort had come from the most unexpected corner. "They sure can."

Shelby shoved away from the door. "Since it looks like neither one of us is going to get lucky any time soon, wanna go find some chocolate?"

"Yeah, hon, I sure do." She hooked an arm around Shelby's shoulders as they walked down the hall. "I think we'd both benefit from eating our weight in M&M's."

"I hear ya." Shelby shuffled to the cabinet, pulled open the door and reached behind the coffee mugs. She tossed two bags of M&M's on the counter, crispy and plain.

Julia's secret stash. She sat at the kitchen table. "How did you know where those were?"

Shelby angled an adults-can-be-so-lame look over her shoulder. "That's a rookie candy-hiding move. You'll have to do better than that when Patrick's older." She opened the freezer. "Let's see what Ivy has squirreled away."

She rifled through the frozen goods, pitching bags of peas, corn and waffles in the sink before sighing. "Ahhh, pay dirt." Shelby spun around, a freezer bag full of Christmas candy dangling from two fingers. "Ivy's learned to hide things a little better than you, but then she's had a lot of practice lately."

Shelby sifted through the bag, nudging aside candy canes, foil-wrapped kisses, a chocolate Santa with his head bitten off. She cocked her head, then resealed the bag. "No need to teach her how to bury them better yet. Let the kid keep her illusions a while longer. She'll learn to hide things as well as I do soon enough."

Julia straightened. Suddenly, their midnight feeding frenzy became about more than food. Like her father,

Shelby hid her deeper feelings and thoughts well behind understatements.

Shelby hitched a knee up onto the counter, hefting herself up until she stood in front of the cabinet. Arching up onto her toes, she peered into the top shelf. She shuffled aside a dusty food processor to reveal a gold box.

The kid was good, no doubt. Julia wouldn't have touched that food processor for another fifty years.

Shelby leapt to the floor, Godivas clutched to her chest, and plopped down to sit at the table. She tugged the red bow and lifted the lid. "Silly to waste Mom's bribes on Aggie anymore, I guess."

Blinking fast without looking up, Shelby dug into the box, picked a white truffle and ate the first bite of her mother's presents in over a year. She chewed slowly, swallowed even slower, a new level of acceptance and maturity marking her face. "Not bad." She scooched the box forward. "Here. Try some."

Guilt hammered Julia in relenting blows. Zach was right that a break-up now would devastate all three of the children.

Julia covered Shelby's hand with her own. "Hon, I'm so sorry you had to hear all of that. Your dad and I really have been trying to do the right thing for you kids."

Shelby didn't look up and Julia suspected she was covering more of those tears she'd hidden from Zach while she let herself soak up the comfort. Julia wanted to hug her and tuck her into bed and reassure her everything would be fine, but she couldn't lie.

Finally, Shelby slid her hand free. "My dad always hides his candy the best of all. He used to keep it in his truck, but I haven't been able to figure out where he hides it since Mom left."

There it was. Shelby's message hidden under all those understatements, but no less powerful for its subtlety.

Julia stacked the empty brown candy papers and thought

of Zach's joking offer of Little Debbie cakes from his desk drawer. The man definitely hid his snacks and secrets better than the girls. He filed everything away in his office, submerging himself in work, tackling the world's troubles as a line of defense against acknowledging his own.

Zach took the needs of so many on those broad shoulders without anyone to take care of his. She wanted to build a real home for him, one where fathers didn't hurt their sons and wives didn't walk out.

He deserved all that and more. He deserved to have someone fight for him. And she wanted to be that someone.

Zach had insisted his actions counted more than words, and if so, then that man loved her. Even if the stubborn guy didn't know how to put the label on his feelings. Yet.

Julia crumpled the candy wrappers. She'd insisted she was stronger and that she loved him. Time for her to prove it by doing exactly what Zach had said. Show him. She would love him enough to put aside her pride and stay.

Shelby scooped up two more chocolates and stood. "Guess I'll try to catch some sleep."

Julia touched Shelby's arm lightly as she passed and counted yet another blessing in the form of this woman-child dispenser of chocolate, hairstyles and wisdom. "'Night, hon."

"G'night."

Julia watched her stepdaughter cross the kitchen and realized more than one Dawson needed reassurance. "Shelby?"

"Yeah?"

"Could you watch Patrick for me for a couple of hours once your dad gets back?"

Shelby blinked fast before shrugging as if it was no big deal when they both knew otherwise. "Sure. No problem."

"Thanks, hon." Julia smiled, knowing full well she couldn't say goodbye to these children any more than she could their father.

Shelby snapped her fingers and Aggie came trotting from under the table to follow her. The Woodworkers Kick Ash shirt blared a reminder Julia desperately needed.

What had she been thinking, demanding some silly words? She'd felt more love in one day with Zach than Lance had given her in six years of marriage.

She didn't intend to throw that away.

Whatever wounds Zach still harbored that kept him from voicing those words, she would heal with time. Starting tonight. She would sit on their front porch until her toes froze off if need be waiting for him. Never again would Zach come home to an empty house.

The seasoned commander might have fought a few battles in his time, but he hadn't seen anything like the siege she planned to wage to win his heart.

Zach roared around the corner. Only two blocks left until home. And he wasn't any closer to easing the frustration churning inside him than when he'd lost control and stormed out. His bike hadn't offered its usual escape—release, relief from the mess he'd made of his life.

At least the time away had given him one answer. He wasn't giving up. Sure, he'd hoped for something more from Julia, but that didn't mean he would roll over and quit. First thing Monday morning, he would park himself in the Wing Commander's office and request a year's deferment of his Air War College slot.

Yeah, it pinched to risk losing out on a career opportunity he'd worked his ass off for, but the regret didn't come close to what he would feel if he lost Julia. He would stomp around on her roof for the next twelve months cleaning leaves out of her gutters until she caved, if that's what it would take to persuade her.

Zach slowed the motorcycle around the last corner, heading home. And tried like hell not to think of how damned empty that house would be without her and Patrick.

He turned into the driveway, the single beam of his bike sweeping across the yard. Revealing Julia. Moonbeams and the porch light glinted off her blond curls.

Zach braced himself. He'd been ready for a confrontation in the morning. He wasn't sure he wanted to finish this conversation tonight, not when they were both still so raw from the flight line, their time in his office, and his damned careless words about his father.

Then Zach looked at her. Really looked.

Julia wore his leather flight jacket, a motorcycle helmet perched on her knee, her invitation for a ride clear.

Zach exhaled a long gust of relief. As far as signs went, hers carried a cargo hold full of hope.

He'd told himself it didn't matter if he had to fight for her a while longer. He would wait. But having her make the first move mattered a helluva lot more than he'd expected.

Zach hit the accelerator and drove across the grass, stopping in front of Julia. She stood, her mile-long legs unfolding. Those incredible legs in stretch pants and red boots made him almost as crazy as the incredible woman inside them.

Julia sauntered forward, winding around a row of empty flowerpots. She didn't hurry or run, but then Julia never rushed through life. She made him find time to take a wild night ride, stop for a nap in a hammock or watch his children play from a purple glider. Julia had given him and his children so much. More than anything, he wanted to be the man she needed. The man she deserved.

She strapped on her helmet. ''Let's go for a ride.''

''Where do you want to go?''

Julia slid onto the bike behind him. Her arms locked around his waist without hesitation. ''Surprise me.''

He lifted one of her hands to his mouth. He pressed a lingering kiss to her wrist before replacing her hand on his stomach. ''I'll do my best.''

Zach cruised out of the yard, easing down the curb to the street. Outside the front gate, he opened up the engine and threw away the boundaries. Highway lights whipped past, sky above, air swirling below under the bridge. The road hummed beneath him with all the ground flight release he'd always enjoyed in the past. And more. The allure of the ride was back, and he knew it wasn't so much the bike as the woman with him.

Now to figure out how to make the most out of whatever miracle had prompted her to give him a second chance. He needed the perfect way to romance this unconventional lady he'd married. The house had too much potential for interruption, and he wanted somewhere more neutral than his office. Then the perfect answer came to him, the ideal offering for a woman who valued a Crock-Pot family dinner more than diamonds.

Returning to base, Zach pulled up outside the gym and cut the engine.

Julia slid off the bike, tugging her helmet free. "Uh, I know I said to surprise me, but what are we doing here? I had a more…" she paused to caress every inch of him with her gaze "…intimate setting in mind."

Zach pressed a finger to her lips. "Hold that thought."

He led her through the lobby, flashing a salute to the uniformed attendant. The subdued echo of a lone late-night fitness enthusiast clanged behind a window. At the end of the hall, Zach swung a door wide and flipped a light switch to illuminate a gaping, empty room.

Julia circled slowly, her brow furrowing as she surveyed the high ceiling. Excitement charged through him, a sense of purpose to meet Julia on their new ground of compromise. God, he couldn't wait to share his latest idea with her, to see her smile and know he'd put it there.

Zach strode past her. "I had a phone consult with the Wing Commander while I was TDY this week."

"About what?"

"About the fact that your base support group needs more room for the children to spread out." His rumbling bass bounced and echoed off the walls. "We're thinking this space may work. It's already slated to be an indoor play gym. The contractor could use your input on designing a section with modifications like you made for the playhouse. You and Rena Price will have to draw up the proposal and wade through a mountain of paperwork. But with luck and decent funding, it should all come together by the fall."

He watched the graceful sway of Julia's hips as she silently walked. Thanks to her, he'd learned to look beyond the mission to the people. But would she understand the message he was trying to send, how he was trying to show her his feelings?

Then she slowed, turning to face him. Her full-faced smile below tear-filled eyes answered his doubts.

He'd hit pay dirt.

"Thank you, Zach, so much." She swiped her wrist over her eyes.

Zach closed the last two steps between them. "Before you say anything more, I want you to know that none of this is contingent on your staying. I can understand if how I reacted back at the hotel might worry you. My father—"

She clapped a hand over his mouth. "Stop. Not another word. My turn to talk now. Okay? No running off before I have my say."

Determination radiated from her in waves that would have sent rebel forces running. Zach raised his hands in surrender.

"You are *not* your father. Sure you have a temper. So do I. So do most people. You had every right to be angry. Mad. All-out pissed at Shelby. Just like I had the right to get mad at you on the flight line tonight. But it's how we handle that anger that matters. When it came right down to it, we both held it together. Angry, sure, but never violent. You are *not* your father," she repeated a final time.

And this time, he heard.

Her words washed over him with a truth that resonated deep inside him. She was right. He'd faced frustrations as a husband and parent tonight that would have sent his dad over the edge. But he'd held it together with Shelby.

With that truth from Julia came a peace he'd never expected to find, a reassurance he could be a man worthy of Julia's love. "You're not leaving me."

She cupped his face, the numb side, but he felt her healing touch in his soul.

"Of course not. I will stay with you. Go with you. Be with you. Wherever you are, I'm right there beside you forever, because I love you. Do you hear me? I love every stubborn, take-charge, drop-dead sexy awesome part of you."

Linking her arms around his neck, she rose up onto her toes and plastered her body to his. He combed his fingers into her tousled curls and kissed her, long, full. A perfect forever fit.

They toppled back against the wall, sliding down together. Julia sprawled on top of him in a tangle of arms and legs…and escalating need.

She dipped her face to kiss him. Or maybe he pulled her head toward him. Who knew? And who cared as long as she kept loving him.

A squeak of door hinges sounded a second before a cleared throat echoed. Julia and Zach sprang apart to find the uniformed desk attendant standing in the doorway.

"Oops, sorry Colonel. I, uh, wanted to make sure you found the lights and to let you know we're, uh, closing in about ten minutes."

"Thank you, Sergeant." Zach nodded.

The door swung shut just before Julia's shoulders started shaking with laughter.

Zach slung an arm around her and tucked her to his chest. "So you like the kid gym idea?"

"Of course I do. I should have known you would find a gift far more special than even a Craftsman ratchet set."

His laugh rumbled free. Lord, he loved the way she made him laugh.

Loved?

The word settled inside him with a rightness much like the feeling Julia brought with her whenever she walked into a room, and his defenses came crashing down.

He loved her.

For the first time, Zach looked at his feelings without the filters of the past. He'd been so wrapped up in comparing her love to Pam's or his father's, Zach hadn't seen his own love for Julia or recognized the value of hers for him.

She'd demanded he push the boundaries of his limited view of relationships and family to build something better with his children. She respected him enough to stand up to him and demand he be the man she deserved. Hell, yes, he loved her. How could he have ever doubted it?

Julia nuzzled her head under his chin. "It really will make a fabulous play area, with a ball pit over there maybe, and a playhouse in that corner. We could plan a family trip from Alabama when they unveil it."

The move. Zach thought of his decision to stay in Charleston another year. He wouldn't have to do that now. He wouldn't have to give up the career opportunity to convince her to stay.

But he would do it anyway because it was the right thing. He wasn't the man who put his job before his wife and family anymore. "Uh, Jules."

"What?"

Her fingers explored the exposed patch of skin at the neck of his flight suit, making coherent thought, much less speech, damned difficult.

"We're not moving this summer."

She gave his flight suit zipper a playful tug, answering absently, "We're not?"

He captured her hands in his before she could travel down to dangerously distracting territory. "I did some thinking while I was riding around tonight." He worked to keep his words coming while her mouth traced a steady path up his throat. "I'm filing a request with the Wing Commander to defer my Air War College slot for a year."

Her lips stilled, and she looked up at him. "Why would you do that?"

"We don't need the upheaval of a move right now. We need the time to settle in as a family."

"But you don't have to do that. We're okay. I'm staying." She gripped his flight scarf and tugged. "This is a once-in-a-lifetime chance for you."

"No, Jules. *You* are a once-in-a-lifetime chance for me." He thought of the reassurance she needed and found it so easy to offer now he couldn't believe he'd ever held back. "There are plenty of times the Air Force won't give me a say in where I go, but I've learned there are also times I do have choices. I want you to know I mean it when I say I'm trying. You come first."

Her eyes filled for the second time in minutes. For a woman who didn't cry easily, apparently she had a well of happy tears just waiting to be tapped. Julia let them flow while Zach held her and counted all those blessings Julia was always talking about.

He liked to think he'd learned a few lessons after nearly seventeen years in the Air Force, ninety-seven combat missions, two weeks as an Iraqi POW and one very speedy divorce. Most important, he'd learned that *being* him was a hell of a lot easier than being *married* to him.

But he intended to spend the rest of his life working on that. Because thanks to Julia, he'd also learned the best lesson of all. He could touch the clouds from his own porch on a purple glider as long as she sat beside him.

He kissed the top of her head. "I love you, Jules. I love the way you make me smile, the way you love our children.

Most of all, I love the way we are together, because together, we can do anything. And if you'll let me, I'll tell you and show you how much I love you for the rest of my life."

"I love you too, Zach." Her words breathed over his skin. "I love how—"

He silenced her with his finger to her lips. "I know."

She smiled against his touch. "Oh, that's right. I already told you."

"Yeah, but that's not how I know."

"Then how?"

He traced the upward tilt of her mouth. "You stayed."

"I sure did. And you don't stand a chance of shaking me lose now." Her arm snaked around his neck, her mouth grazing his with the promise of more to come later. Julia nipped his bottom lip. "I only have one more request."

"Just ask, Jules, and I'll make it happen."

"Will you paint my toenails when I'm old and arthritic?"

His laugh rumbled deep and full between them. "Why wait? I've had a serious hankering to slick some of that Five Alarm Red on your perfect toes."

She scratched a fingernail down every link of his flight suit zipper, trailing lower toward seriously fired-up territory. "Well, Colonel, if you take me home to bed, I think this just may be your lucky night."

Epilogue

Shelby shouldered through the post-recital crush back-stage, her hand linked with John's as he followed her. Weaving around tutus and smiling faces painted with glitter, she followed her dad and Julia while they looked for Ivy. A *Nutcracker* kiddie recital wasn't exactly a rock concert date, but John was hanging tough. He told her it didn't matter as long as he could see her.

Cool.

After the fall-out in the hotel almost a year ago, her father and John had come to an understanding of sorts—family-oriented dates. If John could withstand Dawson picnics, hikes and endless hours of elementary-school children in tutus, then her father would back off.

And he had. Well, as much as any dad ever did.

Three steps ahead of Shelby, Julia tucked Patrick more securely against her shoulder and arched up to her husband. "Can you see her?"

"Not yet." Zach towered over feathery and sequined headpieces. Finally, Ivy's head bobbed above the masses.

Shelby watched as her stepfather swept Ivy up, her mom standing beside them with an armload of roses. Eddie wasn't so bad, in small doses. Even if the guy's tan bordered on tangerine, he made her mom happy, so Shelby put up with him.

At first, she'd been scared spitless Eddie and her mom would start some lame custody battle. Not that Shelby would have gone. Luckily, her mom seemed okay with the weekend parent gig, and the mall trips were kind of fun now that she knew her dad and Julia would always be home waiting.

"Daaad-dy!" Catching sight of her father, Ivy wriggled out of Eddie's grasp and launched forward.

Zach caught her just before she catapulted onto her face. "Hey, kiddo."

"Did you see me? I never stumbled once. Well, once, but I made it look like it was supposed to be there."

"You were perfect. It was a great show."

And it had been. The mouse had found her confidence. Who'd have thought a year ago that she would take center stage at a ballet recital? "Good job, Mouse."

Ivy grinned, "I know."

Her mom and Orange-Eddie could buy Ivy a hothouse full of flowers and name-brand chocolates, but her dad and Julia had given Ivy something a lot more important.

"Julia!" Ivy squirmed down. "What did you think? Huh? Did you see me?"

"Yes, hon, I sure did. You were fabulous." Julia passed Patrick to Shelby before kneeling to hug Ivy.

Ivy patted her netted hair behind the white furry headpiece. "My hair didn't fall down, not a bit. I felt like a real princess."

"And you look like one too, hon."

The crowd milled and pushed and shoved around her, but Julia focused completely on Ivy. Julia had a way of doing that, making whoever she was talking to feel like the most important person in the world.

"Hey, Dad?"

Tugging his gaze from Julia, he looked down at Shelby.

Dad? There'd been a time she didn't think she would ever call him that again.

"Yeah, Shel?"

She wondered what he'd say when she told him she'd been talking to Doctor Bennett about taking an ROTC scholarship when she went to college in the fall. She'd been thinking she might be a pediatrician. She could work at base clinics with Air Force families to make things easier for them, like with the special needs support group. She knew first-hand how tough the military life could be. Maybe she could make her own difference in the world, kinda like her dad.

Shelby scratched her shoulder and also wondered what the Air Force would think of a lady doc with a tattoo?

"Shel?" her dad asked again. "Did you need something?"

"Not really." She'd tell him later. This was Ivy's time. "Just wanted to say I love ya."

Something else she'd thought she might never say to her dad again.

"Love you too, kiddo." He winked before reaching for Patrick. "How about let me take him so you and John can head on out to the movie."

"Sure. Thanks." Shelby passed over her brother with a quick buzz-kiss on his cheek to make him giggle. "Catch you later, Paddy."

Her dad hefted him up onto his shoulders. "Let's go find your mama, Bruiser. Bye, Shel. No later than one o'clock."

Of course, some things never changed.

"Roger that, Colonel." Smiling, Shelby slid her hand into John's, backing away as she took one last look at her family. With Ivy tucked under her arm, Julia tickled her son's nose with a flower. Patrick squealed from on top of her dad's shoulders. Then her dad smiled at Julia. Julia smiled back. Simple stuff. But good, really good.

And Shelby realized something else she wouldn't have thought a year ago.

Her old man wasn't such a nimrod after all.

* * * * *

Don't worry, there are more
WINGMEN WARRIOR
*stories on the horizon, so look for Renshaw's
story PRIVATE MANEUVERS coming in June
2003. But in the meantime, turn the page for a
sneak peek at Catherine Mann's
next Intimate Moments,*

THE CINDERELLA MISSION.

Enter the world of FAMILY SECRETS, *a new continuity series from Silhouette Books. It all starts in Silhouette Intimate Moments this February with...*

Prologue

Dr. Alex Morrow was dead.

Samuel Hatch feared it all the way to his sixty-year-old, ulcer-riddled gut.

The aging operative bolted back breakfast in his office, two antacids with cold coffee. His job as the Director of ARIES came with countless rewards and endless holes in his stomach. Since Hatch had created the secret section of the CIA, ARIES had become his family, his agents the children he and Rita had never been able to conceive.

Now he suspected he'd lost one.

Restrained tension hummed through him, stringing him as taut as the twine he worked to twist around the wilting plant behind his desk. He aimed the sunlamp with meticulous care, grounding himself in the ritual while he plotted how best to utilize his unlimited resources.

One day's silence he could accept, especially given the unstable climate in European Holzberg and neighboring Rebelia. But three days and Alex's tracking device inactive...

Every inch of Hatch's raw stomach burned after ten years of worrying about his pseudo-offspring. Yet their mission was too important to abandon. ARIES operatives embraced assignments no sane CIA agent would touch.

Their country owed these silent knights countless debts that could never be acknowledged.

Hatch anchored the stake on a struggling strawberry plant he'd grafted from home. He mentally sifted through Alex's final transmissions as he would soil through his fingers, looking for the proper texture to bear fruit. Heaven help them all if Alex fell into DeBruzkya's hands. The crazed Rebelian dictator under investigation was a sick bastard.

Heaven help Alex.

His fingers twitched, snapping a limp stem off the plant. He wouldn't let even one of his operatives, especially this one, go down without unleashing the full arsenal at his disposal. Hatch clutched the crumpled leaves in his fist and turned back to his office.

And what a mighty arsenal it was, compliments of the government's blank check.

Large flat-screen monitors lined one wall, glowing with everything from CNN to satellite uplink status. Computers hummed from his desk as well as along the conference table where laptops perched in front of eight seats. Electronic cryptology boxes littered the workspace for encoding and decoding transmissions.

In the midst of it all, he relied on an old-fashioned map of the world with pins marking locations of his operatives. The cover of each agent's private-sector identity offered the freedom to travel anywhere undetected. Already, he'd alerted European operatives to begin searching, but without a narrowed field, there was only so much he could expect.

He needed focus, someone to pull together the minuscule threads of information left behind in a handful of transmissions from Alex. Hatch rubbed the bruised leaves between his fingers like a talisman as he studied the map. Slowly two pins on the board paired in his mind.

The perfect duo for finding answers to the questions left in those last transmissions.

Logical Kelly Taylor would balance well with Ethan Williams, a rogue operative who thought so far outside the box he invented his own rules.

And their personal baggage?

They would either have to work through it or ignore it. He didn't need any fireworks drawing unwarranted—and potentially deadly—attention to this mission.

Hatch reached for one of the seven phones on his desk and punched a three-digit code. One ring later, he carefully placed the mangled leaves on the soil at the base of the struggling strawberry plant. "Taylor, Director Hatch here. I need you to locate Ethan Williams, then meet me in my office with his after-action report from Gastonia."

Her affirmative barely registered. Hatch studied the sole remaining plant from Rita's garden that hadn't been killed by his black thumb. Since Rita's death, that plant and ARIES were all he had left, and by God, they would bear fruit.

Hatch packed the soil around the base of a new sprout and refrained from reaching for the antacids again. Williams and Taylor would find Alex.

Assuming there wasn't—as his roiling gut kept telling him—a Judas in their ranks.

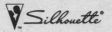

In February 2003

COMING NEXT MONTH